I'M FALLING FOR A LOUISVILLE SAVAGE

DEEANN
KEISHA ELLE

Published by Urban Chapters Publications

www.urbanchapterspublications.com

Contains explicit languages and adult themes

suitable for ages 16+

TEXT UCP TO 22828 TO SUBSCRIBE TO OUR MAILING LIST
If you would like to join our team, submit the first 3-4 chapters of
your completed manuscript to
Submissions@UrbanChaptersPublications.com

To our publisher Jahquel J...
Thank you for believing in us. You've been both positive and encouraging
throughout this entire journey. It's easy to second guess yourself when
you're in an industry filled with so much talent. You push us to new heights;
all while keeping it professional and classy. We appreciate you for that .

To our readers...
Thank you for your support. Enjoy!

ACKNOWLEDGMENTS

DEEANN

First off, I would like to thank God! Without Him, I am nothing. I'm so thankful for this gift He has given me and I pray He continues to work in me.

Thank you to my husband for supporting and believing in me. The hand massages after a long day of writing mean so much; it's just the small things.

To my son, everything I do is for you. I love you so much and I promise I will make you proud.

Mommy, thank you for being my number one fan and always supporting me. I know I can always count on you.

UCP, we are on the rise! You all are great and I appreciate you all.

Jahquel, thank you for believing in me and being such an inspiration not only to me, but to others as well. You're an amazing mentor and publisher. You're stuck with me forever!

Keisha Elle, you are an amazing writer, person and friend! I finally got the collab with you I've been wanting! I truly look up to you and I am so happy of our newfound sisterhood. I can't wait to see what the future holds and I'm happy to be on this journey with you! I look forward to our future collabs!

Readers, thank you for taking a chance and continuously rocking with me! You guys are the bomb!

Let's Chat!
Facebook: Dee Ann, Like page: DeeAnn, Reading group: DeeAnn,
What We Reading?
Twitter: AuthorDeeAnn_
Instagram: Authoress_DeeAnn
Email: authoressdeeann@yahoo.com

ACKNOWLEDGMENTS

Keisha Elle

I tend to be long-winded, so I'll try to keep this short and sweet. Before anything, I thank God. He's my guiding light and the sole reason I am able to do what I do.

Thank you to my husband for holding down the fort while I focus on my craft. Sometimes I don't thank you for all the sacrifices that you make. Just know that its appreciated.

To the young men and women that I'm grooming for greatness...I hope I can make you proud. I love you all with everything in me and nothing will ever change that.

To my mother...You are my heart! Even with your declining health, you keep a smile on your face. There's only a select few that I'd go to war for, and you're at the top of that list!

A special thanks to the authors of UCP! Y'all rock! Our time is coming!

To Jahquel...I'm hard-headed at times, but I'm listening! Thank you for the words of encouragement. It's been a pleasure to be part of the team.

To DeeAnn...Girl...You are wise beyond your years! You're like a little sister keeping me on track. Thank you for the advice, laughs, and even allowing me time to vent. You find a way to turn every negative into a positive. Only a special person can do that. This was my first collab, but you made it so easy. We definitely have to do it again!

To the readers... I hope you enjoy reading this book as much as I enjoyed writing it!

CONNECT WITH KEISHA ELLE!!!

FACEBOOK: WWW.FACEBOOK.COM/AUTHORKEISHAELLE

Twitter: www.twitter.com/keisha_elle
Instagram: www.instagram.com/keisha_writes
Email: keisha.elle@yahoo.com
Website: www.keishaelle.com

Now to the story....

1

AMAYA

*H*is tongue had me climbing the headboard for an escape. The expertise he portrayed every time he spread my lower lips and licked me from the front to the back couldn't be taught in any classroom. It was an acquired skill, and Santiago was a pro. Even if he wasn't showering me with expensive gifts, or paying the bills for my bomb ass crib, I'd gladly fuck him for free just to feel that tongue sliding up and down my wetness.

Watching him sloppily slurp my juices had me ready to bust in his mouth. He flicked his tongue across my hardened pearl, begging my body to release. The pot was stirred, and if he kept doing what he was doing, it would surely boil over.

With a firm grip, he pinned my knees down to the bed, holding my pussy captive. I returned the favor, restraining his fresh locs with both hands, forcing him to drink from my fountain. I was beyond wet, and I was gracious enough to allow Santiago the opportunity to quench his thirst.

"Shit," I moaned, feeling his stiff tongue dart in and out of my opening. "Daddy, I'm about to cum."

"Go ahead," he mumbled, not missing a beat. "Get it."

I got it alright. My breathing picked up as my lower body trembled involuntarily. Santiago took my clit in his mouth, sucking so hard I was sure it would detach. I arched my back, feeling a wave of satisfaction course through my entire body. Santiago didn't release his grip until my legs felt like jelly and gave out from pure exhaustion. That shit was good as hell. Damn good. The wet sheets up under my ass was proof of that.

He stood to his feet and ran his open palm down his glistening face. The glistening face that I was responsible for giving him. That shit was a turn on in itself. As he began to fidget with his belt buckle, I recognized my cue to get in his favorite position – face down, ass up. I pushed myself onto all fours and waited for him to claim what he thought was only his, but he surprised me.

"I'll be back for that."

"Wait. What?" I was confused. Was he turning down this pussy?

"I got some shit to tend to real quick. I'll be back though." He slapped my naked ass with his hand. "Keep it wet for me."

Usually Santiago took his time to clean himself up. He'd gotten smart and purchased the same products he used at home for my condo. He went back to his wife smelling the same way he left; however today, he was leaving with pussy still on his breath. *My pussy.*

Now, before you form an opinion about me, let me say this... I don't care. I've been on this Earth long enough to know that deep down everyone is out for self, and I'm no exception. I wanted Santiago from the first time I laid eyes on him and my friendship with his wife was not a deterring factor. They weren't even married at the time, so technically he was single, which means I did nothing wrong. It wasn't my fault that she couldn't satisfy her man. That was a personal problem that I couldn't relate to.

I didn't have relationship issues because I avoided relationships. Men couldn't be trusted, Santiago was proof of that. All it took was for me to purposely leave the door open while I showered at Marley's house. She went to sleep while trusting me, her best friend, and her man under the same roof. Mistake #1. That nigga stood there rubbing his shit through his pants for the full duration of my shower. I played with my own nipples while he licked those juicy lips of his. Before the night was over, I was sitting on his face, coating his throat with my warm nectar.

Even though I've been keeping her man satisfied for over seven years, Marley is still my girl. I know it may sound fucked up, but there's love there. She's the sister I never had. We met our senior year of high school after my mother uprooted my brother and I from Decatur, AL. She said she needed a change of scenery, and after visiting a childhood friend in Louisville, KY, my mother decided to stay. For me, the transition was hard. My mother's selfish decision to move separated me from both my friends and family. All I knew was Alabama, and I wasn't ready for change.

Then Marley entered my life. I was immediately in awe of her beauty. Niggas flocked to her as if her body were made of gold. She was as close to perfection as one could get, wrapped in a 5'6 frame. Marley was a flawless mixture of both her parents; large almond eyes and a cute button nose. Her full, pouty lips had me questioning my own sexuality, even though pussy had never been my thing. It was just hard not to notice the hourglass shape that was emphasized by everything she wore. I wanted that too; complete with the slim waist, round booty, and thick thighs. I'll admit it, I was jealous. So, when she extended her friendship to me, and took me under her wing, I gladly accepted. With her guidance, I morphed into a close second, but I was tired of standing in her shadow. I wanted people to do a double take when they saw me, just like they did her. I wasn't ugly. I had a smooth, caramel complexion, a narrow nose, and round, heart-shaped lips. I just didn't have the tits and ass to cause a second look. That was, until I learned about a quick hustle called financial aid. I enrolled in community college, registered for enough remedial classes to achieve full-time status, and waited patiently for my refund check. I got a few surgical enhancements on the government's dime, and I started stopping traffic just like Marley, maybe even better.

I stuck around long enough to finish my program. It took me three years, but I walked across that stage and collected my Associate's degree with a firm set of DD breasts, and an ass that remained well after I departed. Marley was right in the front row, cheering me on with a pretty nigga next to her that I couldn't take my eyes off of. She introduced him as Santiago, and I didn't hear a damn thing after that. All I knew was that I wanted him, and I always get what I want.

He began showering her with gifts. I wasn't really fazed by the bouquets he would send with corny 'I love you' notes, but I did take notice when the plants and flimsy paper turned into high-priced jewelry. Marley had more bracelets and necklaces than she needed, which allowed her to freely pass the wealth on to me. She passed her barely used hand-me-downs my way, and I gladly accepted. There was no shame in my game. I rocked that shit like I purchased it from Jacob the Jeweler himself. It wasn't until she showed up to my mother's apartment showing off a new Mercedes Benz and a huge rock on her left finger, that I started seeing red. Why couldn't I find a nigga to take care of me?

It just so happened that luck was on my side. My mother kicked me out because as a grown woman, I wouldn't abide by her 12AM curfew. My girl Marley came to my rescue, offering me a room in her four-bedroom house purchased with Santiago's dirty money. Yes, I said dirty money. It didn't take long for me to find out how he was able to afford the expensive gifts Marley was running around town with. He wasn't just some street thug, pushing drugs on a busy corner. He was the man; the one that made the calls and got shit popping. He had an army of loyal soldiers, with soldiers up under them, all ready to do whatever needed to be done. Santiago was Marley's come up. I too needed a come up. I needed *her* come up.

Marley's loose lips broke one of the cardinal rules of friendship – don't tell the next bitch about what your man does in bed. That was Mistake #2. Like a dummy, Marley told me Santiago's dick game had her limping the next morning. My interest was piqued. I wanted to feel it for myself, and let me tell you; she was exaggerating. He was okay, but I just didn't see myself fucking him again. Marley had me anticipating Thunder Over Louisville; instead, it was more like a single sparkler – the big kind though. I guess it frustrated him when I didn't cum because after he got his, he bent down and worked his magic with his tongue just like he did the first time I rode his face. My sheets were wet before the end of the night, and Santiago's number was added to my speed dial.

We began fucking on the regular after that. I didn't care much for the dick, but I put up with it for the tongue. Every time I laid on my back, I was guaranteed a gift. The best one came after he and Marley set their wedding date. I was in my feelings; worried that my good thing was about to come to an end, but like always, everything worked out. Santiago handed me keys to a condo he purchased just for me. My acceptance gave him 24/7 access to my pussy, and I didn't have a problem with it. As long as he took care of me, I would continue taking care of him – sexually.

I stared at the closed door well after Santiago left. I wasn't sure if he was coming back or not, but I wasn't going to wait up for him. That was Marley's job. Besides, he had a key to open every lock in my condo. What was mine, was technically his.

Grabbing my eye mask from my nightstand, I slid it over the curly mane that I was too lazy to wrap up. Instead, I positioned myself in the center of my king-sized bed, adjusted the mask, and closed my eyes. Sleep was turning into more of a task than it should. For the past month or so, I'd suffered from a serious bout of insomnia. Going non-stop for most of the day, my body refused to relax and wind down. The solution was supposed to be found in a little white pill called Ambien, but as my phone vibrated ferociously and fell off the side of my nightstand, my hopes of a good night sleep fell right along with it.

I lifted the pink eye mask and focused in on the time displayed on my digital alarm clock. Who the hell was calling me at 3AM? There was only one way to find out.

Rolling my naked body to the side of my bed, I reached down and grabbed my phone from the floor. Marley's number flashed across the screen as the phone shook in my palm. I debated answering the call. While I enjoyed my fair share of gossip like the next person, engaging in it with Marley was sure to keep me up. As the phone stilled in my hand, Marley made the decision for me. She hung up.

The phone started its series of vibrations once again. Marley could be relentless when she wanted to. Since she was calling back-to-back, I figured it was important. I answered her call.

"Hello," I said into the phone.

"Hey girl. Was you sleep?"

I don't know why people chose to ask dumb, redundant questions. If I was sleep, I couldn't answer the phone. If I woke up to answer the phone, I was no longer sleep. The question was irrelevant, but I just said no anyway and waited to hear the reason for the call.

"I'm bored," she finally said as her voice perked up. "What are you doing?"

"Sleeping," I threw back at her.

"Well get un-sleep. Talk to me. Help me calm my nerves."

"What's going on?" I probed.

"Santiago's on his way. I have a feeling tonight's going to be the night."

"For?" I questioned.

"You know Santiago and I have been trying to have a baby. Well, I'm ovulating, and—"

I'd heard enough. There was no way I was gonna sit around and let my cash cow give her something he refused to let grow inside of me. My hard-earned money was at stake, and no one messed with my coins. It was bad enough that I had to share with Marley. There wasn't enough to go around for some snotty nose kid, unless of course it was mine. I made up an excuse to get off the phone and dialed Santiago's number.

"Yeah," he spoke into the phone.

"You don't sound happy to hear from me."

"It ain't that. I'm just working right now."

"That's funny, cuz I just talked to Marley and I heard you're on your way to bust all up in her guts. You know, give her the baby she's been asking for."

"She's still on that bullshit?" he asked as if he expected me to answer. When I didn't, he continued. "Good lookin' out, though. I owe you."

"Is that right? Why don't you come back and give me your babies instead," I teased, knowing he would take the bait.

"As long as they're in your mouth, and not in your pussy, you can have 'em."

"I wouldn't want them anywhere else."

"A'ight, girl. You got me out here with my dick hard and shit. Give me about thirty minutes, and you better be ready when I get there."

"Yes, daddy."

I hung up the phone with a smile on my face. Mistake #3 – Don't tell your left hand what your right hand is doing. That baby that Marley so desperately wanted was about to have a final resting place right in the back of my throat.

2

MARLEY

*C*hecking my appearance in the mirror, I nodded my head in approval. Not one to brag, but I was a bad bitch and anyone who laid eyes on me would agree. I turned heads everywhere I went, male and female. I had curves in all the right places and they were all natural, unlike Amaya who paid for hers, but that's none of my business.

Any who, the black and red lace negligee I wore clung to my hour glass shape, leaving little to the imagination. When God created me, He took His time crafting every inch of me. From my head covered in my wild, curly burgundy spirals to my freshly pedicured toes I was banging. Any woman would die to have my body and I took care of it very well; especially for my man Santiago.

Santiago and I have been together for what seems like forever. He's older than me by five years, but that didn't matter to us. We bonded instantly, and our love was undeniable. When I first laid eyes on him, I was in awe. I had never seen a man that fine and confident. His aura screamed that he was a boss and he carried himself like one as well.

Santiago was mixed with Black and Puerto Rican, although the latter was hard to believe just by looking. Standing at 6'1, he towered over my small, thick frame. He had long, brown locs that fell in the middle of his muscular back. Thick, dark eyebrows rested above his deep set stormy gray eyes that creased when he smiled. His eyes were the color of a midday thunderstorm sky that was waiting to open the flood gates of heaven. Captivating. He had thick, pouty heart shaped lips that could suck the soul out of my pussy. He was very skilled with his mouth and tongue. I could cum from just thinking about his competent head game.

I loved him with every fiber of my being and I was ready to bear his children. Santiago and I have been able to enjoy life to the fullest. Traveling out of the country, shopping sprees to no end, just blowing money; now, it was time to start a family. I was tired of feeling lonely when he was out working and I was stuck in the house. I wanted a house full of kids to fill that void of him not being there and I prayed that he would give them to me.

I wanted three children. A set of twin boys and a girl. I grew up with siblings and I loved it. I never felt lonely. I always had someone there no matter what. I wanted my children to have that bond and security like I did with my siblings.

Peeking out the window, I saw our golden gates open, announcing Santiago's presence. Butterflies immediately began to flutter my stomach as I hustled through our room, making sure everything was in place. I could hear the door unlock downstairs, so I positioned myself sexily across our bed and waited for him to enter.

"Ley!" I heard his deep baritone voice call out to me.

"I'm in the room!"

I looked over myself once more in the mirror above our bed. He loved to watch us have sex. We had mirrors in every corner of our room, so he could see us from every angle. I loved that shit too. Watching as he would wrap my hair in his massive hands and pound me from behind always made me cum instantly. The love faces he would make did something to me. Knowing I was the one giving him so much pleasure made it that much more enjoyable.

His *Eternity* cologne by Calvin Klein tickled my nose before he even made it inside the room. He walked in looking like a million bucks and the boss that he was.

"Hey, baby." I cooed, opening my legs wide so he could get a peek of my freshly waxed pussy. "I missed you."

The bulge in his pants made my mouth water profusely, but the scowl on his face made me frown.

"What's wrong, baby?"

"Nothing, just stressed. Some shit happened that I need to handle. I just came home to change then I'm heading back out," he explained, going to one of our multiple closets.

Our bedroom was spacious. It was more like a small guest house. We had four closets; two for me and two for Santi. We each had a closet dedicated for shoes and one for clothes. Upon entry to our room, you're greeted with a living room, bathroom, and mini bar. No one but the two of us venture beyond that point. Guests wait in the living room area, if we feel comfortable enough to allow them into our bedroom. Security cameras were everywhere, so we had our eyes and ears on them at all times.

I got up and followed him while he mumbled something under his breath. I tried to make out what he was saying, but I couldn't. I knew my husband and something was off with him and it wasn't nothing to do with his damn work either.

"Are you sure you're heading back out to work?" I questioned with my arms folded under my bosom and a light scowl on my face. "You've been having to deal with shit every other night and I'm getting sick of you not being home! I've done all this for you and you didn't even acknowledge it!"

"Come on, Ley. Chill, ma. I know I've been gone, but I swear it's all because of my work! Niggas been testing me. I'm having to show my face a lot more than I want to. You know I rather be home with you; cuddled up and all in those guts." He licked his soft pink lips and winked at me. "Nothing you do ever goes unnoticed, I swear baby. I peeped all this when I walked in the house and you saw how my mans reacted. I felt bad as hell for having to tell you I can't stay and enjoy this night with you. Just know I'm going to make it up to you real soon."

"You promise?" I asked skeptically.

"I promise," he repeated.

I walked away and let him finish getting ready. Shit was weighing heavy on me, but I didn't want to speak on it just yet. My woman's intuition was jabbing me in the pit of my stomach, but as usual, I shrugged it off and chose to put my faith and trust in my husband. He had never given me a reason to suspect any infidelity, so I wasn't going to sweat over it.

Stripping from the negligee into an oversized t-shirt, I laid across my bed and scrolled through my social media accounts. I never posted anything. I just liked to be nosey and see what other people were doing. Some people put damn near their entire lives out in the open and I was one of the ones that took it all in.

Amaya was one of those people. She just posted how she was waiting for her mystery man to come over so she could put him to sleep. I promise that girl was something serious. She kept a man at her house.

Santiago emerged from the closet, naked as the day he was born.

"What are you doing?" I questioned as my eyes followed his tight ass to the bathroom.

"About to shower. I've been sweating and shit all day and you know how I am about being clean," he yelled from the bathroom above the shower water.

I waited for a few minutes before I took off my t-shirt and went into the shower with him.

"What are *you* doing?" He smirked, washing his body.

"Nothing, I just figured I could help you out before you go to work."

I fell to my knees as the steaming hot water cascaded on my head and down my back. Santiago's rock hard member was staring back at me, begging me to take it in. I wrapped my small, manicured hand around his thick shaft and slowly massaged it while I kissed his swollen, mushroom shaped head sensually. He let out a low, sexy moan that made my nipples hard.

"Come on, baby. Quit playing," he said, wrapping my hair in his hands.

I gave him some of the best, sloppy head I had ever given him. The way he was moaning out would of had one thinking I was throwing it back at him. Technically I was, just with my mouth. I could feel him growing, letting me know he was about to cum. Picking up my pace, I went hard until I felt his warm seeds spilling down my throat. I smiled in satisfaction as I looked up to see his head leaned back and his eyes closed tightly as he tried to gain his composure.

"I guess I'll let you finish showering now," I smirked, standing to my feet. Before I could even attempt to get out, he roughly grabbed my arm and pushed my back down so my ass was in the air. Ass up, face down. That's how he likes it.

"You know better than to try and leave without letting me get my pussy. You had your dick, right?" He questioned, ramming himself inside of me. Yelping out in pain and pleasure, I nodded my head yes as he worked himself in and out of me.

"Ooohhh, daddy! Go deeper," I begged as he slowly stroked me. I could feel my juices mixed with the now freezing cold water slithering down my legs. The sound of our love making echoed through the bathroom as he slapped my ass and worked me into an orgasm. "I'm about to cum!"

"Don't you cum yet!" He demanded, slapping my ass once. Quickening his pace, he went faster and deeper.

"Pleeeaasssseee!" I cried. I knew if he delivered one more long, deep stroke that I would be squirting all over his abs.

"Not. Yet!" He groaned, slapping my ass harder.

Santiago pushed my head down further, making me touch my toes. He gripped my small waist tightly then delivered two spine breaking strokes that caused my body to start violently shaking and a loud, shrill moan to escape my lips. That still didn't make him stop. He continued until I felt his manhood throbbing inside of me. Before he could pull out and have his kids on my ass; I tightened my pussy and made him cum inside of me mid-stroke.

He was leaned forward with his hands on the wall still inside of me. He was panting heavily, trying to catch his breath. I couldn't help the smirk that tugged at my lips as I thought about what the future could possibly hold for us.

"I have to wash up again foolin' with your horny ass," he chuckled, pulling out of me and turning the water off. "I guess I'll have to do it in the sink since you made the water cold."

"How are you going to blame that on me, Santi?" I giggled, grabbing my feminine wash and getting out. "I tried to get out the shower, but you stopped me and started raping me."

"How can I rape the willing?" He shot back, causing me to laugh harder. "Your sneaky ass knew what you were doing when you came in the shower with me. Now, you got me running behind and shit."

"I don't know what you're talking about," I played dumb, washing myself while he brushed his teeth.

We handled our business in silence. I was tired now and the bed was calling my name. I glanced at Santi through the mirror and the mean mug on his face indicated he was in deep thought.

"You okay, baby?"

"Yeah. Just thinking about all this shit, but I'm good." He answered.

"Do you want to talk about it?" I suggested, turning towards him with my hands on my hips.

"You know I never pillow talk about my work, Ley. I never want you to know anything because the moment you find out; that's when shit is going to change and I don't want that. I can't risk it," he explained.

I just nodded my head and went into the room and got back in the bed. Grabbing my phone, a smirk tugged at my lips as I texted Amaya to let her know I was successful.

Me: Mission accomplished.

I went to my LiT app and tried to decide on a book to read when Santiago's phone started ringing. I figured it was work calling since he was running late. I heard him mumbling something into the phone and then he let out a loud frustrated sigh.

"It's going to be okay, Santi," I reassured from the bed.

He emerged from the bathroom and hurriedly put on his clothes. He went through the room to make sure he had everything and came over and kissed my forehead.

"Don't wait up for me. I don't know how long this shit is going to take," he stated.

"Please, be safe Santi. I love you."

"I love you too, Ley."

3

SANTIAGO

I got the cold shoulder when I arrived back to Amaya's place. Unbeknownst to me, Marley had already disclosed my whereabouts, making the lie that fell from my lips infuriate Amaya even more. She stood inches away from me with her arms crossed over her chest. Instinctively, I stepped back. The look on her face warned me that a swing was coming.

"So you're trying to give that bitch a baby!" she shot at me.

"Calm down. Chill out, ma. No I ain't tryna give her a damn baby."

I thought I was going to lay up with Amaya and get a few hours of shut eye before meeting up with my man Cashmere, but the way Amaya was acting, that plan was about to fall through.

"So why were you over there?" she asked.

"Damn! I can't go home?" I paced the floor, trying to calm my growing attitude. I had genuine love for Amaya, sometimes even stronger than my wife, but the twenty-one questions shit had to stop. I didn't owe her a damn thing. She knew the deal when we got together. Marley was my wife, and nothing was going to change that.

"No one said you couldn't go home, Santi. That's not the problem. You went home and fucked that bitch. You know she's trying to have your baby."

"And?" I countered.

"What the fuck do you mean, *and*?"

"She's my wife, Amaya! Damn! If she gets pregnant, she gets pregnant. Oh well."

The swing that I anticipated connected with my chest and shocked me for a moment. She actually hit me. As Amaya prepared to hit me again, I grabbed both of her wrists and tightly secured them in my firm grip.

"What the fuck is wrong with you?" I barked, inches away from her face. "You hit me again and I'm going to forget you got a pussy between your legs. You hear me?"

"Get off me!" She wiggled frantically, trying to free herself from my grip, but she wasn't going nowhere.

"Not until you calm the fuck down."

Tears fell from Amaya's eyes and streamed down her face. I felt a little guilty. Amaya wasn't one to shed tears. For her to do so now, in front of me, meant much more than I realized.

"Fuck you Santi!" she yelled through sobs. "Just fuck you. Go home to your wife. Lay up with her and have all the babies you want."

That's when realization hit me. I don't know why I didn't see it before. Amaya was in her feelings. Shortly after we started messing around, Amaya became pregnant. I made her get an abortion. How could I explain to my then fiancée that her best friend was pregnant with my child? Three years later, we were in the same predicament. She got another abortion, and Marley never found out.

A few months back, the shit happened again. She claimed to be on the pill when I raw-dogged her ass, but a pregnancy test confirmed that she was indeed pregnant. I gave her the money to take care of it, just like the times before. Instead of getting the abortion, she went shopping, and had the nerve to blast her pregnancy announcement all over social media. Amaya even went behind my back and scheduled a few doctor's appointments. She was smiling ear-to-ear when she showed me the black-and-white sonogram photo of my seed growing inside her. To say I was furious would be an understatement. It was bad enough that I had slipped up, but I had to hear Marley's mouth too. She began nagging me for a baby. I wasn't ready for any of it. I just wanted to get money.

Fate intervened and saved my ass. Amaya had a miscarriage shortly before turning four months. By that time, I had eased out of her life after her refusal to abort my child. When she called me crying, I was back by her side, trying to comfort her broken heart. I, on the other hand, was happy as hell inside. Our secret was still safe, and my wife didn't know that the child she shared tears with Amaya over was actually mine.

As you can see, I continued fucking with Amaya. Call me crazy, but I got feelings for the girl. They aren't strong enough to make me leave my wife, but I do care about her. Seeing her crying in front of me tugged at my heart. I would do just about anything for her, except intentionally reproduce. That's something only Marley could have, when we were both ready.

"Listen to me," I said softly, loosening my grip on her wrists. "I ain't trying to get her pregnant. It was one time. The chances of her getting pregnant are slim, so chill out. Can't you see that this is where I wanna be? I just left my wife's house to be with you. That should tell you something."

I hoped that my words would calm her down. As her face began to soften and her sniffles diminished, I knew that I had done just that. Now it was time for reinforcement. I released my grip and brought my hands down to her cheeks. Smoothing long strands of hair from her face, I wiped the remaining tears away and placed a soft kiss on her lips. She leaned in, deepening the kiss. I had her now. She opened her mouth, allowing my tongue to dance with hers. I took it up a notch, letting my hands freely roam her naked body. Within minutes, we were in her bed. With my hands firmly planted on the sides of her thin waist, I long stroked her; giving it to her better than I ever had before. I came inside the condom when my name left her lips in a high soprano. I was back in. Just to ensure we were all good, I turned her over and buried my face in between her legs.

I didn't stop when her phone began to ring. She answered it;

which turned me on. Let the games begin! I took her clit into my mouth as she tried to talk to the caller on the other end. She gave in to the pleasure and moaned into the phone. I was face deep in her pussy when my conscience slapped the shit out of me.

"Marley, let me call you back."

I was eating her pussy with my wife on the phone. What kind of grimy shit was that? I was all the way turned off. Fuck that!

"What are you doing?" she asked, ending the call. The phone hit the bed and bounced beside me. Sitting up, I wiped her juices from my face and shook my head.

"Why'd you answer the phone?" I questioned. "That shit's foul, ma."

"I wanted to see what she wanted."

"While I'm face deep in ya pussy? Really? You knew what the fuck you were doing."

I stood to my feet and grabbed my clothes. I should've left after the bitch swung on me.

"You act like she knew it was you. She said I sounded busy and to call her back. That's it."

"Yeah, a'ight."

I jumped in the shower and washed her scent from my body. Ignoring her pleas for me to stay, I dressed quickly. That was the problem with females. Once you put the good dick on them, they started doing that slick mess. What if I had slipped up and talked shit while eating Amaya's pussy? There's no doubt in my mind that Marley would have known it was me. That was a risk I wasn't willing to take. Amaya was going to learn today. She could be in her feelings all she wanted, but she wasn't running things – I was. I left her to think about what she did. When I felt like being bothered with her again, I'll call. Until then, she was getting my voicemail.

Thankfully, Cashmere agreed to see me early. I met him in our usual spot right off of Hurstbourne Lane. I was standing outside my red Camaro, enjoying the early morning breeze when a black Range Rover with tinted windows rolled up on me. The back passenger's window rolled down, and Cashmere's dark face appeared. He gave me a head nod and rolled the window back up. I walked to the other side and climbed into the luxury SUV.

"Thanks for meeting me," I mentioned, closing the door.

"It's no problem; as long as you're not wasting my time."

I watched Cashmere twist his signature pinky ring around on his finger. It was massive; with a large diamond encrusted crown atop the letter 'C.' I guess he considered himself *The King* or something, but whatever.

The driver slowly drove around J'Town. I disclosed to Cashmere my dilemma, well aware that there were three pairs of ears listening to me. Cashmere never traveled alone. Both the driver, and the big nigga in the passenger's seat were all part of his entourage. That didn't count the car following two car-lengths behind us.

"Go on," he coached as I swallowed my pride and asked him for a front.

The money that I paid him days earlier was supposed to go toward the next shipment. However, after one of my workers got knocked, the majority of the previous shipment was seized too. I had to come out of my own pocket to pay Cashmere back, and that shit put a serious dent in my wallet.

"Stop the car," Cashmere spoke. His dark eyes narrowed into small slits

The driver pulled into a Meijer parking lot. I nervously waited for Cashmere to speak again. When he did, I wished he hadn't.

"Get out."

Normally I would have protested, but as the driver and the front passenger turned toward me, their stares became enforcement enough. I exited the car and started my walk of shame. I made it five blocks before the Range Rover reappeared.

"We've been dealing with each other for a while now," Cashmere began once I reentered the vehicle. "I ain't never had any issues with you before. You've always been good on your word. So, what kinda numbers are we talkin' about?"

He kept a straight face as I asked for the advance. I over exaggerated my request; aiming high and hoping he would at least meet me in the middle. He did better than that, offering me whatever I needed, along with a verbal promise to pay on my end. Today was my lucky muthafuckin' day!

I would soon have the money to put as a down payment on the dream home Marley had been asking for. Our shit was dope now, but it could always be better. I would give my baby the world if I could; and for the shit I was doing to her, she deserved every bit of it.

I looked down at my ringing phone. Amaya's number flashed across it. I sent her to voicemail. She called twice more and both times ended with the same result. She hadn't learned her lesson yet. I was gonna let her sweat for a few days.

"The Mrs.?" Cashmere questioned, rubbing his large hand over his deep waves.

"Yeah," I lied.

"Women...you can't live with 'em, but you certainly can't live without em'. Remember that."

"Oh I know. Marley's my everything. I love that girl. I certainly don't wanna lose her."

"Just make sure you don't fuck me over, and that will be the least of your worries."

A look crossed Cashmere's face that I'd never seen before. The muscles in his chocolate face began to twitch. I immediately went on edge, positioning my feet so that I could easily push the door open and make a speedy exit if need be. First, I tried to lighten the situation.

"You know I ain't gonna do nothin' like that to you, Cash. We boys!"

He laughed in my face, displaying a set of straight, white teeth.

"Boys? I got all the boys I need; I ain't got no room for no mo'. You my friend, are on borrowed time. You have exactly one week from the time my product touches your hands to pay me my money. I don't take partial payments, and I don't give extensions. If I have to come lookin' for you, it's lights out. Do we understand each other?"

I nodded as my car came into view. Like every other deal we'd made, we shook on the terms, and I turned to exit the vehicle.

"Don't forget what I said."

I was halfway out of the car when I turned back around to face him. "I hear ya."

"Hearing and understanding are two different things. I don't play about my money. I'll text you the pickup location later on today."

The car drove off after I closed the door. He'd have his money well before the deadline. I could damn near guarantee it.

I entered my car and dialed my righthand man. Looney picked up on the first ring.

"What's good, boss man?"

"Round up the squad. We got a big shipment coming in a short timeframe to move it. We need all hands on deck for this one."

"You got it."

A wide grin spread across my face. I was about to be muthafuckin' paid!

4

CASHMERE

"Sss, shit. Work tha- Fuck! Bitch, did you just bite me?" I growled, pushing this broad back and checking my dick. Some of my skin was peeled back and a little blood was oozing out. Anger flashed across my light, toffee colored eyes making them look almost black. I snapped my fingers and my hitter, Murder roughly pulled her back by her long hair and held a knife to the nape of her neck. Her body trembled uncontrollably as if she was having a seizure and I couldn't help the chuckle that escaped my dark pink lips. This shit was amusing.

"I... I'm so sorry, Cash! My teeth scraped you on an accident! I promise I didn't do it on purpose," she cried, begging for her life. "You know I never slip up!"

The gleam of desperation in her eye didn't affect me any. I was cold; made of stone. I was numb to everyone's feelings, including my own.

Allow me to introduce myself. My name is Cashmere Wilson, but everyone calls me Cash. I supply these dirty, grimy streets of Louisville with the finest, purest cocaine that has ever graced this Earth while having two degrees. I deal with other shit too, but the white girl is what makes me the most money. I am very intelligent, but the streets won my heart from the start. Maybe one day I'll put my degrees to use, but as long as there's breath in my body and I'm at the top of the game, I'll remain where I know.

Louisville is my city. Nothing goes on without my acknowledgement; not even with the Feds. The majority of those bastards are on my payroll, so I'm untouchable. Shit, even if they weren't, I still would be. I never leave a trail behind me, not one speck of dust. I've done so much shit in my lifetime that I know I'm going straight to hell. I'm going to take over that muthafucka when I get there too. There's rumors that I'm the devil in the flesh, so I make sure I live up to it.

Don't get me wrong; I'm not all bad. I have a soft spot and that's for my sister, Kensley. She's only fifteen and I'm her guardian. After her dumb ass mama, Kelsie abandoned her I took her in. Her mama was chasing after a man that didn't want her ass and a fuckin' high that I wouldn't give her. There have been countless times she's came to me begging to suck my dick just for a bag. It was crazy how she could ask for coke, but not even fix her crusty, dry ass lips to ask about her damn daughter! Each time she came begging, I would curse her out and send her own her way. It was a secret I would never tell Kensley because all she knew was that her mother was dead and I was going to keep it that way.

As for our father, fuck that nigga too. He's the reason I'm so cold hearted now and I will never forgive him for that. I've been searching high and low for his conniving ass, but I always come up short. My life is dedicated to making sure Kensley is always happy and on top of her shit, serving the streets, and finding our sperm donor so I can send him to his maker. There's no room for any other shit.

Back to the problem at hand.

"Let that bitch go," I demanded. I chose to show some mercy on her because I knew her situation and how much she needed the money, but things in life didn't come for free. Shit always comes with a price.

Murder grilled me like I had lost my mind. "You sure, Cash?"

I nodded my head and dismissed the both of them to clean myself up. Murder roughly jerked her by her hair as she silently thanked me for sparing her life. I shook my head while laughing lowly and proceeded to clean myself up.

Ring! Ring!

Just as I was putting on some new boxers, my personal phone started ringing. I knew it couldn't be anyone but Kensley. She was the only one that called that number.

"Yeah."

"Cash, that is not how you answer the phone. Do you answer like that for everyone? *Yeah?*" She mocked me with laughter in her voice and I couldn't help but to laugh also.

"Yeah, I do. Now, what's up? You're calling me while you're at school, so something must be wrong." I noted with a wrinkled brow.

"I need you to bring me some tampons," she whispered and my eyes bucked. This was the shit I don't think I could ever get used too.

"None of your friends have any?" I sighed, pinching the bridge of my nose in frustration. This little task was going to throw my schedule off track, but Kensley was my number one priority.

"No, they don't," she whined. "I know you don't want too, but I *really* need them." She stressed, pulling at my heart strings.

"Okay," I sighed, giving in as I knew I would and she did too. I heard a tiny giggle escape her lips and I shook my head. "Give me about fifteen minutes and I'll be there. Do you have some in your part of the house?"

Kensley was spoiled to say the least. Together, we lived in an eight bedroom, five bathroom estate. She had half, and I had the other. Kensley never gave me any problems, so she got almost everything she asked for. In addition to being mature for her age, she kept good grades in school and was active in extra curriculum activities. She was in the top ten percent in her sophomore class. I was beyond proud of her for doing so well; especially after all that she's been through.

Another reason I was willing to go the extra mile for her was because I wanted her to know how to love and be loved. I want her to know how a man is supposed to treat her and she never has to settle for anything less. I want nothing but the best for her. Because of that,

I do random shit like buying her flowers and leaving her encouraging little notes to get through the day. She's always getting pampered and going on shopping sprees. I reward her for her hard work. Even with all of that, nothing compares to how I feel about that girl. I love her with everything in me and I will protect her to no end. She's my responsibility and I do my best to take care of her and make sure she stays on the right path. For all that it's worth, I think I'm doing a damn good job.

"Yes. They're in my bathroom in my main room," she explained then thanked me before ending the call.

I retrieved her things and sent a text to my lieutenant telling him to inform Santiago that we would have to meet at a later time. I had shit to handle after I dropped this off to Kensley, and I was going to be later than expected.

My driver, along with my body guards, drove me the ten minutes to Kensley's school. I replied to some of my dealers, letting them know the time, date and drop-off spots for their supplies. I liked to do deliveries every other day, so that I could check all their numbers and make sure everything matched up. I was very critical about the way I handled things. They had to be perfect to the T. If something was just a few numbers off, I would begin an investigation. I didn't play when it came to my operation and everyone knew it. That's why I only fucked with the best dealers around. I appreciated every one of them, so I made sure they were fed and living like the top dogs they were. They would forever be straight as long as they continued to show me consistency and loyalty.

Once we pulled up, I got out with a few of my body guards around me. I wasn't a bitch nigga, but there was a lot of heat for my head because I was the nigga on top. So, I had to be on point at all times. There was no way in hell I was going to let an uneducated, tack head little boy come and take what's mine because he caught me slipping. Trust me, I never got caught slipping.

As we walked to the door, I got a glimpse of someone out the corner of my eyes. Clenching my jaw and gritting my teeth, I had to bite my tongue and stroll inside like I didn't see them. I couldn't show the true, ruthless Cashmere at Kensley's school, but I would if I had to.

Kensley was waiting for me in the office. She was scrolling through her phone with a slight frown on her face as if she were reading something disturbing. I cleared my throat and she glared up at me with eyes matching mine and a smile lit up her beautiful face.

Even though we had different mothers, we shared a lot of the same features. I towered over her small, 5'4 frame at 6'3 with wide, broad shoulders. She had shoulder length caramel highlighted hair that complemented her round, mocha coated face. I had a fade with deep, dark brown waves resting on top. Our light, bright chestnut colored eyes mixed with our warm sepia skin made us look of Haitian descent, much like our sperm donor. We both had entrancing dimples that appeared with even the slightest movement of our mouths. To me, that was one of our best features.

"Thank you so much, Cash!" She exclaimed with a smile, jerking the box out of my hand and hurriedly stuffing it inside her bag. "Did you have to bring the whole box though?" She questioned with a laugh.

"Hell, I didn't know how many you needed, so I just grabbed the whole thing. Next time, be more specific." I stated with a smirk tugging at my lips.

"I'll try. Thanks, brother."

We embraced in a hug then she scurried off to the restroom. Being the overprotective brother that I am, I sent one of my guards to make sure she was fine before I exited out of the school with them in tow.

Please, don't let this bitch still be out here, I mumbled under my breath. Just my luck. Our eyes met and she waved me over. Against my better judgment, I told my guards to stand down while I went to deal with her. I knew exactly what she wanted. I was already prepared to dismiss her.

"What?" I asked with a clenched jaw avoiding eye contact with her.

"Don't what me, Cashmere. You know exactly what I called you over here for," Kelsie spat. "I feel like you've been avoiding me."

"Nah, you just haven't seen me and I don't know what you called me over here for. I don't fuckin' read minds. Now, get down to it. I have some shit to handle."

"I need a bag, Cash. I've been feenin'," she admitted, scratching at her scrawny neck with her boney fingers. "None of your men will sell me shit because of you! I just need a hit, that's all."

"Exactly, that's the point. If I gave my men orders not to serve you, then what makes you think I would? I know that coke ain't fuckin' with your head that bad." I chuckled, shaking my head at how delirious she was.

"Because, Cash. You know how bad I need-"

"Nah, I don't know shit but that you need to get clean, Kelsie! Look at you! You out here begging me for a hit right across the street from where your daughter goes to school! Type of shit is that? You need to get yourself together. You're too old for this shit, man and I'm tired of telling this to you. You're a grown ass woman out here begging. I bet you don't even have a pot to piss in because you spending all your money on a fuckin' high." I seethed. I had to pinch the bridge of my nose to try and calm myself. I hated I let this bitch get to me so bad, but I couldn't help it. The love I had for Kensley made me want Kelsie to do so much better, because then maybe, I would let her be a part of her life. Until then, it would remain the same.

"Whatever," she sucked her teeth and rolled her neck. "I'll find it somewhere else."

"Cool." That was all I said as I turned to run back across the street. Fuckin' with her made me even later than I already was. I hated being thrown off schedule.

"You know I see her every day. I sit here every day and watch as she gets dropped off and picked up. She's so beautiful, Cashmere. I can tell that you're doing a very good job with her. Thank you," Kelsie spoke and then disappeared down a dark alley.

My body guards made sure I was in the truck safely and everyone was in place before we went on about our day. It was time to give Santiago this product and see if he was true to his word. He had never given me a reason to doubt him, so I hoped he could live up to his word. If not, his family would be paying for it with their lives until I was paid back every cent that he owed me.

5

AMAYA

I fixed Santiago's ass. He called himself being slick by repeatedly sending me to voicemail. Soon, I stopped calling all together and then it was Santi's turn to blow my phone up. Two could play that game. I would eventually answer his calls, but first I was gonna let him sweat. I wasn't the type to sit back and take his shit. Hell, I wasn't Marley.

Replaying the scene over in my head, I smiled. I loved the whole thrill of it all. The thought of getting caught stayed in the back of my mind. Friend or not, I didn't care one way or the other. Even if Marley found out about us, I wasn't going to leave Santi alone. My heart was already in it. To me, he was *our* man. If she wanted to get mad and leave him, that was perfectly fine with me. I'd gladly take him for myself and spend all of his money on my own.

I arrived at my condo early in the evening. Most of my day had been spent looking good and pampering myself. The Louisville streets needed a constant reminder of what perfection looked like, and I became the self-proclaimed muse. I cruised around in my freshly washed Camaro, stopping traffic in the process. It didn't hurt that when I stepped out of the car in my five-inch colorful *Brian Atwoods*, my body bore a matching navy blue dress that could have easily been mistaken as painted on. That's how I rolled. I was there to show the broke, jealous bitches how it was done. It was impossible to name a bitch on the planet badder than me because she didn't exist. If you think I'm lying, name one. I'll wait.

When I arrived at my condo, I immediately noticed that something was wrong. I was a perfectionist, and never left my crib in disarray. A plate and cup sat lonely in the sink, while my remote control was tossed on the coffee table. I always sat the remote control on the entertainment center enclosing my seventy-inch flat screen television. Someone had been in my apartment. I only needed one guess to figure out who it was.

I picked up the phone, and dialed Santiago's number.

"You finally callin' a nigga?" he asked on the other end. That boy had issues.

"Cut the bullshit. You already know why I'm calling. What were you doing in my condo?"

"You mean my condo? The one I pay for? If that's the one you're talking about I remember getting a key when I signed the lease."

"This is my shit!" I raised my voice to emphasize the point. He had some fucking nerve. "I let you have your little temper tantrum and I kept it pushing. I didn't go over there bothering you and Marley. Why do you have to come to my spot?"

"Girl, if you don't chill the fuck out. I ain't on that shit no more. I came by to see what you were up to. I waited a while, you didn't show up, so I bounced."

"Next time I would appreciate it if you would call before you just show up to my crib."

"You on one, ma. We'll rap though. My dude just pulled up. I'll catch up with you later. Are you gonna be home?"

"Maybe. Call first."

I ended the call. Hell naw I wasn't gonna be home! What the fuck did I look like sitting back waiting on a nigga? Desperate was not in my vocabulary. Again, I wasn't Marley. She put up with his bullshit and called me crying when he did her wrong. I listened intently, taking a mental note of the issues in their relationship. I made sure I was everything she wasn't. So far, it had worked to my advantage, even though it appeared that he had the upper-hand.

After convincing myself that I was ready to turn-up, I called Marley and told her about my plans. You're supposed to keep your friends close, right? Yeah, I know the saying goes on to mention keeping your enemies closer, but as fucked up as it may sound, I didn't consider Marley an enemy. She was more like competition. Unbeknownst to her, we were playing for the same prize. Anyway, she was dressed and at my place within the hour. She wore a black catsuit that I was positive would have looked better on me. To one-up her, I changed into a barely there romper and over the knee boots. I let my hair hang straight, while Marley beat my face to perfection. She wasn't too bad with a makeup brush. It wasn't long before we were stepping out and turning heads.

Marley picked this afterhours spot, full of tipsy niggas with long money – my kind of scene. We maneuvered our way through the thick crowd and found an empty table in the back. Not so subtle combinations of perfumes and colognes invaded our nostrils, but didn't stop our stride. I don't know about Marley, but I was on a mission. Operation find a horny nigga to keep the drinks coming was in full effect.

I found my target in the middle of the dimly lit room. He was downing a glass of brown liquor while engaging in conversation with another man. The charcoal gray suit, gracing his long body clung to him effortlessly. I could smell his money across the room.

As if on cue, his chocolate face turned my way, and our eyes locked. I gave him my signature smile and grabbed Marley's arm. Pulling her with me, I started in his direction, bypassing tables of patrons in the process.

Ahem.

His guest cleared his throat loudly, gaining the mystery man's attention. I slowly eased into the mix and joined the conversation.

"Hello gentlemen. It's a nice night out, ain't it?"

"Yes it is, but it looks like it might be getting better." His friend smiled widely, licking his lips. The top two buttons of his crisp white shirt were unfastened, displaying an unruly patch of curly taco meat. *Yuck.* He needed to shave that shit.

"What are you ladies trying to get into?" Mr. Sexy asked, turning his attention to a half-naked waitress approaching in our direction.

Marley was always iffy about meeting new people, so I answered for the both of us.

"We're just trying to have a good time. Ain't that right, Marley?"

She nodded, but didn't say anything. Her eyes avoided his gaze and scanned the room. I don't know how she could not be infatuated by the male Adonis in front of us, but she appeared uninterested.

"Marley?" he questioned, cocking his head to the side. "Is your dude named Santi?"

That got her attention, and mine too. How did this dude know *our* man? Well, technically Marley's man.

"Yeah, that's my husband. How do you know him?"

"We go way back," he answered simply. "I'm Cash, and this is my nigga Murder."

Murder, or Mr. Chest Hair, smiled as if his name alone pulled weight. I didn't know who he was. I didn't know Cash either, but if he knew Santiago, it had to be on a business level. It was no secret that Santiago was a big name in the streets. The way Cash carried himself, there was a good chance that he was right up there with Santiago.

My eyes fell to his left hand. There was a large, eye-catching ring on his pinky finger, but nothing indicating he was legally tied to anyone else. *Jackpot!* It was time to make my move.

I eased closer to Cash as the waitress approached. Cash ordered another round for both him and Murder and told Marley and I to order whatever we wanted. It was on him of course.

"We'll have whatever you're having," I mentioned, batting my eyes.

"Aww shit," Murder said excitedly. "Looks like we're about to turn up!"

I smiled, knowing good and damn well that nigga was not gonna turn up with me. First of all, he was bald. That might have been sexy to some, but to me a bald head was not the business. On top of that, every time I glanced in his direction my eyes fell to that shit on his chest. I swear those hairs were growing by the second.

He was big, with milk chocolate skin and large hands. I estimated him to be at least 6'5 and a regular at somebody's gym. Still, I wasn't turned on at all. Even with the black glasses sitting atop his face he just wasn't my type. Cash on the other hand...He could get it. I was sure that he knew it to.

"I don't know what kind of turn up you're talking about Murder, but my girl and I are just looking to have a good time."

"You gonna have a good time a'ight. I can promise you that."

With a chuckle, Cash turned to his boy and gave him a pound. I rolled my eyes.

If those words had fell from Cash's mouth, it would have been cool. As long as he was throwing those Benjamin Franklin's my way, I was down for whatever. And I do mean whatever.

The waitress was quick as hell with our drinks. She arrived with four small glasses on a round serving tray. Cash handed everyone their drinks, and fished in his pocket for his money. He produced a hundred dollar bill and handed it to the chick.

"We want another round," he said coolly. "But you can keep the change."

Her light cheeks flushed crimson. That bitch was blushing. The little attention that he gave her had me seeing red. I was the number one bitch in that place. All attention should have been directed toward me.

She hurried off and I downed my drink. Cash slowly brought his glass to his lips and took a small sip. *Amateur*, I thought, watching his eyes bypass me and focus on Marley. I know she peeped that shit too. With a shy smile, she tossed her drink down her throat in one gulp. Cash watched intently, infuriating me even more. Why wasn't he focused in on me? Murder's eyes sure were. I'm surprised I didn't catch on fire from the hole his eyes burned into me.

"So what are your plans for the night?" I asked Cash, hoping he would break his trance-like stare with Marley.

"You tell me. What do y'all got going on?" Cash's mouth moved, but his eyes stayed fixed on Marley.

"Not a damn thing," a familiar voice said behind me. I turned around to see Santiago making an impromptu appearance. Talk about cock-blocking. What the fuck was he doing there?

"It ain't like that Santi. I know that's you." Cash was smooth. If Santiago wasn't there, he would have been singing a different tune. I'm sure of it.

"What's up, baby?" Santiago wrapped his arms possessively around Marley's small waist and kissed her passionately.

I don't know if he was trying to prove a point to me or Cash, but his actions banned him from my pussy that night. He was usually respectful of my feelings, and didn't engage in PDA. At that particular moment, he didn't give a fuck, which felt like a slap to my face.

"Damn, are you gonna let my girl up for some air? Shit, you're smothering her."

Marley laughed it off. That shit wasn't cute.

Cash finished his drink and sparked up a conversation. It wasn't long before the topic of business made its way to the forefront. Santiago gave Marley a knowing look and she grabbed my arm.

"Walk with me to the ladies room," she uttered.

"What about my drink?" I wasn't ready to walk away just yet.

"I'll keep it cold for ya," Murder insisted.

On second thought, the ladies room didn't sound too bad. Cutting my eyes at Santiago, I followed behind Marley, switching my hips extra hard during my departure.

"Girl, did you see the way Murder was looking at you?" Marley asked when we arrived in the bathroom. Thankfully it was empty and no one else heard that nonsense.

"You mean the ape? That shit on his chest is long enough to braid."

"You're crazy."

"No, I'm serious. I ain't looking at that nigga. But what about you? I saw how you were looking at Cash."

"I don't know what you're talking about." She examined herself in the mirror and averted my gaze.

"Like hell you don't." I joined her side and smoothed my hands down my romper.

What did Marley have that I didn't? Men flocked to her as if she were the queen bee herself. Pulling a nigga was never an issue, but next to Marley, I always fell short. When I didn't get my way, I removed myself from the situation. Petty or not, that's how it was.

"I'm ready to go," I declared, washing my hands in the sink.

"Already? We just got here."

"This place is whack," I lied.

"Okay. I'll let Santi know we're leaving, and we can go."

I walked to the car alone. I didn't need to see anymore kissing, hugging, or anything else Santi wanted the world to see. I also didn't want to see Cash blatantly play me to the left, or Murder for that matter.

I noticed Marley walking toward me as my cell phone chirped. I checked the message. It was from Santiago.

Santi: Sorry about that. I'll be over in a few.

He could lay up with Marley for all I cared.

She hopped in the car and handed me a folded up piece of paper.

"What's that?" I asked.

"Murder wanted me to give you his number." Was she serious? I snatched the paper from her hands and threw it out the window.

"Why'd you do that?"

"I told you I wasn't feeling him."

"You didn't even give him a chance. You're gonna be lonely for the rest of your life with that attitude, Amaya. You ain't getting no younger, girl. Give him a chance. He seems nice."

That did it. Marley wasn't going to talk to me like my standards were too high. There was nothing wrong with wanting a certain kind of man. I didn't know how Murder's finances were set up, but his looks didn't appeal to me. What was wrong with that? I had options, and I had no intention of adding Murder to that list. As she continued to scold me like a child, I responded to Option #1.

Me: Only if I can sit on your face

Santi: Mmm. Leaving now.

Marley was still running her mouth when I placed my phone back inside my purse. She was the last person I needed relationship advice from. It was about to be another long, boring night for her. It would be a long night for me too, but far from boring. The only difference was, while she was sleeping, I was going to be cumming down her man's throat.

6

MARLEY

I was playing it cool on the outside, but on the inside, my heart was beating so hard and fast that I swear Amaya could see it through my tight-fitting catsuit. My body temperature was rising and my suit was starting to stick to me everywhere. And I literally mean *everywhere.* That man had me so hot and bothered and I barely said two words to him.

Cashmere. Lord, that man was fine. He was standing there looking like a tall glass of dark chocolate milk and I was thirsty as hell. The way he was studying me, glaring at me intently with those piercing amber eyes, made me nervous to be in his presence. From the moment we approached him and Murder, I could feel his power. I'd heard of him before. He reigned supreme, more than Santi, so I was intrigued. I wanted to know more about him, but I couldn't. I was a married woman. Married to a man that technically worked for him. I said my vows in front of God and I love Santi with everything in me. I would never want to hurt him. It doesn't hurt to look though and Cashmere was very nice to look at.

"Take me home," Amaya huffed, breaking me from my daydream.

"Home? I thought we were going to another bar. Why do you

want to go home?" I questioned her with my perfectly threaded brow raised.

"I'm just not feeling it anymore," she pouted. "I just want to go home and cuddle up in my bed and watch Netflix."

"Girl, if you don't stop with that shit." I smiled with a hint of laughter in my voice. "What? You mad because Murder was paying more attention to you than Cashmere?"

I was just joking, but how hard she rolled her eyes and the scowl on her beautiful face let me know I had hit a nerve. She was so fuckin' sensitive when it came to men. She thought that every nigga was supposed to fall at her feet because she had a cute face and fat ass. I hated to break it to her, but life didn't work that way.

"I'm not worried about Cashmere's wannabe ass. He probably a fake thug, anyways." She stated, rolling her neck. We glanced at each other and fell out laughing.

"Now, bitch! You know that nigga is dripping money! I could literally smell the Benjamin's when we strolled over to the bar. You know he's getting paper if he's fuckin' with my baby. You and I both know Santi is paid!" I bragged, flashing off all my diamonds, complementary of my husband. I swear that man had me spoiled. I was always laced with the best of the best. Not like any of the material things mattered. It was just nice having them and my baby had the means to provide me with anything I wanted.

"Don't I know it," Amaya made a sly remark with a smirk. She made slick little comments like that all the time, but I just ignored them. She was always trying to get under my skin, but I wouldn't let her get the satisfaction. I knew she was secretly jealous of what I had, but I was her best friend. What's mine is hers. Well, all except for Santi. He was off limits and I dare a bitch try to him.

"Don't get slapped, hoe," I snapped playfully, muffing the side of her head. "Let me call and tell my man I will be home earlier than expected. Maybe I can get some of that long, thick snake tonight."

Amaya let out a long, exaggerated sigh as I dialed his number. The phone rang twice before Santi's sexy, deep voice came over the loud car speaker, causing my insides to quiver. I couldn't wait to feel him massaging my insides.

"Hey, Ley. What's up, beautiful?" He spoke and I blushed. No matter what, he always made me feel warm and gushy inside.

"Nothinggg," I sang. "I'll be home earlier than I expected. Amaya wants to be a party pooper, so I thought we could have a little fun tonight. I still have tags on some of the lingerie you brought me the other day. Maybe I can try them on for you."

"Mmm, I would love to see all that ass in barely anything, but I can't." He sighed.

The huge, cheesy grin I had before was wiped from my face and replaced with a sad frown.

"Whhhyyy, Santi?" I pouted, hitting the steering wheel.

"I have some shit to handle, Ley. You know how this shit goes. Sometimes I have late nights and early mornings, but it's all for us. I swear," he explained, but I wasn't trying to hear it. I was getting fed up with coming second to the streets.

"You know what; it's cool. I'll see you when I do," I barked then hung up and blocked his number before he could call again. Call me petty, but it is what it is. He wanted to choose the streets over me, then I didn't have shit for him until he got his priorities together with me at the top of the list.

"Trouble in paradise?" Amaya questioned, rubbing my arm.

"I'm just so tired of this shit, Amaya! Yeah, I understand that him being the big time man that he is requires a lot of time and hard work, but DAMN! Where do I come in? I'm getting sick of coming second," I cried with shaky hands.

"Don't cry, Marley. You know everything he does is all for you. Look at you. You're laced with the best! Any bitch would want wha-"

"Material shit does not matter! His time, his love, and his attention is what matters to me and he's not giving me that! I'm not the type of bitch that will sit around and act happy because I have the finer things when in reality I'm miserable as fuck because my man is never there! I'm just fed up." I expressed, pulling up in front of her house and throwing the car in park. I closed my eyes as I rested my head on my seat. I was trying to control my emotions in front of Amaya. I didn't want her to see me break down because deep down I know Santi was hiding something from me. What was it?

"Do you think he's cheating?" Amaya asked in a shaky breath, barely above a whisper. She looked over at me with concern evident in her eyes. A lone tear slid down my rosy cheek as I thought about all the late night's he has been having. Hearing her ask me my biggest fear caused me to shudder.

"No," I lied. "I know it's all work. You and I both saw Cashmere and I can tell that he means business. I just wish he didn't have Santi doing all this shit late at night, but I guess it is something I will never understand."

Amaya's phone chimed, indicating she received a text. She checked her phone and wiped that one little tear away with a smile tugging at her lips. She locked her phone and threw it back in her purse.

"Just try to talk to him and get him to see things your way. Maybe he will try and work something out." She tried her best to encourage me.

"I will. Thanks, Amaya."

We embraced each other in a sisterly hug and I watched as she went inside of her home. Backing out of the driveway, I contemplated on my next move. I didn't want to be alone at home without Santi and the night was still young. I figured I could go to the bar, have a few drinks and go home and finish off the night with a glass of wine and a hot, steamy bubble bath. Just because Santi was out working didn't mean I had to sit at the house and wait up on him. He would probably be pissed, but at this point, I didn't give two fucks about his feelings. He didn't care about mine.

I typed my destination into my GPS and turned up Sirius radio that was playing *Unappreciated* by Cherish. I sang along feeling each word deep in my heart. Santi really had my emotions fucked up tonight. What I didn't understand was; how was he at the club, but couldn't come home because he had shit to handle? It wasn't sitting right with me, but what could I do?

I pulled into *The Silver Dollar* and parked close to the door. I checked myself in the mirror; fixing my hair and makeup. I unblocked Santiago and powered my phone completely off. I placed it in my clutch and got out to go enjoy a few drinks at his expense.

I strutted into the bar, turning heads immediately. I tossed my hair over my shoulders and found a seat in the back far away from anyone else. Men were eyeing me hungrily as I studied the bar menu. I just continued to sit pretty and ignore them. I may be mad at Santiago, but I wouldn't dare disrespect him. Everyone knew whose woman I was and if the thought of entertaining one of these clowns crossed my mind, Santi would go ballistic. I knew where I belonged and everyone else did too.

"What can I get for you?" The overly enthusiastic bartender questioned with a huge grin. I couldn't help but smile back at her happiness. It was contagious and exactly what I needed at the moment.

"May I get a cranberry and vodka with a shot on the side?" I asked politely.

"Would you like anything else?"

"Let me get a shot of Remy," a vaguely familiar voice demanded. His scent greeted me and I knew who it was before I looked over.

Cashmere.

"If I didn't know any better, I would say you were following me." I teased, casually glancing in his direction. His presence made me nervous, but I wouldn't dare let him know that.

"I could say the same about you, Marley. It's quite a coincidence, isn't it?" He chuckled and I could feel his gaze fixated on me. I wiggled around in my chair to get comfortable and hide my nervousness. I guess I wasn't doing a good job because he sat beside me and scooted close with his thick, juicy lips grazing my ear. It caused a chill to slither down my spine; deep into my woman parts. "Do I make you nervous?"

"Why would you make me nervous? I don't even know you."

The bartender came and sat our drinks down in front of us, but Cashmere didn't budge. I could feel his icy cool breath blowing on the side of my face and the light scent of mint and alcohol crept up my nostrils.

"You may not know me, but you know what I am capable of."

"And what exactly does that mean?"

"It means I can have you if I want you to." He eased into the seat next to me and let his words sink in. "I'm a powerful man and I get what I want and you, Marley... You just so happen to be someone I find very intriguing." He admitted smoothly, placing his strong, masculine hand on my thigh and squeezing it firmly.

"I'm sorry, but I am happily married." I dismissed him, shoving his hand off me.

"Are you?" He pondered, taking a sip of his drink.

"Am I what?"

"*Happily* married."

The emphasis he put on the word happily made me stop and think for a second. Of course I was happily married. Santiago may piss me off sometimes, but that's just something that comes with marriage. We fight and bicker, but all the good times outweigh the bad and that's all that matters. There's no question that we love each other.

"Yes, I am." I answered proudly. "Why wouldn't I be?"

"I see you're here alone instead of home with him," Cashmere observed.

"That's because he had business to handle. You should know since you're keeping him busy," I muttered, rolling my eyes in annoyance.

He smiled a bright smile, showing off straight, pearly whites and the sexiest dimples I had ever seen on a man. The way they sunk into his cheeks so perfectly caused me to cream in my thong.

"Listen, that's not on me. My job is to make sure my men have their supply and they have my money. I don't go digging around in how they do their job. Whatever he's doing is his business. So, understand this...The way Santiago is running his shit is on him. If he's staying out late or coming home early, I don't have shit to do with that." He informed me with a shrug.

Now, my mind was in overdrive. Santi always made it seem like Cashmere had him working all night long when in reality, Cash had nothing to do with it. Why would Santi lie to me? What was he really out here doing? Once again, my woman's intuition was pounding away at me. To make it go away, I downed my drink and ordered another one. I would drink until I was numb if I had to in order to get this feeling to go away. I didn't want to believe it. Was Santi actually cheating on me?

"Where's your friend?" He asked, breaking me from my thoughts.

"I took her home. She wasn't feeling it anymore since you wouldn't give her the time of day," I giggled as my mood perked up. I was happy to discuss something other than Santi.

"She's not my cup of tea. If I were you, I would watch her. I can spot a snake from a mile away and she is one. She's not your friend like you think," he warned looking deep into my eyes. The way he said it and the way he was looking deep into my soul made me want to believe him, but how could I? I didn't know him at all and Amaya had never did anything to make me question her loyalty. She was my best friend, my sister even. Why would he think otherwise when he didn't know her?

"Look, I appreciate your warning or whatever, but Amaya is my best friend. She would never do anything to hurt me or jeopardize our friendship. Trust me, I know her well."

"I was just warning you, beautiful. You'll see for yourself one day," he stated, finishing off his drink as I started on my third. "I think you may need a ride home after that."

"No, I will be fine. Thanks anyway." I declined his offer. I could feel myself growing tipsy and Cashmere was starting to look even better. My teeth sank into my bottom lip as I eyed him hungrily. He licked his lips and I swear I felt like my insides were going to explode.

"That wasn't debatable, Marley. Finish up so I can take you home. Don't make me have to repeat myself either."

"I said I-"

"I said don't make me repeat myself," he barked in a low tone, clenching his jaw. "I'm ready when you are."

I was speechless. I finished my drink and let him help me outside where a car was waiting for us. His authority and protective instincts turned me on. There was nothing like a man who knew his place at the throne and didn't take shit from anyone. I could feel his eyes on my ass as I entered the car. He took a seat next to me as the driver closed the door behind him.

"Where to?" The driver questioned.

"My-"

"Santiago's residence, please." Cashmere instructed. The driver nodded his head and took off in the direction of my home.

The bumps and dips in the road caused my body to sway instantly making me nauseous. I was doing my best to contain my composure and keep the alcohol down, but dizziness swept over my body and I was done.

"Stop the car," Cashmere demanded with his eyes glued on me.

Cashmere opened the door just in time as I spilled my guts all over the grass right outside the door. I was beyond embarrassed as the contents of my stomach continued to spew from my mouth and nose. To my surprise, Cashmere held my hair out of my face while rubbing my back. His touch was welcoming.

"I'm so sorry," I apologized as he handed me a damp towel and a bottle of water. "I guess I had a little too much to drink."

"That's exactly why I insisted on driving you home, Marley. You're welcome. We'll work on getting your car tomorrow."

The rest of the ride to my house was silent. I couldn't help but think about how attentive he was to me. He had a hard exterior, but I could see he had a soft side as well. That small gesture made me want to get to know him more and see what he was all about. Little did I know, I was going to get to know him very well.

7

SANTIAGO

*M*an, Marley was pissed! I could tell from the way she ended the call. I tried calling her back, but my calls went straight to voicemail. She was on one, but I'd much rather feel her wrath than Amaya's any day. Unlike Marley, Amaya had leverage. With a slip of her tongue, she could fuck around and end shit for the both of us. That was a risk I wasn't gonna take. Call me what you want, but I chose my side bitch over my main. Marley would get over it; she always did.

A loud, orgasmic cry escaped Amaya's lips as soon as I opened the door. I guess my arrival wasn't fast enough. She got her own self off with the help of her battery-operated friend. That shit had my man jumping in my pants. With her legs spread-eagled, I could see her juices dripping down toward the sheets, creating a puddle under her ass. Mmm mmm mmm. My turn! All she needed to do was get my guy wet.

I unbuttoned my pants and leaned toward her. Fast as shit, she sucked my pole into the back of her throat like a straw, taking me all in. I bitched up, letting out a moan that should have come from a female, but I wasn't ashamed. Good head will do it to ya. If you can't relate, you don't know good head like I know good head. Anyway, I pounded her walls for a good hour before my soldiers finally decided to make their appearance. I got mine, so I let her get hers – again. As usual, I finished up with her clit in my mouth, allowing her to get off on my tongue. I tell ya, she can't get enough of that shit.

I wasn't trying to stay the night, but that's exactly what happened. Before I knew it, the sun was up and my phone was ringing out of control. *Fuck*, I thought, realizing my mistake. I was alone, comfortably under Amaya's thick comforter. The smell of bacon filled the air. She was in there cooking, which meant she was up. She didn't have to let my ass sleep. If I didn't know any better, I would think that this was Amaya's plan all along. Since I did know better, I knew it was her plan. Typical, Amaya. She knew I was supposed to go home. Marley was gonna flip.

My phone stopped ringing as I reached for it. I assumed that there were a few missed calls from Marley, but you know what they say when you assume. She hadn't called me even once. Yep, she was beyond mad. I was gonna need the help of that Crocodile Birkin she'd been eyeing to get me out of this one. What I did have in my hand, was a call log full of missed money. The word got out that all owed money was due to me by 6AM that morning - no exceptions. As I watched the clock in the top right hand corner of my screen turn from 8:58AM to 8:59AM, the muscles in my jaw began to twitch. In my business, missed calls were missed opportunities. If the number one guy wasn't available, you go on to the number two; until someone answered the call. That somebody needed to be me. It was time to make moves.

I dressed quickly, and returned my first missed call. It was to Charlie who agreed to meet me in twenty minutes to deliver the ten grand he owed me. The next call was to Donovan, who didn't answer my return call. A quick check of my visual voicemail displayed his number. I listened to his message, giving excuse after excuse as to why he didn't have my money. It was cool. I knew where his bitch lived and after I finished doing what needed to be done, I was gonna pay her lil triflin' ass a visit. Donovan stayed knee deep in that bitch's pussy, and if he wasn't on the block, he was resting his head in her dingy Park Hill apartment. I was gonna get my money one way or another.

Amaya was all smiles when she entered the room. In her hands sat a wood serving tray, topped with a covered plate and a glass of orange juice. The smile disappeared when she saw me, preparing for my exit. It smelled good and all, but I had shit to do.

"Where are you going?" she asked, sitting the serving tray down on a nearby desk. She placed her hands on her hips, and started pouting like a child.

"I got moves to make, sweetheart. Thanks, but no thanks on the breakfast. I ain't got time."

"I've been up all morning cooking for you. The least you can do is eat it."

"Girl, I said I don't have time," I repeated.

"Damn, Santi. Why do I even try with you? Every time I do something nice, you disregard me like I don't even matter. This shit is getting old and fast."

She was out the room before I could protest. I wasn't going to stop her anyway. It was a known fact that women were nuttier than fruitcakes, and nothing I said was going to change that. I quickly glanced over the room to make sure that I hadn't left anything. On my way out, I grabbed two pieces of bacon and stuffed them in my mouth.

Amaya was blocking my exit with her arms crossed over those big titties of hers. She had on one of my old t-shirts that almost reached her knees. Even under the thick material, her hardened nipples made an appearance. Her hair was discreetly tucked under a silk scarf. The disappointed look plastered on her face told me I wasn't going to be going anywhere anytime soon. Why were women so damn difficult? I already had World War III to deal with when I got home, now Amaya was in her feelings too. I just couldn't win.

"Don't do this, Amaya," I warned. "I told you I got somewhere to be."

"I drop everything for you. Whenever you call, I'm there. The only thing I ask is that you give me the same courtesy. When you're here, I should be the only thing on your mind. Not Marley. Not work. Not nothing. You shouldn't be rushing outta my house to meet nobody. When you're with me, everything else can wait."

Was this bitch serious? If I hadn't fucked her the night before, I'd swear her pussy was bleeding. Women got a pass for being on their period; their hormones were all fucked up and shit. Amaya wasn't on the rag though, she was just talking crazy. The kind of crazy that made me wanna forget I didn't put my hands on females, and knock her little ass out the damn way. Money was waiting.

"Amaya, move!"

"No! This is *our* time."

"What the fuck is wrong with you? I'm here with you damn near every night. I spend more time with you than I do my own wife."

"I want more. I deserve more."

"What more do you fuckin' want?" My nostrils flared as I spoke. I took a step back to create distance between us. I was liable to lunge forward, and put my hands on her.

"Take me with you."

"Hell naw."

"Please. Take me with you. Let me see what it feels like to be by your side and not hidden in the background. Take me with you, Santi."

"And what if somebody sees you with me? You ain't thinking straight. I can't risk Marley finding out, especially like that."

"My car broke down, and you gave me a ride home." The lie fell from her mouth so smoothly it almost sounded believable. "It doesn't have to be all day. Let me go on a few runs with you and then you can bring me back home. I just want to spend some more time with you, Santi. Is that too much to ask? I love spending time with you."

Deep down, I knew those words were true. Even when she was playing hard, that girl loved my dirty drawers. I ain't gonna lie, I had feelings for her too; a lot more than a married man should. Since Marley was stuck on having that damn baby, it pushed Amaya and I even closer. She didn't hound me like Marley did and up until recently, she played her role. All she wanted was more time with me.

Hell, it's not like Marley wanted it. I accidentally slept over at my side bitch's house and Marley hadn't so much as called my ass. I could've been in somebody's jail or the city morgue, and how would she know? She wouldn't. Her actions showed that I was the last thing on her mind. I flipped the script and made Amaya the first thing on mine.

I let her ride with me to meet Charlie. Money discreetly changed hands, and before long, we were once again back on the road. Her straightened hair flew with the wind as she rolled her window down and took in the morning air. It was against my request to keep the windows up, but it put a smile on my chick's face, so I lightened up.

I was just about to round the corner, and hit the highway back to Amaya's spot when Cash hit me up. He had a few samples of some new shit, and wanted to see how the streets liked it. I agreed to be the guinea pig, and take on the free product. Free was right up my alley.

Knowing Cash's time was precious, I let Amaya stay along for the ride. I pulled into our meeting spot, and hopped into Cash's parked Escalade. I swear, every time I met with that nigga he was in a new whip. I eased into the back seat and was greeted with an interrogation.

"Who's in the car?" Cash asked cautiously.

"Oh, she's just a friend," I explained, waiting to see what he had for me.

"You know I don't like you bringing people along. Who's to say they ain't gonna run their mouth? How much does she know?"

"She don't know nothing."

"Oh, she knows something. Only a fool would get in the car with a complete stranger. What does she think you're here doing?"

"She knows what I'm doing. I mean, she knows I'm here to see something. She knows-"

"Too much. Bring her here."

"What?"

"Nigga, you heard me. Tell her to get in the car. I need to see the face of everyone I'm dealing with."

"But Amaya ain't got nothing to do with it."

"Amaya? The broad from the club?" He didn't even wait for my response before continuing. "What the fuck is wrong with you? She don't need to know nothing about what we got going on, but since she does, she needs to be sitting here right next to your dumb ass. Go get her, and it better not take you all damn day."

I quickly climbed out the ride and power walked to my car, mumbling expletives under my breath. I wasn't a bitch, and for Cash to talk to me as if I were one didn't sit well with me.

Amaya was in the mirror, freshening up her makeup when I opened her door. She jumped, but didn't dare drop the matte lipstick in her hand.

"What are you doing?" she asked.

I didn't have time for the small talk. I pulled at her arm, and told her what was up.

"Come on. You wanted to come, so I guess you're gonna hear this too."

She stepped out the car way too eagerly in my opinion. I think she enjoyed being a part of what I had going on. She wanted to be right there with me; side-by-side. I almost never took Marley out on runs with me, so Amaya felt as though she were superior. The petty, one-sided rivalry she had with my wife was getting old. Still, I entertained it, and walked side-by-side with my wife's best friend.

"So, we meet again." Cash repositioned himself in his leather seat. With an elbow perched on the armrest, he eyed Amaya skeptically. "I wasn't expecting to be graced with your presence today."

"What a coincidence," Amaya mouthed sarcastically. "I wasn't expecting to see you either. I guess Louisville's not as big as I thought."

"You're right about that."

With a smirk, he turned his attention to me.

"Back to the business at hand. Murder..." He snapped his fingers.

I watched a neatly wrapped brown package pass over me, and land in Cash's awaiting hands. It was another reminder that although the front seat was quiet, Cash had eyes and ears on him at all times.

The wrong words or movements on my part could prove fatal, and Cash wouldn't even have to lift a finger.

Accepting the package that Cash extended toward me, I took my time and carefully reviewed the outer exterior. I could feel Cash's eyes on me, but it was Amaya's gaze that made me uncomfortable. Her eyes darkened, and her dilated pupils anticipated the big reveal. She was excited, fidgeting in her seat as if she couldn't sit still. Seeing a brick of cocaine never had me acting like that. She was more like a kid in a candy store, fucking up my vibe. I should've left her antsy ass at home.

"Calm down, ma."

I caught Cash's gaze out the corner of my eye. It was in Amaya's direction, who didn't even seem to notice. I sped things up, quickly opening the package and checking the quality. I ran my index finger along the side and stuck it in my mouth. The bitter taste instantly numbed my mouth. I had some good shit on my hands.

"Hell, yeah. I can get rid of this shit in no time."

"Good, that's what I wanna hear. I'm sure you'll be in touch soon."

"No doubt."

I turned to Amaya who was doing everything she could to be invited into our conversation. After clearing her throat loudly, she tried leaning forward in her seat, until she eventually leaned onto me. We were talking business, and her voice wasn't a part of that, so I ignored her antics. But when she started inching closer to me, and leaned her head onto my shoulder, it was time to cut the conversation short.

"You ready?" I asked, flexing my shoulder. Once she sat up, I readjusted the rubber-band holding my dreads out of my face.

"Yeah, I'm ready. It was nice seeing you again, Cash."

"Likewise. Oh, and by the way, tell Marley I said what's up."

I could feel my blood boiling at the mention of my wife's name. The guilt that should have set in from me being out with my wife's friend was replaced with my male ego. It didn't matter who I had on my arm, Marley was my bitch. Point blank. Period. End of story. If

Cash wanted to send my wife a message, it would have to go through me.

"She don't need to tell Marley nothin', that's my job."

"My bad, you're right." He held his hands up in defense. "That's all you, playboy."

He chuckled as we exited the car. I didn't see a damn thing funny.

8

CASHMERE

I sat outside of the salon that Marley attended and waited patiently for her to come out. Ever since that night I took her home, I couldn't get her off my mind. Especially after my meeting with Santi. I couldn't say that I was shocked to see Amaya with him, because I wasn't. Like I told Marley, I knew Amaya was a snake from the moment I laid eyes on her and she proved me to be right. As for Santiago, he was fucked as far as I was concerned. He left the door wide open for another man to come in and get close to Marley and that man was going to be me. He had always been a very loyal worker of mine, but when I had my mind set to something I always fulfilled it.

"How much longer would you like to wait? You have a meeting in an hour," my driver, Toney spoke up, staring at me through the rearview mirror.

"As long as I have to. It's my meeting, so I'm the only one who can be late. They know to wait if I'm not present."

He nodded his head in understanding. We waited five more minutes before Marley emerged from the building. She was stunning to say the least. She was wearing a scarlet red plunging neckline *Alice and Olivia* romper that looked painted onto her curvy body with nude Balenciaga heels on her feet. Her usually curly, burgundy hair was now jet black and bone straight resting just above the perfect arch in her back. Big, round gold Chanel shades were covering her face as she walked towards her car scrolling through her phone.

Toney rolled down my window and I cleared my throat to get her attention. She glanced up and did a double take when she realized who I was. A smile tugged at her lips, but she did her best to hide it. She took off her shades and rolled her eyes as she strutted over to the truck.

"If I didn't know any better, I would say you were following me. *Again.*" She stated with a smirk. The scent of *Coco Mademoiselle* invaded my nostrils and I inhaled deeply. I made a mental note of it.

"Can we not be at the same place at the same time?" I questioned with a raised brow and she broke free of the smile she had been holding.

"No, we cannot. This," she waved her index finger between the two of us, "is called stalking. You are being a stalker, Cashmere."

I let out a low chuckle and shook my head. "A man like me doesn't stalk, Marley. I prey."

She placed her sunglasses back on her face to try and hide the fact that she was blushing. Throwing her hair over her shoulder, she placed her hand on her thick hip and glared at me. "And what exactly are you preying on, Cashmere? It can't be me since I am a married woman; in case you forgot."

"How can I forget? Your husband works for me...In case *you* forgot."

The mention of Santiago must have hit a nerve because she smacked her lips and shrugged her shoulders. If she only knew what I did, but I wasn't going to tell her. It wasn't my place too.

"Come take a ride with me," I suggested. "We can go grab lunch or something. Your choice."

She was hesitant to answer. She was nibbling on her juicy, gloss covered bottom lip with the cutest scowl on her face. Glancing down at her phone, she opened her mouth as if she was about to say something, then closed it back. She pressed her phone to the tip of her nose and smiled a little.

"You do know I'm a married woman, right?" She questioned with laughter in her tone.

"Yes, I do. You know I prey, right?" I asked in a serious tone. She stared at me with excited, lust filled eyes. I had noticed when I talked to her with authority, her eyes would flash with excitement, as if she got a thrill from me speaking to her in that way. She liked the controlling side of me and I didn't mind displaying it.

"Yes," she answered just above a whisper. Pressing my fingertips together, I nodded my head slowly and told her to get in. She obeyed.

"So, Marley...Tell me where you would like to go? It's still a little early and I know Santiago won't be home anytime soon. We can always retreat to my house and I can have my chef whip us up your choice of a meal and a few drinks." I suggested, gazing at the side of her face. She was avoiding eye contact with me; staring straight ahead as if she were in deep thought. I knew she was contemplating on whether she should take me up on my offer or not. I was leaving the decision in her hands. If she didn't, then we could go wherever she wanted. But oh, if she did...

"Sure. That's sounds nice," she decided with uncertainty in her voice.

"Are you sure?" I quizzed. I didn't want her to feel forced.

"Yeah. Why not?" She reassured me with a smile. "I don't have anything else to do. Besides, it'll give me a chance to learn about the man who coincidentally keeps popping up around me."

I laughed when she rolled her eyes in my direction. "Well, what do you want to know?"

"Tell me about yourself."

"I'm twenty-eight. I don't have any kids, but I do have a younger sister, Kensley that I am the legal guardian of. You already know what I do. I run an empire behind the streets, but I have a variety of businesses that cover my tracks." I paused to gage her reaction. "I'm a boss. Louisville is my city and everyone knows it. I hardly ever show my face and when I do, it's for a special reason. Oh, and I always get what I want. *Always.*" I clarified with a wink. She blushed and looked away from my gaze. "Now that I'm not a stranger; how about you not be one?"

"Well, I won't disclose my age. A woman never tells." She smirked and then added, "I'm younger than you though. I don't have any kids either, but I do want some soon. I've been begging Santiago to have kids, but he refuses. I-"

"He's crazy as hell! I would give you whatever your heart desires," I said, cutting her off. The way she moved in her seat let me know she was uncomfortable. "Sorry about that. I'm straight forward. I speak my mind. You can continue."

"Let's see...I run my own business. I design jewelry and have my own store. I'm wearing some of my custom pieces now," she noted, sticking out her wrist to show me her bracelet. It spelled out her name in small, clear diamonds with a gold background. I spun it around and on the other side, it spelled out Santiago's name. A jealous rage shot through my veins causing me to clench my jaw and look away. She pulled her arm back and fiddled with the bracelet.

"Anything else you want to know?" She questioned.

"How long have you known Amaya?"

"Since high school."

"Has she ever brought a man around? Like a boyfriend or some-thing?" I interrogated and she frowned.

"No. She's always had different male friends she would talk to from time to time, but that's about it. Why? You interested in her?" She pondered with a hint of jealousy in her tone, causing me to laugh.

"And if I was?" I challenged and she didn't like it. She sat back hard, rolling her eyes and poking out her bottom lip. The funny thing was; she didn't even realize she was doing it. It seemed to be a natural thing and that let me know she was spoiled.

"Then I would relay the message and see if she was interested," she tried to convince me, but it wasn't working. I decided to play along and see if she would break.

"Call her then." I demanded.

"Call who?" She played dumb.

"Amaya. Call her up and let me talk to her. I want to see if she would like to go on a date with me Sunday night."

Marley grilled me with jealousy sparking in her big eyes. Her gorgeous face scrunched up in a frown. With much attitude, she pulled out her phone and began scrolling through it, mumbling obscenities under her breath.

"Put your phone away. I was just fuckin' with you. Amaya's not my type of woman," I informed her. "I already told you how I felt about her. She's not my cup of tea."

"What is your type of woman?" She pondered with a quizzical expression.

"I like a woman who is head strong. A woman who knows her worth and doesn't let a man bring her down. A woman who has her own, but doesn't mind being spoiled by her man. A woman who caters to her man, but doesn't lose herself in him. A woman like you, Marley."

My last statement caught her off guard. Her eyes bucked and her cheeks flushed red from blushing. Her mouth was slightly agape as if her words were caught in her throat. I couldn't help the smirk that tugged at my lips as I watched her struggle with what to say next. It was cute how I could leave her speechless.

Her phone began ringing and she glanced at it and shook her head while ignoring the call.

"Hubby finally calling?"

She nodded her head as her phone started ringing again.

"What, Santi?" She answered with annoyance in her tone. She listened to what he was saying before she spoke again. "Well, if you would have come home last night, then you would know where I was." She paused again and rolled her eyes after a few seconds and took a long, deep breath. "I don't have time for your excuses anymore! Here lately it's just been all about work. What about me, Santi? I have needs too!"

Hearing her get frustrated and seeing the tears in her eyes enraged me. I could see that she was a good woman and really loved

Santiago, but he was too stuck up Amaya's ass to see it. I studied Marley's face as she continued to listen to whatever bullshit Santiago was feeding her. A tear finally escaped from being captive in her eye. That was it. Scooting closer to her, I snatched her phone out of her hand, powered it off and threw it in the front seat with Toney.

"Keep that with you until we escort Marley back to her destination," I instructed Toney who put his thumbs up in understanding. I made a mental note to put a little extra on his paycheck.

"What in the hell did you do that for?" Marley questioned in a high pitched voice. "He's going to come looking for me now!"

"Sit back and relax, beautiful. He will never get to you while you're with me. I promise you that. You will always be safe with me," I stated, gazing into her eyes to let her know I was serious. I was untouchable and I moved under the radar. Even the Feds couldn't find me when I was in plain sight. That's how good I am at what I do.

"I... I'm not so sure about this anymore, Cashmere. I think I should just go home," she stammered with a gleam of fear in her eye. She was scared, but of what?

"What are you afraid of?"

"Huh?"

"What are you afraid of? I can see it in your eyes; you're afraid of something."

"You," she admitted barely above a whisper. "This isn't right."

"Me?" I chuckled. "Why are you afraid of me? I won't bite. That is, unless you want me too." I whispered into her ear and she shivered. I rested my face in the nape of her neck and breathed deeply; inhaling her intoxicating scent. "Talk to me."

"I've never showed interest in another man since I've been with Santiago, but you... I'm intrigued by you. It's something about you that I find myself wanting to know more about and I know it isn't right." She confessed, fondling with her massive wedding ring. "I'm married and I shouldn't even be entertaining you."

Leaning back, I ran my hand across my head and thought about what she had just said. If she wanted to leave, then she could. I wouldn't force her to be here with me. Trust would come in time.

"Who are you trying to convince? Yourself or me?" She didn't answer. "Would you like for me to take you back?" I questioned and she nodded her head yes. "Turn around and take Marley back to her car."

"Yes sir."

The ride back was silent as she sat there in deep thought. Every so often, she would steal a glance at me and when she noticed that I was looking back, she would turn her attention to something else.

We made it back to the shop she was previously at and waited for Toney to open the door for her. She scurried out without uttering one word. Laughing to myself, I rolled down my window and called out to her.

"Marley?"

She spun around on her heels with her hands on her hips. "What?"

"Here," I tossed her phone and she barely caught it. "You forgot this."

"Thank you," she muttered. Embarrassment was written all across her face.

"No problem."

I watched as she switched to her car and got inside. I leaned back and I could still smell her perfume lingering in the air. I would be seeing her again soon.

9

AMAYA

I never thought Santiago would fuck up as bad as he did. In the middle of our lovemaking, he did the dumbest thing possible. I pushed his sweaty body off of me and covered my nakedness with my thick comforter. I was beyond pissed, and he knew it.

"Amaya, I'm sorry," he pleaded, edging closer to me.

"You sure are. Sorry as hell!" I barked. I didn't want to hear anything he had to say at that moment.

"I didn't mean it, I-"

"You what? Forgot? It slipped? Nigga, please! Every excuse you try to think up won't change the fact that you called me another woman's name."

"It ain't like that, Amaya. I swear. I'm sorry, baby."

"Don't you mean, Marley?" I shot back in all seriousness. "Cuz that's who you were calling out to when you were inside of me."

Santiago sat there with a confused look on his face. I guess he thought I was overreacting, but fuck that. Marley and I may have been friends, but we looked nothing alike. We acted nothing alike. Hell, I knew for damn sure our pussy wasn't alike. My shit's A1. Santi knows it too. If it wasn't, he wouldn't stay face deep in my hot spot every chance he got.

"You know the shit I'm going through. I made a mistake. I said I was sorry."

"And I said nigga please! You can get your shit and go."

He didn't budge, so I took matters into my own hands. I stood from the bed, grabbed his clothes from the plush carpet, and threw them in his direction. Now he had his shit. It was time for him to go.

"Damn. Can I at least shower first?"

"No. Shower at home with your wife."

That hit a nerve. He roughly tossed the cover off his body and dressed quickly. He mumbled something under his breath, but I didn't give a damn. It served him right.

He didn't say a word, look back, or even acknowledge me as he exited my condo. When he was gone, I slowly made my way to the front door and added the chain lock to prevent him from reentering. The all night fuck fest that I planned was officially ruined.

I plopped down on my bed, allowing my 'just fucked' hair to fall every way but right. Santiago had my blood boiling, and as I stared at my white ceiling, I became madder by the second. Whatever Santiago had going on with Marley manifested into my bedroom, and that just wasn't right. He actually called me her name. That was the ultimate disrespect. I'd bet my life that he hadn't done that shit with Marley. If he had, she would have been knocking at my door, ready to kick ass and take names later.

Subconsciously, I blamed her. She had a hold on him that I couldn't seem to break. No matter how hard I schemed and connived, she still ended up on top. What was so special about her? Even Cash seemed to be more interested in Marley than me. I just couldn't understand it. Was I losing it?

Cash came to mind as I slid my body over my silk sheets to the other side of my bed. He had an aura about him that I dug the shit out of. He was a bosses boss, and although I didn't seem to capture his attention, he sure captured mine. He had that 'take charge' mentality. Santiago had it too, but on a much smaller scale. I thought Cash may have come to his senses while we sat in the back of his Escalade. I peeped his eyes zooming in on all of my assets. I just couldn't let Santiago know that I saw. While keeping a straight face, I maintained eye contact with Santiago and the package he was playing around with. When I finally looked up, and met Cash's gaze, I was confronted with a hard side-eye that I read loud and clear. He *still* wasn't interested.

I picked up my phone and invited Marley over. I made it seem as though I'd been wanting to kick it with her all day. It sounded nice and Marley agreed without hesitation. I wanted her to come over, but for a different reason. In addition to ensuring that Marley wouldn't be getting the dick that I turned away, I also wanted the tea.

I showered quickly and slipped my body in a simple pair of black leggings and a t-shirt. I ran a wide-tooth comb through my hair, and settled on a loose ponytail. Turning on my seventy-inch television, I scrolled through the channels until my friend arrived. It took Marley almost forty-five minutes to get to my place. Santiago strategically set it up that way. It gave him enough time to dip out if he knew Marley was on her way.

I opened the door when she knocked and was greeted with both Marley, and my brother Armando.

"Look who I found," she said, leaning in for a hug. I embraced my girl, and showed the same love to Armando.

"Hey bro, what are you doing here?"

"I saw Marley at the gas station. She said she was coming to see you, so I tagged along. I hope you don't mind."

"Of course not." I painted on a fake smile and invited them both in. As Armando walked past me, I tapped the back of his shoulder. He turned around, and smirked at the scowl on my face.

Armando and I were only a few years apart. Technically, he was my baby brother. You just couldn't tell by looking. His frame was much larger than mine, although we shared the same mother and father. I was on the shorter end, while he stood at an average height for a man. He was 5'11, with a smooth milk chocolate complexion. His hair was short, black, and wavy; just like most of the men on my mother's side of the family. He had a nice smile, but fucked it up with his collection of gold grills. The deep dimple in each cheek more than made up for it though.

Like me, Armando went to school, and eventually graduated. Instead of putting his business degree to use within the corporate world, he put it to use in the streets. A few of the knuckleheads he used to run around hustling in the streets with had really made a name for themselves. While Armando received rejection after rejection during his job hunt, their pockets were increasing. When one of them pulled up to a car lot, and bought a brand new car with cash, Armando wanted in. Unbeknownst to him, he was teaming up with the biggest boss in Louisville – Santiago.

Santiago and I had already been messing around for years at that point. Whenever I came around, Marley was with me, so it didn't raise any eyebrows. That was, until Armando walked in and caught us in a compromising position. I couldn't deny it if I wanted to. I was ass up on Santiago's desk while he ate me from the back. Respectfully, Armando turned away, but he sure tore into my ass the next time he saw me.

"What the fuck are you doing sis?" he questioned.

"Nothing. Just mind your damn business." I left it at that.

There were a few more times that Armando caught the two of us. One of those times involved Marley, and if it wasn't for my brother, we would have been cold busted. She was out running a few errands, and I decided to be petty and fuck her man right in her bed. Her neck teased my eyes with a new blue sapphire necklace. I wanted one too. After giving Santiago some of the best head of his life, I knew that I would be getting an even better version.

Armando came over shortly after we finished. They spoke briefly about business, before changing the subject to sports. I made myself at home in the kitchen and grabbed a bottled water out to the refrigerator. Santiago followed behind, grabbing a beer for both he and Armando. When he turned around, and our eyes met, he gave me *that* look. Within seconds, I was leaned across the table, my skirt was hiked up, and my panties were pulled to the side. My moans were muffled by Santiago's hand, firmly clasped around my mouth. He was giving it to me good with long, hard strokes. I don't know if it was the noise from the table or my brother's thirst, but something guided him to the kitchen. There I was, getting fucked by his boss and thoroughly enjoying it. Santiago didn't even stop. He maintained his rhythm as Armando turned around and disappeared back into the living room.

Then I heard Armando's voice a little *too* loudly, "Hey Marley!"

Santiago's dick was back in his pants within record speed. I readjusted my skirt, and patted down my hair. Santiago grabbed the two beers sitting on the table and entered the living room. Waiting a few seconds to gain my composure, I clutched my water bottle and joined the trio. From that day on, fucking was strictly limited to my place.

I couldn't help but notice Marley's attire. Her body was tight in a sleek jumpsuit and high heels. Her hair was long, and black; a stark contrast from the burgundy ringlets she previously sported. She looked cute, I'd give her that. I wasn't a hater all the time.

Marley and Armando followed me to my bedroom and pulled the two chairs accompanying my wood desk to the middle of the floor. Once seated, I played hostess and retrieved bottled waters for everyone. When I returned, I was all ears. What was going on in Marley's world?

"Does Santi know you're out here looking like this?" I teased, patting her jokingly on the arm. "Looks to me like you're trying to find a man."

"Girl, he better hope I ain't out here trying to find nobody. Let me tell you what this fool did."

I listened intently from my position on my bed as she outlined Santiago's sketchy ways. He wasn't coming home every night. He was spending more time out in the streets than usual. She even suspected that something was up. I tried my best to ease my friend's reservations, all while ignoring the numerous eye rolls from my brother. The conversation was headed in a direction he wasn't comfortable with. He asked if we needed anything from the store, and excused himself. I turned the conversation up a notch.

"Have you talked to Santi about how you feel?" I quizzed.

"I hardly ever see him. He told me that he's been putting in more hours for Cash, but I know that ain't true."

"How do you know?" I took a sip from my water bottle. My interest was piqued.

"I saw Cash at the bar. We talked for a minute, and I found out that Santi's been lying to me."

My face scrunched up at the mention of Cash's loose lips. What a fucking pussy! For him to not vouch for his worker was a bitch move and made me lose respect for him.

"When did you see Cash?" I wondered if he had mentioned seeing Santiago and I together.

"I've seen him a couple times. Ever since we saw him at the club that night, he's been popping up everywhere."

"Is that right?" I crossed my legs and shook them nervously. "That's some coincidence. Sounds to me like he's following you."

"At least somebody is. Santi doesn't want to come home, but now that I'm avoiding him, he's blowing my phone up. This is him now." She held up her silenced phone, going off in a bright array of colors.

"Answer that man's call. He's probably worried sick about you."

"I ain't answering shit. When I'm ready to talk, I'll call him. Until then, I'm going to let him see how it feels to be ignored."

I changed the direction of the conversation. "So what are you trying to do? You wanna go out tonight?"

"I can't. I have plans."

"What kind of plans do you have?" Crossing my arms over my full breasts, I scooted toward the edge of the bed. "Spill it."

Instead of hearing Marley, the bass in Santiago's voice rang throughout the condo. "Amaya!"

The color drained from my face. My heartrate increased as I jumped from my bed. Marley matched my speed, exiting my room before I did.

"Amaya! Amaya, where you at girl? I hope you ain't still mad."

Marley rounded the corner and was met by Santiago.

"What the fuck are you doing here?"

"I was looking for you," he lied, creating a story in his mind as he spoke. "I wanted to see if Amaya knew where you were."

"And you just bust in here like you own the place? You didn't even knock. What would she be mad at you for? What's going on?"

"Nothing."

"So why's she mad at you? If anyone has a right to be mad, it should be me. You're out here running the streets, and now I catch you over my best friend's house. You two must really think I'm stupid."

She turned toward me and I stepped back. Only a few feet separated me from the cold glare in her eyes. Her chest heaved up and down in anger. I knew how it looked, and I could only imagine what was going through her head.

"Amaya. What the fuck is going on?" The harshness in her tone didn't match the sadness in her face. She was hurt. The tears forming in her eyes only confirmed it.

"It's not what it looks like," I pleaded, slowly inching backward.

"Well, what is it then?" She took a step toward me, and a look that I'd never seen before crossed her face. I was scared. Scared of what she might do to me. This wasn't the Marley I knew. This was a woman out for blood, and at that time, I was her target.

"Marley, baby listen to me. I told you why I'm here. We can talk about this at home." Santiago advanced toward her turned back and wrapped his arms around her waist. "Baby, I just wanted to know where you were."

She pushed his arms off her waist with enough force for the both of us. "Don't fucking touch me!" She turned her attention back to me. "I thought we were friends."

"Damn nigga, you flew over here didn't you?" Armando reentered my condo, with a plastic bag in hand. "I left the store before you did. How'd you get here faster than me?"

"Wait. You saw Santi at the store?" Marley quizzed.

"Yeah." Armando advanced further into the room as if he hadn't just walked into a tense situation. "He told me he was looking for you. I told him you were here. I hope you ain't mad at me. He said he called Amaya earlier looking for you, and she gave him an ear full. You know how my sister can be." He chuckled, and sat the bag on a nearby end table. "By the way, here's your beer bro."

Armando retrieved a bottled *Dos Equis* from the bag and handed it to Santiago. "Look what else I got." He held up a brand new pack of playing cards. "Who wants to be my partner?"

"Me!" I yelled, a little too excitedly.

I tried to quickly walk past Marley, but she managed to grab my arm. Pulling me close, she wrapped her arms around me and whispered in my ear. "I'm sorry, Amaya. I should have never questioned you."

"It's okay."

"No, it's not. I should have known that you would never do anything like that to me. I'm so sorry. I love you."

"I love you too, Marley."

Tears filled my eyes during the exchange. I was emotional, and trying to calm myself down from almost getting caught up. Once again, Armando was my life-saver. He walked in at just the right time and deescalated what could have been a tragic situation.

I held on to Marley much longer than I needed to. It was the guilt in me. I needed her to know that I was there for her, and nothing was going to change that. She loved me like a sister. Fucked up or not, I really did love her too.

10

MARLEY

*C*ashmere and I had grown close over a short period of time. He was always popping up on me; wanting to give me all his time and attention. I didn't mind. Cashmere was giving me the attention that my husband refused to. I was starting to enjoy spending time with him; maybe a little too much. I did miss my husband, but it was nice having someone show some interest in me.

I was driving around town trying to calm my nerves before I headed to Cashmere's house. He was tired from working all night and wanted to see me. I can't lie; I wanted to see him too. He had become a constant thing on my mind and it scared me. I found myself thinking about him when I should have been thinking about Santi. Damn. What am I getting myself into? I love the feeling that Cashmere gives me. It's so fresh and new and I've been welcoming it with open arms.

My thoughts drifted to the other night at Amaya's house. I trusted Amaya and Santiago, but once again, my woman's intuition was saying otherwise. Why did this feeling keep coming back? I just wanted it to go away so I could be happy and content. Maybe I need to dig a little deeper and listen to it.

I haven't talked to Santi all day. He said he had some business to handle and he didn't know what time he would be back. Like always. Usually, I would whine and cry and throw small fits to get him to come home earlier. But, not today. Today, I was just like cool. I'll see you when I do. I was tired of sitting at home while he was out all day. Cashmere got me out of the house and my mind off all the 'what ifs' about where and what Santi was really doing. I had my doubts, but I had to keep reminding myself that I trusted him and that he would never cheat on me. At least I hope not.

My phone rang loudly and I knew who it was. I was running a little behind and Cashmere didn't like waiting. He was all about punctuality. I smirked as I glanced at my caller ID and saw his name flashing across the screen. Taking a deep breath, I pressed the button on my steering wheel to answer the call.

"Hello?" I sang.

"Where are you?" He questioned with a pinch of irritation in his voice.

"I'm close."

"Don't keep me waiting much longer, Marley. I hate waiting," he stated and I laughed.

"Yes, daddy." I joked in a flirtatious tone.

"What I tell you about that?"

"About what?" I giggled, playing dumb.

"Don't start anything you can't finish, girl. You don't want me to get my hands on you. I can't promise you I won't be able to control the beast once you wake him," he stated in a cocky manner; instantly making me gush. Santi and I haven't had sex since the shower episode and the more I was around Cashmere, the harder it was to contain my sexual attraction to him.

"I can tame him," I challenged just as I pulled into his estate. "I'm here." I informed him and then hung up. The gates opened and I drove up the driveway to his front door. The outside of Cashmere's house was absolutely breathtaking. I couldn't wait to explore the inside.

Two men greeted me and led me inside the house. Cashmere was leaning against a wall, watching me intently. I bit down on my bottom lip as I lustfully gazed at him. He was comfortable; completely different from what he usually wore. He had on some black basketball shorts that hung loosely at his hips and showed off the waistband of his *Tom Ford* boxers. His blood red V-neck shirt clung to his body; showing off the veins in his muscular arms. Damn this man is fine.

"Welcome to my home, Marley." He greeted me, reaching for my hand. I happily placed it in his as he gave me a tour of the house.

"Your house is beautiful. I bet your sister loves staying here," I complimented as we went inside of his home movie theater.

"She does," He chuckled. "She's spoiled, but she's the reason I go as hard as I do. She doesn't want or need for anything, but at the same time I taught her to value what she has. Nothing in life is free. I work hard for everything I have and I try to pass that same thought process on to Kensley."

"I'm sure you're doing a great job."

"I try. How has your day been? You're looking very sexy today," he approved, licking his thick lips sexily. I could picture myself sucking his juicy, succulent lips right off his face.

"Thank you," I blushed, spinning around to let him get a better view. "My day has been good. Seeing you has made it better."

"Is that right?" He quizzed with a raised brow, grabbing me by the waist and pulling me into his body. His hands traveled down my back and rested on the top of my ass while mine rested lightly on his shoulders.

"Yes."

"You've made mine a lot better also. If you didn't get here soon, I was coming to find you. I've been working nonstop. Now that I have a free moment, I'd rather spend it with you. Come sit." He motioned for me to sit down in one of the fluffy, plush chairs. I sat down and he snuggled in close to me; his face only inches away from mine. I held my breath as he lightly kissed my cheek with his hand resting on my thigh. Clearing my throat, I scooted away from him a few inches and blushed.

"Can I tell you about what happened the other day?" I asked in all seriousness. Santi's pop up at Amaya's house went off like a light bulb in my head and I wanted to get Cashmere's opinion on it.

"Why not?" Cashmere said, pulling his right ankle on to his left knee. "Speak."

I told him everything from Santi running into Armando at the gas station to us all playing cards at the end of the night. He looked me in the eyes and listened intently as I rambled on about how I was suspicious of what was going on; nodding his head every so often. I felt so comfortable and open with him. It felt good to know that he was genuinely interested in what I had to say.

"So, what do you think?" I asked him after I was done explaining.

"You want me to be honest?"

"Of course. I wouldn't have asked for your opinion if I really didn't want to know," I said with an attitude and he laughed.

"Damn, Marley. Stop being so feisty, girl." He chuckled and those sexy dimples appeared. "I only asked because I'm brutally honest. I don't bite my tongue or sugarcoat a damn thing for anyone. I will give it to you straight like a shot of liquor and won't give you time to let the burn go away. I'm harsh and I just wanted to make sure you could take it."

"I'm a big girl. I can take it."

"What else can you take?" He pondered with lust in his tone and hunger in his bedroom eyes. My eyes traveled down to the bulge trying to break free from his basketball shorts. My mouth watered as I thought of how he tasted. Probably like some creamy dark chocolate. Delicious!

"Stop being nasty," I giggled while trying to hide my true emotions. "I want to hear your opinion."

Cashmere sat up and his shirt clung to every vein and muscle he had. He was flexing his hands; making his veins appear and then disappear. I found myself drooling over his masculinity. He was so damn sexy.

"Something is going on between them two. I know it." He stated with such confidence that it frightened me. Did he have some sort of proof? Was there something he knew that I didn't. Oh, fuck. It's getting hot in here.

"How…" Gulp. "How do you know?" I stammered. My mouth was dry and I was getting dizzy. I wasn't prepared to feel another heart break.

He gazed at me out the side of his eyes and sighed. "You said Santiago always has to work late nights and you know for a fact that it's not because of me, correct?"

I nodded my head yes.

"You said that Amaya always posts about some nigga that you've never even met and that y'all don't hang out like y'all used too, correct?"

I nodded my head yes again.

"Did you ever hear Amaya's phone go off when Santiago came barging inside? She had it, right?"

"Yes, it was right beside… her…" My voice trailed off as I thought back to that night and remember her phone being right beside her the entire time. Not once did it ring.

Cashmere shrugged his shoulders and threw his hands in the air. "Just pay attention to your surroundings, Marley. Shit can be happening right in front of your eyes and you are too blind to see it. Pay attention."

He lifted my chin so I could raise my head. We gazed at one another for what felt like an eternity before his soft, succulent lips came crashing into mine. I tried to resist. I continued to repeat to myself over and over that we were just friends. This wasn't right. But damn, it sure did feel good.

His tongue parted my lips and danced with mine. He pulled me in close; gripping my thighs and placing me on his lap. My sundress came up and he roughly massaged my bare ass and a low, breathy moan escaped my lips. His thick, hard member rubbed against my sheer thong; tingling my insides and it gently rubbed against my swollen, tender clit.

His strong, coarse hands roamed my body as I grinded myself against him. Our kiss deepened and I was soaking wet. I knew his shorts would have a stain from my juices. He kissed me with so much passion; like he had been waiting to do that from the moment he laid eyes on me. His kiss made me weak. Weaker than I expected. That's how I knew I was falling for him.

My phone rang loudly and the ringtone signaled it was Santi. Breaking away from Cashmere, I leaned over and answered the phone.

"Hello?" I answered, trying not to sound out of breath.

"Where are you?" Santi asked.

"Out."

"Well, come home. I need to talk to you," he demanded and I could hear the smile in his voice.

"About what?" I tried to get up from Cashmere's lap, but he pinned my thighs down. He lifted my sundress and used his thumb to rub my clit. Leaning my head back and sinking my teeth into my bottom lip, I fought hard to suppress the moan tickling the back of my throat. I was going to kill him.

"No questions, Ley. Come home." He stated firmly then hung up.

"Are you leaving me for him?" Cashmere pressed with a smirk on his face.

Before I could answer him, he flipped me on my back and pinned my legs to the chair. In one swift motion, he pushed my thong to the side; revealing my dripping wet, pink pussy. Hungrily licking his lips, he smirked before diving in and devouring my hot spot.

He should have given me a warning or something. The way he was eating me had me climbing the walls. I was speechless. I couldn't even moan as I felt his stiff tongue deeply penetrate my love box; in and out, in and out. My breathing quickened. I was on the brink of a strong orgasm. I thought Santi's head game was fierce, but Cashmere had him beat by a long shot.

Just as I was about to release my phone blared Santi's ringtone again. I tried to get up, but Cashmere glared up at me with my juices covering his mouth and shook his head no.

"I have to finish my meal first," he stated firmly and picked back up where he started.

He flicked his tongue across my clit and my juices oozed out of me. He licked me clean then kissed my lips softly.

"You better go before he calls you again and I answer the phone. I don't think he would like that too well, do you?"

I shook my head no and tried to get my breathing under control. I was still on cloud nine from my amazing orgasm. I wasn't ready to come down just yet, but I had to get home. Damn! Why did Santi have to be early today of all days?

Cashmere disappeared and came back with a warm, soapy wash cloth. He took his time cleaning me; inspecting my body.

"You are one fine woman, Marley." He complimented me and I blushed.

"Thank you."

"You know what this means, right?" He questioned with laughter in his voice.

"What?" I raised my brow and cocked my head to the side.

"You're mine now. You better not go home and give Santi *my* pussy? Do you understand? Trust and believe that I will find out if you do. Nothing gets past me."

11

SANTIAGO

*M*arley came home and went straight to the bathroom. She bypassed me and the meal I had prepared for her without as much as a second look. Water shooting out of the shower-head could be heard shortly thereafter. I tried to open the door, but it was locked.

"Marley!" I said, pounding my fist on the door.

"What?"

"Whatchu got the door locked for?"

"I'm taking a shower. I'll be out in a minute."

Now, I can't even begin to describe what was going through my head. Usually when I came home and strolled straight to the bathroom it was due to one of two reasons: I needed to use the bathroom, or I needed to wash something off of me; if you know what I mean. I didn't hear the toilet flush, so that could have only meant one thing. I gritted my teeth and knocked again, this time with more force.

"I said open the fucking door!"

Click.

I turned the knob and pushed the door open. I caught a glimpse of her naked ass stepping back into the shower. When she tried to close the glass door behind her, I stepped forward, grabbing a firm hold of the handle.

"What are you doing?" she asked.

"Looking at my wife. Is that a crime?" I actually waited for her response. Instead of answering me, she acted as if I wasn't even there, positioning her body under the stream of water. "Ley...that was a question."

"Look all you want. It's a free country." She turned her body toward me, allowing the water to saturate her hair. I focused in on those hardened nipples of hers, begging for my attention. When I grabbed one, she slapped my hand away.

"Will you stop?" she whined, rolling her eyes.

I didn't know whether to be offended, or turned on. Either way, she was my wife, and I could touch her if I wanted to.

I took off my shirt and shorts before freeing my growing erection from the confines of my boxer briefs. It was hard for me not to notice a beautiful woman, and at that moment, my wife was the most beautiful woman I'd ever seen. Her beauty was natural and effortless. Marley could step out in an oversized shirt and sweats and still be the baddest on the block. That's what drew me to her in the first place. I knew I hit the lottery when she became my wife. Now, I wanted to reap my reward.

She didn't protest when I joined her. I slid right on in behind her, where I belonged. I allowed my hands to explore her back and shoulders. She tensed up, but didn't ask me to stop. That was, until my hands ventured from the back to the front, and cupped her firm breasts.

"Santi, come on now. Stop."

She had to be playing. I mean, Ley had never turned me down before. I ignored her, and allowed my hands to fall to the sud-filled entrance to her paradise.

"I said stop Santi," she warned.

With my index and middle fingers, I parted her lower lips and exposed her clit. I rubbed her hardened pearl and whispered in her ear. "Do you really want me to stop?"

Her silence was confirmation for me to continue. She leaned back into me as I touched the private spot that was mine, and mine alone. She was super wet, and as I inserted 2 of my fingers inside her, she backed it up right on me. I wasn't the best at a lot of things, but I sure could please a woman.

I fell to my knees and slurped up her juices, suds and all. My baby must've been feeling some kind of way because her shit was steadily flowing in my direction. I lapped it up, allowing my wife to release right on the tip of my tongue. It was quick. Damn quick. I ain't gonna lie, it pumped my head up a little bit. I still had it.

Standing, I allowed her to return the favor, but she blew me off with a simple, "thank you." My dick was as stiff as a pole and Marley was playing.

"Come on Ley," I urged, holding my erection in my hand. Maybe if she got a good look at what I was working with, she would change her mind. I was so horny, pre-cum oozed from the tip. Still, she paid me no mind.

She lathered her body again and rinsed herself clean. I grabbed her arm as she shut the water off and attempted to step out.

"Marley," I pleaded, looking into her eyes. I tried a different tactic, "Baby, come on. I want to be inside you. I miss being inside you."

"And I want you to come home every night," she snapped. "Looks like we're both out of luck. Excuse me." She stepped out the shower, leaving me standing there with a hard-on and a bruised ego.

Her statement grabbed at my heart and twisted it in my chest. Everything that I had done to make the day special for my wife didn't negate the fact that she felt neglected. I was her husband, her provider, her protector. I was supposed to be the one that she confided in, and told her inner most secrets to. Instead, I was slipping. As my life became complicated juggling two women, my main chick's needs weren't being met. I had to do something about that. Unsatisfied woman usually sought comfort elsewhere. I learned that lesson from my parent's divorce. My father ran the streets and in return, my mother let his friends run up in her. I guess you could say it was an even trade off. I didn't want that to be the outcome for me and Marley. I needed to make some changes, and soon.

I grabbed a towel, drying my naked body as I walked to my room. Marley was sitting on the bed, applying her favorite floral scented lotion to her already smooth skin. I was tempted to reach out, and help her. I wanted to feel those fireworks that went off every time we touched. Unfortunately, the doorbell rang, interrupting the mood. Marley was on her feet within seconds, grabbing a silk robe from the back of her vanity chair. I kept it gangsta, wrapping the towel I used to dry off my body snuggly around my waist. Curiously, I followed Marley to the door. Cash stood on the other side in an all-white linen shirt and matching pants.

"Aww, shit. Am I interrupting something?" he asked, watching Marley tighten her robe's belt around her waist.

"Not at all, come in," Marley reassured.

He entered the house, and stood in the middle of the floor. I couldn't help but notice him checking out my wife as she passed by. He wasn't even trying to hide it. His eyes followed her jiggling ass as she disappeared into the bedroom, leaving us alone.

"So what brings you by? And unannounced, I might add."

"I was in the area. I thought you might wanna join me for a drink or two. One of my boys popped the question to his chick the other day. They're going to the courthouse tomorrow, but he's trying to get loose tonight. You should roll with us."

"Where y'all going?" I questioned.

"The Godfather."

"Y'all have fun." I wasn't interested in seeing stiff, flat asses. There was enough of that showing for free on basic cable.

"You sure? I know a few of the dancers." He pulled his phone from his pocket and scrolled through the screens as he spoke. "They're coming in just for the night."

"Yeah, I'm sure. I'ma chill with Ley. She's mad I ain't been home much lately."

Cash passed me his phone. All I saw was ass and more ass. Two brown-skinned cuties graced the screen, sticking their fingers in the intimate cracks and crevices of each other's body. The homemade video wasn't the best quality, but I saw enough to make me change my mind.

"What time should I be ready?"

Cash chuckled and took his phone back. "My man...I see we got the same taste. My driver's out in the car. I'm ready now. How long's it gonna take you?"

I told him to give me 10 minutes. He chose to wait for me in the car, and I entered my bedroom to get ready. Marley was in her night-gown, sitting on the bed, with a book in her hand. I entered our large walk-in closet and chose a plaid button-down shirt, and black Dickie shorts. I slipped my feet into a pair of all black Js and walked back into the room to add my jewelry. Marley was now laying in the bed, but that damn book was still in her hands.

"I'm about to step out," I mentioned, placing my gold rope chain with a large cross pendant around my neck. "Dinner is in the oven."

"Ok," she said simply.

"I'm not sure what time I'll be back."

She turned the page to her book and kept reading.

"Ley, did you hear me?"

"Yeah, I heard you."

"You ain't gonna ask me where I'm going?"

"No."

I hesitated before placing my newly purchased diamond studs in my ear. "You don't care that I'm going out?"

Her eyes lifted from the pages of her book and found mine. She gave me a long, bored look. "You work late with Cash almost every night, remember? What makes tonight any different?"

Damn. She had a point. I probably should've stayed, but tempta-tion wouldn't allow me to. I needed to see those bitches on Cash's video in the flesh. A threesome with one of them riding my face and another riding my dick was calling my name; even though they didn't know it yet.

I attempted to kiss her goodbye, but she turned her head and my lips grazed her cheek instead. I told her that I loved her, but she didn't reciprocate a response. I made a mental note to take my girl out tomorrow. Everything would be put on hold; Amaya, Cash, the streets, other bitches, everything. Tomorrow was going to be her day, but tonight was mine.

THE DISAPPOINTMENT I felt when I found out that the two hoes I was trying to see were a no-show was short lived. The packed house had an array of beautiful women, both on stage and off. It wasn't the typical scene for the Godfather and I was actually impressed. Women with various colors, shapes, and sizes took their turns shaking their money-makers, some better than others.

We arrived late, and as I sat with Cash and his friend Tyrone at one of the back tables in the large, dimly lit room, I was immediately approached by a fiery red head with a pair of oversized titties.

"You want a dance?" she asked, running her soft hands along my shoulders. Vanilla wasn't my preferred flavor, and her capital 'P' shape didn't warrant a second look. I gave her a once over and passed her off to Cash's friend. "He's getting married tomorrow," I said pointing to Tyrone. "I think he needs the dance more than me."

She was on him in seconds, and I directed my attention to the dark-skinned beauty walking toward our table. I definitely wasn't gonna pass her up, but as she bypassed me and approached Cash, she made the decision for me.

I hid my jealousy by walking away. I muscled my way through the thick crowd until I reached the bar. The announcer came on the loud speaker and introduced the next act. Her name was Odyssey and I don't remember anything the announcer said after that. The room went black and a spotlight shined right in the middle of the stage. She sashayed to the spotlight wearing only what she came into the world in. Ole girl wasn't playing around. Enough money to leave her satisfied for the night was thrown on stage before the music even started. I fully intended to add to her collection, but the citrus scent that hit my nose demanded my attention.

"April, I need a rum and coke," a scantily dressed dancer requested with her hand on her hip. I eyed her seductively. "Oh, I'm sorry. Did you order yet?" she asked, turning to me.

"Nah. I'm still deciding."

"Sorry about that. It's been a busy night. I ain't trying to be rude. Take your time." She turned back to the bartender, "Hold up, April. Go ahead and take his order first. I'll be back. Let me see if anyone else at the table wants anything. It'll save me a second trip."

I watched her as she hurried off to an awaiting table. She said something to the group, and a big nigga with a low cut fade pulled her onto his lap. He whispered something in her ear, and she got up with a scowl on her face. Tuning out the howls for Odyssey on stage, I was more interested in the cutie headed back in my direction.

"April, make that 2 Bud Lights, a Long Island iced tea, and a rum and coke."

"So that's 2 rum and cokes, Nina?"

"No, just 1."

I smiled when the girl turned to me and added, "You did order, right?"

"Nah, but go ahead. Ladies first; especially when they're as beautiful as you." I licked my lips and pushed my dreads off my shoulders.

"Those tired lines don't work around here, but thank you anyway." Nina gave me a wink and took the large serving tray handed to her by the bartender.

For the second time that night, I was in my feelings. I tried to relax with a shot of Hennessey straight to the head. 5 minutes later, Nina was shaking her ass on the guy with the fade and I wasn't even buzzed yet. I ordered another shot and downed that one just as quickly as the first.

I began walking back to my table. I inadvertently bumped into several people making their way to the stage. Someone grabbed my arm, and when I turned around, Nina was standing behind me. She used her index finger to gesture for me to follow. She pulled me into a corner and began gyrating her ass against my dick.

"Let's get outta here," I said, wrapping my arms around her waist.

She removed my hands and spun around so fast I was sure her neck caught whiplash. "I don't get down like that. I ain't no prostitute."

Nina had the nerve to look offended; like I said the worst thing in the world. We were in a strip club after all. Pussy was on the menu. That's what the niggas and a few bitches came for in the first place.

What she refused to do, the red-head I'd met earlier gladly did. She was done teasing Tyrone, and now she was back on to me. I flashed a couple hundred in her face and she fell to her knees and took my dick in her mouth. We were behind the building, and I wanted to see if she could make her mouth do what her body couldn't. After all, she wasn't my type.

I don't even remember her name. Was it Karen? Or Lisa? Who knows. Don't get me to lying. All I know is that she eased the head of my dick into her mouth, and struggled to take in the rest. Licking the sides of my shaft did nothing for me, but she made noises like she was giving me the best dome of my life. Her head game was garbage. I returned my dick back to my pants without even busting a nut. Throwing a single dollar on the ground, I paid her what she was worth and met up with Cash and Tyrone in the front.

"Where you been, man?" Cash quizzed, watching me fumble with my zipper.

"Wasting my time. Y'all out?"

"Yeah. Tyrone's girl just hit his phone. It's past his bedtime."

Two red blotches formed on Tyrone's cheeks. "I'm a grown-ass man. I ain't got no bedtime."

"Yeah, right. When Nay calls, you know it's time to get your ass home." Cash chuckled, and I joined in.

Tyrone was the color of sand, with brown hair and light eyes. His glasses gave him a dorky appearance. He was cool though; he just didn't look cool.

"Fuck you. You too, Santi. I see you over there laughing."

I laughed even harder. Tyrone was a funny looking mothafucka.

Cash and I rode around town for a while chain smoking 2 blunts. It was after 2AM when Cash's driver dropped me off. Marley was snoring softly when I entered our room. I pulled the thick comforter back to join my wife in bed. That's when I noticed that the silk night-gown she wore conveniently hiked up, exposing her full, heart shaped ass. It was a sign. The tease I received at the club was nothing compared to the treasure I had laying in my bed. I was horny as fuck. I wanted to release. I needed to release, but I didn't want to do it solo.

Marley didn't wake up when I eased her onto her stomach. I positioned myself on top of her, and spread her cheeks with my hands. Her opening glistened. My girl was already wet; another indication that I was giving her exactly what she wanted. I slid my stiff pole inside her slowly, careful not to wake her. With each thrust, her pussy muscles contracted, pulling me in deeper. She could pretend to be mad at me all she wanted, but her pussy didn't lie.

Her warm nectar coated my dick as I slid in and out. It was hard to contain myself. Just when I had my own rhythm going, Marley started fucking me back! I don't know how she did it, but somehow while still sleeping, she managed to throw it back at me. That shit turned me the fuck on. I removed my shirt and really gave it to her. I pounded that pussy with no mercy. As my body tensed and stilled, I tried to pull out, but it was feeling too damn good. My soldiers released right inside her. Damn. I should've used a condom.

12
CASHMERE

*I*t was the night of prom for Kensley. She wasn't quite old enough to be taking a date herself, but some little nigga she called herself liking asked her to go and I couldn't say no to her. She begged and pleaded for a few days and I caved. We spent countless hours picking out the perfect dress, getting her pampered and ready. Since she didn't have a mother figure in her life, I had to do all the stuff mothers were supposed to do for prom. I didn't mind. Anything for my baby.

Now, grilling this little nigga, I was regretting even saying yes to Kensley's spoiled ass. His name was Tobias. He was about six foot even and had the aura of a player. His demeanor was cocky and that wasn't allowed in my presence. He had a fake, wide smile plastered on his face and he was trying to show that he was a respectful, young man, but I could see right through him. It was easy for me to read people.

We were waiting downstairs for Kensley and her friend. Like all females they were taking forever, so I decided to text Marley and set up a date while Kensley would be out. I needed to know what happened when Santiago made it home last night.

Me: Hey, beautiful. How are you today?

Marley: I'm good. How about you?

I glanced up at Tobias who was texting on his phone and smiling a little too hard for me. He would peek up at the stairs every now and then to see if Kensley appeared. The more I studied him the heavier the feeling of deadin' this prom shit weighed on me.

Me: I'm good. Will I see you today?

Marley: Only if you want to.

Me: Of course. Would you like to see me?

Marley: Yes.

Kensley cleared her throat and my attention went straight to her. My little sister was absolutely gorgeous. She wore a teal mermaid dress with slits on the side and a split that stopped at her knee. We had gotten her jewelry and shoes custom made just the way she wanted them. Diamonds graced her ears and her neck that damn near cost as much as our small city house we were in.

The house was in Fern Creek. It wasn't anything elaborate or fancy. In fact, only minor changes had been made since I purchased the foreclosure. The sole purpose for the house was to keep people out of my business. I didn't like strangers knowing where I laid my head. In my business, that could be the difference between life and death. After meeting Tobias, I'm glad we met him at the staged house instead of the main house. Something about him was off.

"You look gorgeous," I complemented Kensley with a smile as I helped her down the stairs. Tobias was just standing there with his mouth slightly agape and wide eyes. He could look and drool all he wanted, but he better not lay a finger on her. Hell, I didn't even want them holding hands or dancing, but I couldn't be like that.

After we got a few pictures at the house, the photographer took us to a park to take some more. I instructed Toney to follow close behind them since Kensley didn't want me to ride with them. I told them I could ride in the backseat and just have Toney come pick me up once they were done, but Kensley gave me one of the meanest of mugs, so I backed off. Homeboy just better watch himself.

"I'm going to be fine, Cash." Ken tried to reassure me. "Don't worry. I'll be home on time. Not one second late. I promise."

"I don't know, Ken. Something about that little nigga ain't sitting right with me." I informed her with a scowl. "I just can't put my finger on it."

"I think you're just being paranoid," she admitted with a laugh. "You always get like this when I'm going out."

"Not always. Just when I know something isn't right and I'm always correct, aren't I?" I questioned with a smirk and she rolled her eyes. She knew I was right. Hell, I knew I was right but I always let her con me into seeing her side of things.

"Whatever. You're not always right," she spat. "It's my first prom, Cash. Just let me go out and have fun with my friends. That's all I want to do."

See what I mean?

"Alright," I gave in with a sigh. "If something starts not to feel right with you, you better call me."

"You know I will. I love you, brother."

"I love you too, baby girl."

I watched as they walked away, hand in hand. He opened the door for her and once he closed it he glanced over at me. I held a cold, hard stare. He was up to something. I could see it in his movements. Like I told Marley, I am a good judge of character. Amaya isn't her real friend and Tobias isn't what he trying to show me he is.

"Follow them," I demanded Toney as Kensley and Tobias drove away. I jogged and got in the passenger side of the truck. "Close, but not too close."

We weaved in and out of traffic while staying a few feet behind. My gut was telling me something was about to go down, but I didn't want to ruin the night for Kensley if I was wrong. So, like the overprotective big brother I was, I staked out a few feet away from the school and texted her randomly to see if she was okay.

I wanted to see Marley, but I couldn't risk anything going down. Since it was just Toney and me, I called her up to explain why I hadn't reached out anymore.

"Hello?" She answered with attitude. I chuckled because I loved that shit. It done something to me.

"Is that how you greet me now, Marley? I thought we were better than that."

"I thought so too," she snapped back.

"Watch your tone when you're talking to me. I don't want to have to punish you. Now, what are you doing? And that attitude better be gone when you answer me," I demanded and I could picture her face now; biting down on her soft, juicy bottom lip with gazing at me with lust-filled eyes.

"I'm waiting on Amaya. And you?" She answered with a little more perkiness in her voice.

"That's better," I acknowledged. "I'm sitting in front of Kensley's school."

"Why?"

"She's at the prom with some little nigga and I'm not feeling him. He was rubbing me the wrong way," I admitted with my eyes glued to the doors of the school.

"Let her breathe, Cashmere. I'm sure you're just worried about her. She will be fine," Marley tried to convince me, but I wasn't hearing it.

"Nah. Like I told you before, I can read people and he didn't sit right with me. His background check came back clear, but he presence said otherwise."

"Wait," she giggled. "You did a background check on him?"

"Hell yeah. I do one on everybody. I know people before I know them, understand?"

The line went silent.

"Marley?"

"I'm still here."

"When can I taste you again?"

Before she could answer, Toney tapped my shoulder to get my attention and pointed. I followed his finger and had to do a double take. It was Kelsie. Well, at least I thought it was. She looked different, but in a good way. Her usual dirty, tattered clothes were clean and free from holes and stains. Her hair was braided into two big braids and she had gained some weight. I can't lie; she looked like she was doing good for herself. I wonder what made her have a change of heart.

Something in the alley must have caught Kelsie's eye because she stopped in her tracks and studied whatever it was before taking off running full speed. Curiosity got the best of me. I ended the call with Marley and told Toney to keep an eye out for Kensley.

I got out the car and jogged towards the alley when I heard someone yelling and crying. The voice was all too familiar. It was Kensley. I ran full speed around the corner just in time to see Kelsie knock Tobias over the head with a plank while Kensley held onto her ripped dress with black tears streaming down her face. After that all I saw was red.

Pow! Pow! Pow!

"Cashmere!" Kensley screamed, snapping me from my trance.

"Ken, go and get in the truck! NOW!" I demanded and she obeyed. Kelsie was right on her heels, rubbing her back to console her.

My mind was a blur. I was enraged. I don't know what the fuck this little nigga done to my sister, but he was about to feel my wrath. He laid there on the ground, holding his ears with blood leaking from an open wound. I didn't shoot him; just fired off warning shots. I wouldn't ever do anything like that in front of Ken because she was too delicate. If she saw something like that it would traumatize her. She knew what kind of work I was into, but not everything and I wanted to keep it that way.

Kneeling down beside him, I pressed the gun to his head and watched as he began to sob like a baby.

"Pl... Please don't kill me. I'm sorry!" Tobias cried, begging for his life.

"What in the fuck did you do to my sister?" I interrogated, pushing my piece deeper into his temple.

"I... I'm sorry! I... I just... please, don't kill me!" He pleaded with sincerity in his voice. "I'm so sorry, man. I...I promise I'll do whatever you want me to!"

"You better be glad you're just a child or I would have your brain matter splattered all over this fuckin' wall. Now, what you are going to do is go home and stay the fuck away from my sister. If I even think you glance her way, I'm coming for you and I mean that shit. I don't make any promises that I don't keep. Get the fuck on before I change my mind."

In one swift motion, he hopped up and dashed down the alley and around the corner. My blood was boiling over and my trigger finger was itching. He had fucked with the wrong one. I was going to wait a few years until he got older to put a hot one in his dome. I let him go today for the sake of Kensley and his age. I didn't do harm to children, but he had to grow up one day and I was going to be waiting for him. Ready.

Damn! I got myself together and ran back to the truck where Kelsie was still comforting Ken. Kensley's wet face was pressed against Kelsie's as she rocked her back and forth, lowly singing a song. It would have been a beautiful moment if Kelsie had actually been a mother to her.

"You okay, baby girl?" I asked Kensley, pulling her away from Kelsie and wrapping my arms around her. She covered her face with her hands and laid her forehead against my shoulder blade. The soft sound of her weeping only infuriated me more. My finger was itching so bad to kill Tobias now that it was burning. Fuck, man.

"H... he tried... to rape me, Cash! I kept telling him no, but he wouldn't stop! He kept touching me and pulling on my dress. I fought him off long enough to run away, but he caught up to me in the alley. Everything from there was a blur until she came along and saved me," she explained, pointing to Kelsie. "I would have had to kill him if she didn't come."

That was why she was so upset. She almost had to catch her first body. Kensley was soft, but gutter like me. I had taught her how to kill someone with her bare hands for shit like this. She hated the thought of killing someone or seeing someone killed/ It bothered her in the worst way, but with the work I do I had to make sure she could protect herself. I was open with Ken, but I kept a lot of shit from her too. It was complicated, but somehow we managed.

"Thank you so much for saving me," Ken thanked Kelsie.

"Anytime," she smiled and glared at me. I hit her with a head nod and helped Kensley into the passenger seat of the truck. I made sure she was secure and shut the door before turning my attention to Kelsie who was standing there with her hands on her hip.

"Thank you. I really appreciate you doing that," I said honestly. "I don't know what I would have done if something happened to her."

"You don't have to thank me. She's my daughter," she had the audacity to say.

"I wouldn't say that," I chuckled to keep from getting mad. "She's my sister. That's all."

"Don't do that, Cashmere. Look at me! Can't you see that I'm trying? I've been clean for a month now. I'm going to rehab and classes to help me get through this. They're even trying to help me get a job. I... I just want to be in her life," she admitted on the verge of tears. "I didn't even know it was her when I looked down the alley. I just saw a young girl needing help and I went to rescue her. When I saw it was her, that's when the mother in me came out. I did the first thing that came to mind and that was protect my child. For the first time in forever I felt like a mother."

I laughed deeply and started slow clapping. She was putting on one hell of a show.

"Don't feed me that bullshit, Kelsie. You've done this exact shit before, so why should I believe you this time? I love Kensley too damn much to put her in the position to get hurt anymore. Tonight was already too much on her. She can't handle anything else so soon," I paused to reach in my pocket and peeled off two racks for her. "Here, stay clean and don't backtrack. Go get you some professional help and get your shit together, Kelsie. Once I start noticing some change in you, then *maybe*, I will allow you to be a part of Ken's life. Until then, work on you."

I stuffed the money in her hand and hopped inside the truck, leaving her there with a lot of shit to think about. I was going to let her actions do the talking for her.

13

AMAYA

I was sitting on the couch when Santiago strolled in. He held a nice sized box in his hand. Immediately, my interest was piqued. A bright red bow sat atop the white box. I loved gifts!

"I got something for you," he said, sitting down next to me.

"What is it?" I leaned into him and kissed him on the lips.

"Open it."

I took the box from him and felt movement inside. What the hell? Unraveling the bow, I slid the top off to see an energetic Maltese puppy. It was hard to hide my disdain. Marley came by earlier in a new whip and I got a damn dog. Talk about disappointed.

"You don't like it?"

"It's nice," I downplayed. "I was just thinking you would get me something more...you know, useful."

"It's the thought that counts."

I grabbed the puppy out of the box and examined between its legs. It was a male, and he took an immediate liking to the remote control next to me. I swatted his nose when he began chewing on it.

"Don't hit him." Santiago placed the dog in his lap and rubbed him lovingly.

"Don't tell me what to do with *my* dog." I reached out my hands for Santiago to return the dog back to me, but he didn't.

"He's just a puppy. He doesn't know any better yet."

"Give him here."

"No."

"I thought it was a gift." I rolled my eyes and scooted to the edge of the couch. "You know what, if you're going to tell me how to discipline my dog, maybe you should keep him."

I stormed off, pulling my small, boy shorts down as I walked. I let my frustration get the best of me. The past few days, Santi had been spending more time with Marley. He'd been sending me to voicemail, showing up at my place whenever he felt like it. Up until recently, he felt like it almost daily. Now, I was seeing him for the first time in almost 3 days. To make matters worse, Marley was now driving the car of my dreams.

"Amaya, what's up?"

Santiago followed me to my bedroom. I eased into my king-sized bed, hoping that he would get the message. I didn't want to be bothered; at least by him.

"So, you're gonna act like you don't hear me talking to you?" he barked, walking over to my side.

I shifted my position; turning away from him.

"It's like that, hunh? I bring you a gift and now you're mad? Spoiled bitches," he mumbled, sparking my anger.

"The spoiled bitch is at home!" I sat up in my bed and peered at him with malice in my eyes. He had some nerve.

"There you go! Why you gotta bring Marley into this?"

"How are you gonna buy her a new car and bring me a dog? Where's my car? I do just as much for you as she does. Maybe even more."

He sat the dog down, allowing him to freely roam my room.

"So that's what this is about? You're mad because I bought my wife a car?"

I knew it sounded crazy, but that's exactly how I felt.

"Yes!"

He walked the perimeter of the room and stopped in front of my large window. Pulling the curtains to the side, he peered out into the half-full parking lot.

"This shit gotta stop. You can't be mad at me for taking care of Marley. That's what I'm supposed to do. She's my wife!"

"And what am I?" I shot back. Tears streamed down my face as I stood to face him. "What am I, Santi? I've been riding with you for just as long. So what if she met you first. I don't care that you married her. I'm the one you want to be with. You lay in my bed and fuck me almost every night. That has to count for something."

"What the fuck do you want from me? I'm here ain't I?" he picked up the dog just as he was squatting to saturate my Persian rug with his urine. "I don't need this shit. I'm out."

That mothafucka had the nerve to take my dog with him! I followed behind, grabbing the nearest object within reach. It just happened to be my shoe, and I flung it in his direction. Missing his head by about two inches, the shoe hit the front door instead.

"Crazy bitch!"

"I got your bitch!"

He opened the door to leave. I ran toward him like a mad woman anyway, only to be greeted by Armando trying to enter at the same time. He had someone with him that I'd never seen before. I stopped suddenly, and tried to regain my composure. I was a lady after all.

"Yo, Armando, get your crazy ass sister. She's on one." Santiago briefly glanced in my direction before leaving all together. Armando and this new man stepped in my apartment and closed the door.

"What are you doing here?" I crossed my arms over my chest. He could've at least called first.

"I wanted to talk to you."

"Talk."

"Can you at least put some fuckin' clothes on first. I don't feel comfortable talking to my sister half-naked."

I looked down at my attire – boy shorts, and tank top. My hot spots were covered, but out of respect for my blood, I went to my room and slipped on my robe. I returned to the same spot, re-crossed my arms, and repeated, "Talk."

"This is Koda," Armando mentioned, pointing toward his friend.

"And?" I wasn't trying to be rude. I just wanted to know what everything had to do with me. I wasn't done with Santi yet. I still had to blow up his phone and make him feel guilty about the way he treated me. Dealing with my brother wasn't the best use of my time.

"Well, my man wanted to meet you in person. You're all over social media, and you caught his attention. I told him you were my sis, so here we are." He smiled as though he had just given some big speech. Give me a break.

"Why didn't you hit me up yourself?" I grilled, giving Koda a once over. I had to admit, he was cute, damn cute in fact. He was shorter than I liked, about 5'10 with skin the color of butter. Hazel eyes accented the dimple in each cheek. His shiny black hair was cut low, and was naturally wavy. He was a combination of Black and something else. Maybe Hispanic? I don't know, but the way he licked his lips and took a defensive stance had me intrigued.

"I thought about it, but I wanted to see you in person. You look good, ma. You got a man?"

What kind of tired line was that? Yes, I had a man. His name was Santiago, and unless Koda's money was as long as Santi's we had nothing to talk about. It was time to cut this conversation short.

"Look, Koda. It was nice meeting you, but I'm taken. My brother knows that." I eyed Armando suspiciously. "I'm sorry that you wasted your time."

He gave me a look that made me question my decision. He smiled, showing off a set of straight white teeth, surrounded by full, juicy lips. Damn. Why did he have to smile at me?

"I hope we didn't bother you. I'm sure I'll be seeing you around. Come on Armando. Let's get back to this money."

Money? Now he was speaking my language.

"Where y'all headed?" I tried to sound uninterested, but failed miserably.

"On the block. Why?" Armando hissed, turning his back to me. He gave Koda a nod, and they walked toward the door.

"Just asking." I chickened out at the last minute. Armando was angry that I dissed his boy. I could hear it in his voice.

They left, leaving me with my conscience. Maybe I should've given Koda a chance. It wasn't like Santi was leaving Marley. He was bouncing between 2 women. Why couldn't I bounce between 2 men? I quickly shook off that notion. I talked a good game, but the only dick that had been inside me in the last 7 years was Santi's.

I walked to my bedroom window and peered out of it. Armando and Koda were walking side-by-side until they reached a sporty, newer model Maserati. I knew that trident emblem well, and as Koda hopped in the driver's seat, my perception of him quickly changed. I grabbed my phone and sent Armando a quick text asking for Koda's number. There wasn't any shame in my game. His money was obviously longer than I thought.

I took a catnap and woke up feeling refreshed. Surprisingly, I didn't have any missed calls from Santi, but I did have 2 messages that needed my attention. I opened my brother's text first, and locked in Koda's number. I gave Koda the typical, "What's up?" text, and responded to Marley's text while I waited for his response.

Marley: Wanna get a pedicure with me?

Me: Sure. When?

Her response was instant.

Marley: Now. I sent that text an hour ago. I'm already here.

Me: Same spot?

Marley: Yes

Me: Be there in 15

I dressed quickly and combed my hair into a messy bun. I didn't throw on anything fancy; just fitted jeans and a halter. It was just going to be me and Marley. Besides, I'd yet to find anyone who could compete with me, even on my worse day.

It wasn't long before I was parked beside Marley's car, and strolling into the nail shop. I was greeted upon entry, and seated next to Marley.

"I didn't think you were coming," she said watching her toes being painted a fluorescent pink color.

"I told you I was." I leaned down and hugged her before unlacing the straps of my heeled sandals. "I was just a little – occupied."

"Occupied?" I had her full attention now. "Do tell."

I turned on the chair's massage mechanism after I sat down. The pressure from the jets blowing toward my ankles felt good. Damn good. As I closed my eyes, and allowed my body to fully relax, I almost forgot Marley was there.

"So, you're being secretive now. Is that for us?"

"Oh, girl. I'm sorry." I opened my eyes and turned my head toward her. "It ain't nothing like that. I met this dude today. His name is Koda. He came by with Armando."

"I know Koda."

Her pedicurist applied a clear coat of polish to her toe nails, and paused to allow her to view the finished product.

"How do you know Koda?" I sat up in my seat. I can't explain why I was irritated; I just was. Was there anyone in Louisville Marley didn't know?

"I know all of Santi's workers. I'm surprised you're just now meeting him."

Call me crazy, but I felt like she was bragging. Bragging about the fact that she knew more about Santiago and his work dealings than I did. My conscience told me that I was overreacting, but I oh well.

"If I was all up in Santi's ass, I'd probably know all his workers too."

"And what is that supposed to mean?" Marley became defensive. She whipped that neck of hers around so fast, I thought I her head would detach from her body.

"Exactly what I said. No offense Ley, but you follow that nigga around like you're attached at the hip. I mean, damn. He can't even take a shit without you being there."

Okay, I was exaggerating, but you say things you don't mean in the heat of the moment. I wouldn't be in the picture if they spent all of their time together. My words were fueled by the anger brewing surrounding her new car. It was invading my mind to the point of becoming obsessive. From my position within the nail shop, I had a perfect view of the sleek body and custom wheels. I wanted that damn car!

"For someone that's supposed to be my friend, that's fucked up for you to say. How did we go from Koda to me being all up in Santi's ass?"

"Just forget it. I was out of line," I conceded, watching Marley's face go from calm to bitchy in record speed. "You know I don't mean no harm. I just be saying shit sometimes."

Marley just rolled her eyes and crossed her arms over her chest. She was mad. She didn't even try to hide it. Thankfully, my phone chirped, redirecting my attention. It was Koda, wanting to meet up. Damn. It hadn't even been a full hour yet, and he was hitting me up. A girlish smile spread across my face. I gave him the address of the nail salon. With Marley giving me the side eye, I knew our outing was going to be cut short. She was in her feelings. I guess the truth hurt her deeper than she was willing to admit.

After finishing up with Koda, I put my phone to the side, and tried to start up some small talk with Marley. She wasn't hearing me though, only responding to me in simple, one word answers. That was, until Cash and another girl walked up in the spot.

"Oh shit." Marley lowered her head as if she could hide out in the open. We were the only two people in the eight pedicure chairs lining the wall. We couldn't hide if we wanted to. "What's he doing here?"

"I don't know, but he's walking in our direction."

"Ladies," he said smoothly.

"Cash. What a pleasant surprise." My smile was just as fake as his. Something about his presence was making Marley visibly uncomfortable. I didn't know if it had anything to do with his guest or not, but I probed to find out. "And who is this lovely lady?"

"This is Kensley, my lil sis."

I looked her over. She was cute. She shared features similar to her brother, but had her own distinct look. She gave me a shy smile and sat in the chair next to me. Marley and Cash were locked in some sort of trance that only they were a part of. Quite frankly, I found it pathetic. It seemed as though no one else mattered when they were in the room together.

"Shouldn't you be with Santi?" I asked Cash, interrupting whatever they had going on.

"Shouldn't I be asking you the same question?"

Wait. Was he trying to call me out? And in front of Marley? I guess I underestimated Cash. As Marley's eyes burned a hole right threw me, Koda's message came in right on time.

Koda: I'm outside

I smiled, but didn't respond to his text. The length of time Koda was willing to wait determined how much play he was going to get. As I averted Marley's gaze, and focused in on the woman working wonders on my feet, I could feel the growing tension between the two of us.

"Was that Santi?" Cash just couldn't let it go. He was just as messy as a fuckin' bitch!

"No, it wasn't." His sister lowered her head in shame. She already knew what her brother was on. Unfortunately for him, I was on the same shit. "Santi is the least of my worry; just like his wife should be the least of yours."

I must've hit a nerve, because Marley high-tailed it out of there without even saying goodbye. It didn't stop my observation though. I saw Cash reach in his pocket and pay for Marley's nails. In addition, I peeped the twenty dollar tip he left the pedicurist. Whatever they had going on was more than just friendship. I wasn't stupid. There was more going on between them than they were willing to admit. I asked his sister straight up once he followed Marley outside.

"What is your name again?"

"Kensley."

"Do you know that woman your brother left with?"

"No."

"Are you sure?"

"I'm sure."

Kensley had one of those unreadable faces. Her expression remained cool. I couldn't tell if she was lying or not.

As Marley stood outside the glass window, and spoke to Cash, she eased onto the hood of her car. Cash stepped in, dangerously close – relationship close in my opinion. There was no denying it now. Something was definitely up.

I turned on my phone's camera function to collect proof for when I ran this bit of tea past Santiago. That's when I realized Ms. Kensley wasn't so innocent after all. She knocked the phone out of my hand, causing it to fall into the water.

"What the fuck did you do that for?" I didn't give a damn about her age. She was interfering in grown people shit. For that, she could catch these hands.

"Don't spy on my brother," was all she said before she turned away. Boldly, she closed her eyes and leaned back into her seat like I was a non-muthafuckin' factor. At that point, I guess I was.

That lil meddlin' bitch owed me a new phone.

14

MARLEY

"What is all this?" I questioned Santi as I walked inside the house. There was a beautiful assortment of flowers and balloons everywhere. I sat the keys down to my new Porsche that Santi had just purchased me when a small, cute little chocolate colored dog came running to my feet and I squealed in excitement. "Oh my gosh! You got me a dog?"

"It's never too early to start celebrating your birthday, right?"

That explained my new car. Santi always went all out for my birthday. Ten days before my birthday, he would shower me with gifts, time and sex. It would be the best days of my life, but the day after my birthday, things would go back to normal. Actually, he would be gone more often than usual. I wasn't ready for that same ole shit of being alone, so I was about to show him how it felt and take advantage of being spoiled to no end.

"Never," I giggled, petting the dog while she was cradled in my arms. "Coco. That's what I'm going to call you." I cooed in her face.

I pulled out my phone and took a selfie with Coco and sent it to Amaya. She knew I loved small dogs, so I wanted to share my excitement with her. I don't know if it was just me, but our friendship didn't seem the same anymore. Something was off about it, so I made a mental note to chat with her about it later.

"Can I have some love too?" Santi asked with a fake pout. I switched my way over to him and pecked his soft, thick lips. He pulled my body into his and held me tight. "How was your day?"

See, this was the Santiago I fell in love with. The kind, attentive and loving man. The one who made time for me and not just on special occasions. The one who came home to me every night and gave me his undivided attention. That was the man I fell in love with and I was beginning not to know who this man in front of me was.

"It was good. Busy, but good. I'm surprised you're home so early in the day," I threw some shade and he most definitely caught it. He inhaled deeply and chuckled lowly.

"It's your birthday month; you know how I do. I dedicate every second of the day to you," he defended himself.

"So, I guess the other 11 months of the year don't matter. Right?"

I could feel my body temperature rising. I was speaking my mind for the first time in forever and it felt good as hell, but I was pissed. Pissed that I hadn't done this a long time ago. I should have been got everything off my chest. I knew my honesty was making him upset, but I didn't give a fuck. He needed to hear what I had to say. It was my birthday month, right?

"Ley, chill." He lowly growled.

"Why, Santi? You don't want to hear what I have to say? You don't want to hear the TRUTH?" I barked back and Coco trembled in my arms. I put her down and she scurried off into another room.

"Ley, listen. Can we just enjoy today? Please?" He pleaded, reaching out to me and I stepped back.

"I'm done not talking about this shit. You and I both know there's been some distance between us for some time now."

"I don't know what you're talking about."

"Don't play dumb, Santi! We used to have sex almost every night and now, we only have sex maybe once or twice every two weeks and you want to know why? Because you are never home! We hardly ever talk, a whole week could go by before we actually see one another.

You cater every damn second of your life to the streets and you're neglecting me," I exclaimed with tears staining my cheeks.

"Everything I do, I do for us and you know that. Every second I put into my work is because I know that I have to provide for us. I'm not neglecting you. I'm being a provider; what a husband is supposed to be. I can't help it that Cashmere has me out here working these late nights. If I-"

"No, he doesn't. You chose to be working the late nights," I corrected him before he told another lie.

"What makes you think that?" He quizzed with a raised brow.

Your boss told me.

"I'm not stupid, Santi. I know you're probably out here laid up with some other bitch!" I blurted before I could stop myself. Saying out loud that I assumed he was cheating was heartbreaking for me because I had been convincing myself that he wasn't. Tears rapidly spilled from my eyes as I came to terms with my true feelings; Santi was cheating on me.

"Really, Ley? You think I'm cheating on you?" He faked hurt and I could see right through his shit. Why was I so blind before?

"I know you are. It's a gut feeling," I expressed while trying to shake off the tears. "I need to go clear my mind." I mumbled then grabbed my keys and ran out the door. Santi came running after me, but I tuned him out and sped out the driveway.

Tears blurred my vision as I drove with no particular destination in mind. I needed to clear my head and process all of this. I wanted to talk to Cashmere, but I knew he was busy. Amaya crossed my mind, but I didn't feel like hearing her mouth right now. What was a woman to do?

I was cruising around for five minutes when my phone rang and I was grateful for the smile that tugged at my lips. As if he could see me, I tried to fix my face and wipe the tears from my cheeks before answering.

"Hello?"

"What's wrong?" Cashmere questioned with concern dripping from his tone and a lump immediately formed in my throat.

"N... Nothing," I croaked as I tried to fight the tears that wanted to fall.

"Where are you?" He quizzed and I heard some rustling in the background.

"Uhm, just driving around."

"Go to my house; I will meet you there. Kensley is home, so you can go straight in and wait for me. It should only take me thirty minutes to get there." He instructed and hung up.

I did an illegal U-turn in the middle of the street and sped down the side road to Cashmere's mansion. It was crazy how when he asked if I knew where I was that I didn't realize I had drove in the direction of his house. I knew where I wanted to be.

The guard at the gate allowed me access and I crept up the driveway to find an unfamiliar car parked off to the side. I slightly tilted my head as I studied it while trying to figure out if it was one of Kensley's friends, but I didn't recognize the car. *What is this girl up too?*

I parked my car in Cashmere's side of the garage and took a deep breath before getting out and preparing myself for what was about to happen. The only reason I suspected that Ken was up to something is because I had been there. I was her age one time and I knew what was on my mind; boys. When I was 15, I snuck two boys in and out of my house while my parent's where gone. The last time I almost got caught and decided to just starting sneaking out instead. Thankfully, I never got caught. But, Kensley's living situation was a lot different than mine, so how was she able to sneak?

I walked inside the house and into the kitchen. The house was quiet except for music coming from Kensley's side of the house. Placing my things down, I took off my heels so she wouldn't hear me coming. The closer I got to the room she was in I could hear things more clearly and only heard her laughter. Her door was cracked, so I peeked inside but couldn't see anything. I braced myself and counted to three before opening her door and my mouth hit the floor.

"Marley!" Kensley squealed in shock as she covered up her bare body. "What are you doing here?"

"Question is, what are you doing, Ken?"

Kensley was naked in bed with another girl. Well, at least I think it was a girl. She had breasts with a boyish appeal. When I walked in, the girl and Ken were making out and when the girl took one of Ken's breast into her mouth I almost fainted. It took her a second to notice me, but when she did, she pushed the girl off her and the color from her face drained.

"I can... I can explain," she stammered in embarrassment.

"I think you'll have to explain later because," I stopped to look at my watch. "Your brother will be here in fifteen minutes." I informed her and she jumped out of bed in a hurry.

I excused myself from the room as her and the girl got dressed. I tried to wrap my head around things, but it was all just too much. I needed a strong drink; maybe two.

Kensley and the girl emerged from the room fully dressed and dashing to the garage. They embraced one another and kissed as the girl went to the unfamiliar car. I watched as Ken pulled out her phone to make a call.

"Nate," she stated. "I thought I heard something around back and it sounded like it was outside of the gate trying to get in. Will you go check it out for me?"

There was a pause before she thanked him and hung up. She glanced back at me while rubbing her arm with a somber look on her face. I stared past her and watched the gate open and Nate run around the corner with a gun in his hand. Out the corner of my eye, I saw the girl's car back out of the driveway and sped off down the street then Ken's phone rang.

"Hey, Nate." She answered.

Pause.

"Okay, thank you. I guess I'm just hearing things. Thanks again," she said then hung up.

The gate closed up and I just shook my head.

"You don't have to explain now. I don't think I want to even know right now," I admitted as we walked inside the house.

"Please, don't tell Cash. He would kill me," she begged with a pouty lip.

"I'm not," I sighed. "But, we need to talk about this. Are you scared to tell him you like girls?" I quizzed, trying to get a better understanding of it.

She lowered her head and nodded yes. I heard the garage open back up and headlights fill the door window.

"We'll talk about it later," I stated and hugged her before she ran to her side of the house. I went to the refrigerator and opened it just as I heard the door open.

"Hey, baby." Cashmere breathed with a smile as he made his way over to me. "What's wrong?"

"I don't want to talk about it," I mumbled. The situation with Kensley made me forget my problems, but now I remembered and didn't want to talk about them. I just wanted to lay up with Cashmere and take a nap to temporarily forget about it. "Can we just lay down? I'm tired and just want to sleep."

Cashmere was hesitant, but agreed with a soft peck on the lips. I gave him a weak smile and turned to go to his master suite. I loved the California king bed in there. It had soft, plush sheets that felt heavenly against my body.

I could feel his eyes trained on my ass. I was dressed down today in some black leather tights with a fitted half-shirt that exposed my small waist and toned stomach. I was braless, so my nipple piercings were on full display. My hair was natural in big spiral curls resting in the middle of my back. Today was one of them days that I just didn't care.

We made it to his room and I wanted to shower before I laid down. It would help me sleep better.

"I'm going to take a shower," I informed Cashmere while walking inside the bathroom. I shut the door and turned the shower on before stripping from my clothes and stepping inside. I let the hot water massage my body as I tried to wash all the pain away. I was so hurt and confused and I just wanted to forget about it all.

I heard the bathroom door open and close. I could see Cashmere, naked, watching me through the glass and he stroked his long, thick shaft. My body tingled all over as I watched him intently and thought about our last sexual encounter. I could feel his tongue flicking over my clit and I moaned lowly. I was horny and my body was on fire. I wanted him so bad.

I began to massage my breasts while fondling with my nipple rings. A smirk tugged at Cashmere's lips as he began to work himself a little faster. My teeth sank into my bottom lips as one of my hands traveled down my torso and found its way to my swollen, throbbing clit. Spreading my legs a little, I inserted one of my manicured fingers into my wet canal. Damn, it felt good.

"Can I taste you again?" Cashmere breathed as he continued to stroke his pole. I nodded my head yes and closed my eyes and anxiously waited.

In one swift motion, he got in the shower and lifted me up with my legs pinned against the wall by his strong hand. He planted kisses along the inside of my thigh then some to my lower lips.

"Mmm," A moan escaped my parted lips.

"Open them up for me," he demanded and I obeyed.

I spread open my second set of lips and felt his tongue graze my clit. He sucked it lightly causing me to squirm.

"Be still."

I was thankful that Kensley had her own side of the house because the way Cashmere was devouring my pussy had me moaning loudly. My legs began to shake violently as I was on the brink of a powerful orgasm.

"Not yet," Cashmere stated as he pulled me off the wall and onto his hard dick. The feeling of him filling my insides sent me over the edge, but that didn't stop him. He worked himself in and out of me with force, tapping the right spot every time.

"Shiiittt!" I cried as my muscles tightened around him.

"Whose is it? Whose pussy is this?" He grunted while slapping my ass.

"Yours," I breathed lowly.

"Whose?" He demanded, pounding harder.

"YOURS!" I screamed.

He latched on to my nipple ring, sucking with light forced.

"I'm about to cum, daddy!"

He picked up the pace and seconds later my juices were streaming down his legs. My body went limp just as he filled me with his seeds. He let me down and wrapped his arms around me as we tried to catch our breath. I was on cloud nine and felt as if I could go a second round.

"Let me clean you up," he said and I let him.

We took turns washing each other up in the now cold water before getting out and cuddling in the bed together. At this moment, everything felt so right and I knew where I wanted to be. Hopefully I would feel the same when I woke up.

15

SANTIAGO

*S*ee, this is the shit I'm talking about. When I try to be a good guy, things blow up in my face. Marley and her antics were getting on my *last* nerve. I don't know where this bitchy attitude of hers derived from. Every year, I go all out for my wife's birthday, and this year...well, we all know how that turned out. Maybe this whole baby thing is clouding her judgment. She hasn't mentioned it in a while, but that's the only thing I can think of.

I sat in my car and stared off into space. The sun was starting to set, adding to my somber mood. Where did I go wrong? For seven years, I've been able to read Marley like a book. I knew what she needed before she even opened her mouth. Now, we can't even be in the same room together for an extended period of time without us arguing. I don't know what she wants for me. She claimed that she wanted more of my time. I tried giving her that, but hell, she didn't want it. Does she even know what she wants? Fuck it! Her indecisiveness already ruined my high, but I refused to let it ruin my day. Today is all about me.

I strolled the block and hollered at a few of my workers. As usual, they were on their posts, doing what they were supposed to do. That's one thing I was proud of. My crew, kept shit straight with minimal supervision. They stayed busy, so I didn't have to.

I rode around listening to a beat that I had created. It was a past time of mine, mixing beats for sale. I was nodding my head to the hardcore sound vibrating the inside of my new Porsche. I got one to match Marley's, which was the thing that got Amaya mad in the first place. Wait. Why was I thinking about that bitch?

Maybe it was the fact that she was on Broadway, chopping it up with Koda. As I turned right from Southwestern Parkway and slowly rode past Shawnee Park, there she was, all out in the open. Koda was standing a little too close for comfort. I made an illegal U-turn in the middle of the street and rolled up on them.

I pulled behind Koda's Maserati and shut off the engine. The last remnants of the sun bounced off the hood of Koda's ride and accented the metal flakes in the black paint. He was a typical nigga. I rewarded him for his hard work and he went straight down to the dealership. He got him a car he couldn't afford. It looked nice and all, but unless he backed up off my bitch, he wouldn't have the funds to continue to pay for it.

"What's good?" I eased in between the two of them and cupped my chin. "You on the wrong block, ain't you Koda?"

"I got a little sidetracked." He turned toward Amaya and looked her up and down. I knew what it meant when he licked his lips and smiled. He wanted what was mine, and that wasn't happening.

"I don't pay you for being sidetracked. I pay you for putting in work."

"Oh, lighten up Santi." Amaya side-stepped me and joined Koda at his side. She looped her arm in his and leaned her big titties into him. "We're just enjoying the rest of this beautiful day. There's no harm in that, right? Maybe you should call up your wife and join us. We can all enjoy it together."

If she was a nigga, I would have knocked that sarcastic grin, right off her face. Lucky for her, I didn't hit women.

"Listen. I ain't addressing you." I tried to speak as calm as I could, but Amaya was working my nerves. "I'm talking to Koda right now. I'll deal with you later."

"Please." She took her slim hand and began rubbing Koda's chest. He stood there with a sly smile across his pink lips. He liked the fact that Amaya was standing up to me. "There's nothing you need to say to me that you can't say in front of Koda. Besides, if you check that fake Rolex on your wrist, you'd know what time it was. Fizz took over, which means Koda is off the clock. Now, unless you have some business to discuss, you're killing our vibe right now."

That bitch! She knows I didn't rock knockoffs. That wasn't my style. My shit was a real as it came. She was trying to play me, and that wasn't going to happen.

I grabbed her arm and pulled her toward me. I wanted Koda to object, so I'd have a reason to knock his fucking lights out. Like the bitch he was, he stood silent as I tightened my grip on Amaya's arm and manhandled her in my direction.

"Santi, you're hurting me."

"Shut the fuck up! You ain't seen hurt yet."

I waited until we were out of earshot to unleash my fury.

"What the fuck are you doing, Amaya? Why are you out here with Koda? You got your titties all out and shit. Are you trying to make me mad?" I examined the short dress damn near painted on her body. She looked good, but her body should have been for my eyes only.

"Is it working?" She pushed her straightened hair off her shoulders and waited for my answer.

"What the fuck do you think?"

"Good. It serves you right. You're not the only man out here with a dick, Santi. You're not my only option."

I closed my eyes and silently counted to ten. It's something I saw Marley do a lot, and at that moment, I needed some sort of restraint. Like I said, I didn't hit women, but I wanted to choke the shit out of Amaya at that moment. She was going too far.

"That's right, I have options," she continued, taunting me. "Koda is a nice guy. And guess what...he's single."

I opened my eyes and laughed in her face. Single? Yeah, right. "That nigga got a bitch and a baby on the way. Single my ass."

"He ain't married, so technically he's single. Besides, as you can see, he doesn't have to hide me like you do. We're in a park, out in the open. I don't have any crazy wives to worry about."

"More like a crazy baby momma. Just wait 'til you meet Shay. She ain't nothing to play with."

"It hasn't stopped me yet," she challenged. Slowly, she turned her attention to Koda, pretending to appear occupied. He held his phone is his hand, but every so often, he glanced up in our direction. "So, are you done? I don't want to keep him waiting."

It wasn't the right moment to get into with Amaya, especially when there was an equally attractive woman jogging in our direction. Two could play this game.

"Yeah, go on." I dismissed her and stepped toward the front of my car. She joined Koda's side and I waited until the woman was close enough for me to speak. "Aye, you want some company? I'm trying to get my body right too."

The woman stopped and blushed. She fell for it. I worked my mouthpiece and it wasn't long before the woman, who identified herself as Talia, was sliding her slim body into my passenger's seat. I waved to Koda and Amaya as we peeled off, taking notice of the scowl on Amaya's face. It served her right. She had options, and I did too.

Fifteen minutes later, we were fucking in the back of my ride. I pulled off in the cut, and she hopped on my dick. She sucked it first, but didn't really know what she was doing. I wasn't in the teaching mood, so I tapped her shoulders, and motioned for her to climb up on my stiff pole. Lil momma had skills. She twisted and contorted her slim body in the cramped space, but never once did my dick slide out. Her warm, slippery walls gripped my dick for dear life. She rode me like her life depended on it. Did I mention that she had some good pussy? Miss 19-year-old Talia was one of those undercover freaks. You know, the kind that look sweet and innocent, but will have a nigga singing soprano in the bedroom. Yeah, that was her; and I was the one hitting an octave that was well above my range.

"Damn, girl," I moaned, not wanting the moment to end. As my nut slowly began to rise, my body had other plans. "I'm about to cum."

"Come on, daddy. Give me that nut."

I don't know if it's the way she said it, or the way she bit down on her full, bottom lip, but uncontrollable convulsions overtook my body. I pushed her back forcefully, and she dropped to her knees and sucked my dick with enough force to drain all my soldiers from my testicles. I came in her mouth, and she swallowed like a pro. Yeah, I needed to get her number. 5'5, smooth almond skin, round ass, and a tight pussy...she was a keeper.

I pushed my dick back into my pants and readjusted myself in the back seat. For the life of me, I couldn't tell you where her shorts and panties were. She pulled them off so fast, they kind of got lost in the heat of the moment, if that makes sense.

"Do you see my shorts?" she asked franticly.

I was more worried about her underwear. It wouldn't be a good look if Marley found them bitches. Leaning forward, I quickly scanned the floor. Her green thong came into view once I shifted my body toward the door. I was sitting on them. How did that happen?

She returned her garments to her body and we sat there in an awkward silence. I just wanted to fuck, but it turns out that I actually liked it. I liked her. She was something new. Something different. Something that wasn't Marley or Amaya for that matter.

"So, tell me about yourself," she began, patting down the stray hairs of her twist out.

I couldn't help but chuckle. We'd already fucked. No need for the small talk, but I entertained her anyway.

"What do you want to know?"

"You got any kids?"

"Nope. You?"

"I got a son. He's six."

I did the math in my head. She was only nineteen. She started early as hell, but who was I to judge? "That's cool. You live around here?"

"Yeah, on 47th Street."

"That's what's up. You need a ride home?"

"That would be nice."

It was at that moment that I noticed the sparkle in her hazel eyes. Talia was bad as fuck. And she was young. That means she was trainable. If Amaya didn't stop her jealous ways, her replacement was already in the works.

"It's the second house on the corner," Talia directed.

I pulled into the driveway of a red, brick house. It was much too big for a single woman and a baby. My curiosity got the best of me.

"Do you live here alone? I mean, just you and your son?"

"No," she said simply, flashing a sly smile.

"With a nigga?" I inquired.

"Something like that," she hinted. "I'm sure you understand."

It took a minute for me to realize what she was talking about. As I followed her gaze, my eyes fell to the platinum and diamond wedding band gracing my left ring finger. I was busted. How did I forget to take my ring off?

She eased out the car, giving me a nice view of the back of her sports bra and short shorts that had found their way into the crack of ass. I was ready to fuck again.

"So, do you want my number or what?" She leaned onto the opened door for support and waited for my answer. Hell yeah I wanted her number! I responded by picking up my cell phone and accessing my contacts. When I turned in her direction, she recited the digits.

She didn't ask for my number, so I sent her a quick text so that she would have it anyway. Talia told me not to be a stranger, and sauntered her pretty ass up the stairs leading to the front porch. I pulled out of the driveway, and started in the direction of my house. I called Marley to let her know I was on my way.

"Baby," I said when she answered. "You home?"

"No. Why?"

I hated when she did that shit. Why? Because I asked. That's fucking why!

"I'm on my way to the crib. I wanted to know if you needed anything."

"No. I'm good. I guess I'll see you when you get there. Don't wait up."

I told her I loved her, but she hung up before I could get it all out. Fuck that shit. I wasn't going to wait up anyway. Who the hell did she think I was? I had options. Wait, now I was sounding like Amaya's crazy ass.

She called me as I pulled onto the Watterson Expressway. I sent the first two calls to voicemail and lowered the volume on the radio to answer the third.

"What up?"

"Oh. So, you finally decide to answer your phone?"

"I can always hang up." I challenged.

"Why would you do that?"

"Cuz I ain't got time for your bullshit. What the fuck do you want, girl?"

"I'm sorry, Santi." She overexaggerated her sniffles into the phone.

"Are you?" I continued on the highway, exiting at Bardstown Road. It was beautiful out, and the breeze was just what I needed to clear my mind. I decided to take the long way home.

"Of course. I shouldn't have snapped on you like that."

"You damn right! How you gonna play me? And for Koda? I'm good, Amaya."

"I said I was sorry. I was just mad. That's all. Do you forgive me?"

Her question lingered in my mind. Did I forgive her? A part of me would always have love for Amaya, but another part of me was getting tired of her bullshit. When we started messing around, it was supposed to be just sex. I bought her a few things, but the basis of our relationship was centered around our own sexual desires. I wasn't supposed to catch feelings, but I did. I fucked up. I had a wife; a good one at that. I just needed more. The emotional disconnect between me and Marley lured me into the arms of another woman. It just happened to be her best friend. Seven years later, the shit was still going on.

I shouldn't have cared how Amaya felt. She had more than enough time to get her act together and play the role that she signed up for. Still, her cries for forgiveness tugged at my heart. I had a soft spot for the girl. As much as I hated to admit it, I was feeling her just as much as she was feeling me.

"Yeah, I forgive you."

The tone of her voice changed immediately. She was happy, and she displayed it in her new perky, upbeat tone.

"Good. Why don't you come over, so I can show you just how sorry I am?"

Marley wasn't gonna be home. Sliding through and kicking it with Amaya didn't sound like a bad idea. That was, until Talia sent me a text that had me changing my direction.

"Not tonight," I mentioned, reentering the highway.

"Why not?"

"I got plans. Maybe tomorrow night."

"Ok."

I heard the disdain in her voice, but the naked pic of Talia with her fingers teasing the opening of her pussy had me thinking with my other head.

"I'll call you tomorrow," I promised.

"You don't have to call, just come."

I smiled at the irony of her statement. I was about to do just that – again; just not with Amaya. Didn't I say today was all about me?

16

CASHMERE

"What's up, man? You look like shit," I noted as Santiago sat at the chair in front of my desk. He looked sick, like he had lost his best friend or some shit. Maybe his wife.

"I feel like it," he said, placing a duffle bag on my desk, "Here's the money from my work. I need to re-up ASAP. Niggas feigning for this."

"You sold all that already?" I quizzed and snapped my fingers for my money counter. I liked to count my money by hand and then run it through the counter. You could never be too safe. One of my workers placed it on the desk and stood beside me while I examined the money inside the bag. From the looks of it, he was being honest but, your eyes can deceive you.

"All of it. They wiped me cleaned," he boasted with a Kool-Aid grin on his face. "They couldn't stop coming back for more."

I pressed the tips of my fingertips together and nodded my head with a smirk tugging at my lips. See, this was the shit I loved. Knowing that my men were out here doing the work to bring in my paper was enough to make me nut. That's how good it felt. It almost made me feel bad for Santiago knowing that I was fuckin' his wife and slowly falling in love with her, but I shrugged that shit off. He was fuckin' her best friend, so someone has to keep her happy; right?

I instructed for Santiago to move to a chair in the back while I counted the money. I wasn't for any funny shit. Usually, I liked to count my money in peace, but since he needed to re-up? I decided to let him stay and observe. I emptied all the money on my desk and inhaled deeply. I loved the smell of money. It took me an hour and a half to count all of it and run it through the machine. I was impressed to say the least. One million dollars. Santiago had to work his ass off to get this. With the amount of money he was about to receive off this, he could buy his side piece whatever her heart desires while I take care of Marley.

"Your money should already be in your account." I informed him with a smile.

"I appreciate the swiftness."

"Well, let's not keep them waiting long." I stated as I rose to my feet and walked around my desk. "Follow me." I instructed him.

Santiago followed close behind me and my guards were in tow. They were on his ass so hard that I knew he had to feel their heavy breathing on his neck. My niggas didn't play about me. Not only did I pay them good, but I had bonded and formed a relationship with all of them. I made them feel like family and showed it with my actions. If you were loyal to me then I would always make sure you were straight.

We strolled down the long hallway to the room where I kept some of my supply for emergencies like this. The next shipment wasn't coming in until Thursday and it was Tuesday. There was no way I was willing to take a chance to let the next nigga come in and try to take my throne. Not having any supply meant you weren't making any money and I cannot have that. I made money in my sleep. I placed my thumbprint on the scan then opened the door. I made sure everyone was in before shutting it and making sure it was secure.

"Have a seat," I offered Santiago who was eagerly waiting to see what was behind the large safe on the wall. He was rubbing his hands together with a sly grin etched on his face.

"Nah, I'm good. I'll just stand right here," he declined.

I nodded my head and proceeded to unlock my safe discreetly.

Niggas weren't that trustworthy. I had two guards positioned on my sides and two behind me. Santiago couldn't even see me. I couldn't even let him get a glance at it. He may be a hard worker, but that didn't mean he was loyal and wouldn't rob me after seeing this. I made a mental note to have this room transformed and my safe moved.

I was in and out in a matters of seconds. I got him some work that should last him until Thursday and locked my safe back up. I cleared my throat for my guards to move and rolled the cart of drugs over to him. When his orbs observed the cart, he swiftly rubbed his hands together while smiling wide and hard. I knew that would be his reaction.

"This here is some of best I ever made," I boasted with a smirk and picked up a brick. It was perfectly wrapped and the color of the whitest snow like you see on Mount Everest. "It's so pure that I put all of it up for rainy days quite like today. You will sell out of this fast, so that's why I'm supplying you a lot. I expect my money to be accurate Thursday just like it was today. Understood?"

"Understood," he repeated back.

He was eyeing the product with a gleam in his eyes. He wanted to taste it. I whipped out my pocket knife and slit the one that was in my hand. I stuck my pink inside and scooped some out then rubbed across the top of my mouth. A chill slithered down my spine as my taste buds tingled. This was some good shit.

"Would you like to try?" I offered while holding the brick out to him. He accepted happily. He did the same as I did and let out a loud squeal. His pupils grew wide and the hairs on his arm rose and I laughed.

"That's some of the purest, rawest white I have ever sampled. This shit about to make the streets go crazy. I hope you have a lot more than this," he stated excitedly. "I'm about to fill your pockets up, Cash! Wooh!"

"Let your actions do the talking." Was all I said. My phone chimed and I knew exactly who it was. Marley had her own special ringtone, so I knew it was her. It was ironic that she would be calling while I was standing here with her husband. I decided not to answer and let it go to voicemail. I was still conducting business.

"Will do. I'm about to go get down to business. I appreciate this," he thanked me while dapping me up.

"I'll have my assistant contact you about pick up and drop off time as usual. Until then, get that paper."

"WHERE ARE YOU GOING?" I questioned Kensley as she came skipping into the kitchen with her keys in hand. She went to the fridge and got a bottle of water before turning her attention to me.

"Marley is taking me out to lunch," she answered with excitement in her tone. "I really like her for you, Cash. I can see that she makes you happy."

I nodded my head and smiled as I thought about Marley. Ken was right; Marley did make me happy. I haven't felt like this about any woman, so it was something I was still getting used to. The only thing wrong with our situation is that she's married. Ken didn't know that and I planned to keep it that way. She would be livid if she knew.

"I'm glad you like her," I admitted with a smirk. "We're still getting to know each other, but I'm really feeling her. She's definitely wifey material."

"I agree. I can picture us being the best of friends and her being the sister I never had." Ken giggled as her imagination ran wild, but I had to agree. I wouldn't mind Marley sticking around and eventually becoming my wife. I was falling hard and I was just going to continue to go with the flow.

"Me too."

"Can I ask you a question?" She took off her shades and her expression turned serious. Something was bothering her. I could tell by the way she slightly frowned and her brows turned in. I knew my sister better than I knew myself, so her facial expressions were telling off on her.

"What's up?"

"Who was that woman that saved me that day? The one who hit my prom date?" She asked.

"Just some woman," I answered and shrugged my shoulders. "Why?"

"Because. I've been seeing her a lot lately. She's always standing outside of my school in the morning as if she's waiting on me. When she sees me, she smiles real big and waves at me. I always smile and wave back, but it's getting weird, Cash. It's an everyday thing and it's creeping me out now. It's as if she has some sort of obsession with me." She muttered.

I was livid. I knew exactly what Kelsie was doing. She's trying to inch her way closer and closer to Ken. I meant was I said and I wasn't ready to bring her into Ken's life yet. She still needed to be protected until I saw fit. I was going to have a talk with her ASAP!

"Boss? Some woman is trying to get in. She said she's family," One of my guards informed me.

"Stay right here," I instructed Ken and jogged to one of my rooms. I glared at the monitor to see Kelsie outside going at it with Nate. Shaking my head, I threw on a t-shirt and my flops then went outside to handle her.

"I just want to see *my* daughter!" I heard her yell as tears streamed down her face. I had no sympathy for her whatsoever.

"What in the fuck are you doing at my house?" I growled as I pushed her to the side and grilled her. "How do you know where I lay my fuckin' head?"

"I want to see my daughter, Cash! You've been holding her from me for too long and now that I'm clean I feel that I deserve to see her! She needs me and I need her!" She screamed while pointing her finger towards my house. "I'm getting clean for *her!* Do you know how hard it's been not to come begging and kissing your feet for a hit? I crave it every second of the day, but when I stand outside that school and see her smiling and talking with her friends, it makes me fight even harder! She's the only person that is saving me from myself! I just want to be in my daughter's life, Cashmere. That's all I ask of you."

"Where was all this talk about being here for her when I took her in? Huh? You haven't paid one doctor bill, been to one school function, or even offered money to help! Yes, you may have birthed her, but you are not her mother! She may be my sister, but she is *my* child! I raised her! I put my life on pause to make sure she never had to want or need for anything! I chose *her* over EVERYTHING! You know why? Because I love her more than life itself. Unlike you who couldn't even stop shoving shit up her nose or sticking a damn needle in her arm to catch a fuckin' high instead of taking care of her daughter! She doesn't need you; she needs me!"

How dare this junkie bitch come to my house to demand to see Ken? She hasn't been here for her for sixteen years, so why in the fuck did she think it was okay to pop up when she was damn near grown? I had to admit that it was good finally seeing Kelsie try to get clean and go on the right path, but that didn't have shit to do with Ken. I told Kelsie that I would let her know when *I* was ready for her to meet Ken, but she must be hard of hearing. I had to step away and count to ten before I approached her again. She was crying hysterically while cradling her body. A part of me felt bad because she is Ken's mother, but she's not mine.

"Can't you see I'm trying to change, Cash? I'm doing better; I swear. You don't even have to tell her who I am. I just want to get to know my daughter," she pleaded in between her sobs. "I know you have a heart behind that hard exterior."

"Cash? What's going on?" Kensley questioned as she tip toed down the driveway slowly with a worried expression. When she laid eyes on Kelsie, her pupils widened and she glared at me. "What is she doing here? I told you she was following me!" She yelled and ran and hid behind me like she did when she was little.

Kelsie grilled me with teary eyes that were silently begging me to introduce the two to one another. My mind was heavy as I weighed my options. I knew that Kensley needed a mother figure in her life because it had just been me and her for as long as I can remember. But, I didn't know if her mother was the right one to be there for her. I much rather Marley take on the responsibility, but nothing between us was promised. I turned around and stared into Ken's bright eyes as she waited for me to answer.

"She is following you, Ken. But, she has a reason." I started. How was I going to tell my baby sister that I had been lying to her about her mother her entire life? She was going to be pissed at me, but maybe she would understand after I explained everything to her.

"What reason does she have?" Ken asked as her eyes shifted back and forth between Kelsie and I.

Sighing heavily and secretly praying that Ken would forgive me, I grabbed her hand and led her to Kelsie who was trying to straighten out her clothes and look presentable. I could see the twinkle of happiness gleaming from her eyes as we approached her. Damn. Here goes nothing.

"Kensley, this is Kelsie. She's yo-"

"My mother!"

17

AMAYA

I felt sick to my stomach. No matter which over-the-counter product I tried, nothing was giving me relief. It was hard to keep food down. As much as I like to eat, that alone was pure hell.

My queasy feeling was further elevated by the unknown. There was something different about Santiago. He had this cocky aura about him that seemed to get worse by the day. It pissed me off, really. I was no longer the number one priority in his life. He was spending more and more time in the streets, breaking promise after promise to come see me. I didn't know what to think, so I decided to get to the bottom of things.

Her name was Talia. She was the little tramp I saw him flirting with right in front of me. I played it cool while he drove off with her in his car, but I was positive it wasn't nothing more than a ploy to make me jealous. It worked, but I didn't let Santi know it.

The next day I found her jogging through Shawnee Park again. She was too consumed with the headphones in her ear to notice me following her. The dumb broad led me right to her house. I staked out the place for a little while, sitting quietly down the street in Koda's car. Sure enough, Santi pulled up shortly thereafter. He didn't take her to some rinky dink hole in the wall spot. Nah. He took her to the Galt House, a twenty-five story luxury hotel sitting right on the Ohio River. They weren't even there a good hour before they were reentering his car. He retraced his route and drove back in the direction of her house. I was so mad I couldn't see straight. I could only imagine what she was doing in that room with *my* man.

The next day, I was parked down the street before she even left the house. I timed my arrival to coincide with the time I thought she would leave for her 'daily jog'. I was right on the money. Raising my binoculars to my eyes, I got a good look at the bitch replacing me in Santi's bed. She wasn't even on my level, which further irritated me.

She was half-way down her driveway when a chocolate man, who appeared to be a little older than her, entered the doorway and called out to her.

"Talia!" She turned in his direction. "I got somewhere to be. I'ma take the baby over my momma's house."

She nodded and continued on, placing her earbuds in her ears. I assumed the guy talking was her man, and the baby he was talking about was their son. I didn't really care one way or the other. That big head nigga had nothing to do with me, but it did provide me with a vital piece of information. Her name. Talia. Sounded just like a hoe, don't you agree?

She followed her normal path, and circled the perimeter of the park twice. I watched carefully, trying my damnedest to see what the hell my man saw in her. Her lopsided ass had me nauseated. Seriously, I was nauseated. A queasy feeling almost made me abort my mission, but I didn't come this far for nothing. Talia was young, dumb, and officially at the top of my shit list. I had to continue on, regardless of how I felt.

As expected, Santiago picked her up, and once again took her to the same hotel. I pulled my hair back, and tucked most of it under a Cleveland Cavalier Snapback. There were a pair of Oakley's in the glove box. I threw them on my face and exited Koda's ride wearing a pair of fitted jeans, one of Armando's shirts that he had left at my place, and black Nike's that were reserved for beatdown sessions like the one I planned on giving Talia.

Bypassing the check-in counter, they took the stairs to the second floor. I trailed them, leaving just enough room to not look suspicious. They entered the third door on the right, and closed the door behind them. After counting to one hundred, I knocked on the door, covering the peephole with my finger. Talia's face slowly appeared, and I unleashed on her ass.

"Can I hel—" was all she managed to get out before my fist connected with her face.

"Stupid bitch!" I yelled, knocking her into the door. It fell open, giving me more room to work with.

I mounted her and assaulted her face; right there in the doorway. My hat slipped from my head, releasing a head full of loose curls. That didn't stop me though. I wasn't stopping until I saw blood, and lots of it.

"Amaya!" Santi hollered, grabbing my arm mid-punch.

He pulled me toward him, but I wasn't done yet. This was a fuckin' fight and I was as under-handed as they came. I didn't play by nobody's rules but my own. I raised my leg and kicked toward her face. As her jaw dislocated from the socket, I lost my balance. Santiago was right there to save me.

"Are you fuckin' crazy?" He snatched me up roughly and scolded me; squeezing my shoulders with his vice-like grip. "What the fuck are you doin'?"

"What does it look like? You keep promising to come see me, yet you're here at a hotel with some bitch! What do you expect?"

"Not for you to run down here like some mad woman! Damn, Amaya."

He turned his attention to Talia, moaning in pain. Like a child, she had to take Santiago's attention off of me and divert it to her. She was a'ight. It wasn't like she was dead.

That was a couple days ago, and Santiago hadn't spoken to me since. I got the hell out of there before security came and locked my ass up for assault. I'm guessing that I scared the girl enough to prevent her from calling the law. Or, maybe Santi got in her head. Either way, I was off scot-free.

In the days since seeing Santiago, the origin of my nausea and vomiting revealed itself. I had a little 'Santiago' growing inside me. Yep, that's right. I was pregnant. Five weeks to be exact. The few times Santi slipped up and raw-dogged me resulted in this new person using my body as an incubator.

I was excited, nervous, and scared all at the same time. My emotions were all over the place. Those pregnancy hormones were causing havoc early. One minute I wanted to laugh. The next minute I wanted to cry. Regardless of how I felt, I was sure that once Santi found out, he would send me straight to the clinic to terminate yet another pregnancy. This time, I was putting my foot down. I wasn't terminating anything. My baby was my meal ticket, and I stayed hungry!

Armando called me over to our mother's house. He was a grown ass man, content with living with his mother. Sad, but true. I thought something was wrong when he called based on the tone of his voice. After running a red light that was taking too long to turn green, I arrived only to find out that he called me to take Koda off his hands. Apparently my brother was trying to slip into some gushy stuff, but Koda acted like he didn't want to leave.

I agreed to take Koda off his hands, only if Armando promised to bring Santi to me. I was convinced that Santiago had my number blocked and it was important that I get in touch with him. After all, I was having his baby. I didn't wanna have to do a popup at his wife's house. Then again, that didn't sound like a bad idea.

Koda and I hung out together for a few hours. He was cute, but annoying as hell. I wasn't feeling him like that, but he was cool to hang out with. I hadn't given him the goods yet, and I didn't plan to. I kept him around simply for what he could do for me. He was generous with his funds, and when I flirted with him, he spent it on me freely. Today wasn't an exception. We held hands as we walked together through the mall. His free hand held a bag containing a pair of knee length boots and *Jackie O* sheath dress – things he had bought for me.

My eyes found a store advertising sunglasses in the window when I noticed Marley and Kensley walking by. *Great.* I didn't expect to see Marley there, and with Cash's sister of all people. I still had my suspicion that something was going on, but Marley was close-lipped about the situation. Koda and I kept it moving as she laughed with Kensley and walked in the direction of the food court.

I pulled out my phone and sent her a text.

Me: What are you doing?

Marley: At home. Chilling. What's up?

Lies, I thought, looking over my shoulder. She blatantly lied to me about something so minor. Why didn't she want me to know she was at the mall? Now I was convinced something was going on, and I wanted answers. Answers that I intended to get.

Me: I'm in the area. On my way.

She didn't respond, but the way she grabbed Kensley's arm and hurried toward the exit was all the response that I needed.

"Who are you texting?" Koda asked, noticing the wide smile forming across my face. He was oblivious to what was going on, and I wanted to keep it that way.

"Nobody important. I do need to get home though. Do you mind taking me back to my momma's house so I can get my car?"

"You done shopping already?" His smooth face scrunched up in confusion.

"For now, but there's always later." I grabbed his arm and rested my head on his shoulder. "Are you gonna be busy later?"

"Never too busy for you."

Lame. I wasn't calling that nigga back unless I needed something. It was all just a ploy to get what I wanted. He was wrapped up in trying to the pussy that he'd inadvertently wrapped himself right around my little finger. I had him just where I wanted.

We arrived back to my mother's house and Koda had the nerve to lean in for a kiss. I pecked him on the cheek, but he hungrily released his tongue and forced my mouth open. I don't know why I didn't stop him right away, but I didn't. Something about his roughness reminded me of Santi. The way his tongue danced around mine had me wondering what else his tongue was good for. Umm umm umm. Maybe I needed to give Koda some after all, but today wasn't the day.

"I'll be waiting for that call," he mentioned, standing in the driveway as I pulled off. He was going to be waiting for a while, because I was off to Santi's house.

Marley had more than enough time to drop the little brat off. The mall wasn't too far from her house, but my mother's crib was across town. A whole hour passed before I was knocking at her door, posing with my hands on my hips.

"Whatchu lookin' like that for?" She quizzed, stepping back to allow me to enter.

"No reason."

I passed her, looking as if I had just stepped off a runway. I always dressed to impressed, and as I outshined her in a lace romper and five inch heels, her upturned nose told me that she knew it too. Marley was far from ugly, but clothed in a simple t-shirt, Bermuda shorts, and gladiator sandals, let's face it...There was no comparison.

I confidently walked through her house as if I owned it. I had been there more times than she knew about and as I eased onto her leather couch, I was reminded of memories of Santi and I sexing each other into multiple orgasms. I slid back in my seat, and relished in the moment.

"You okay, girl?"

Marley wasn't privy to my little secret, and that made it all the more amusing.

"I'm fine, but what about you?"

"What are you talking about?"

I was going to lead into my interrogation with small talk, but the way Marley stood over me as if I was a bitch with a problem sped the process up.

"What did you buy at the mall?" I crossed my hands over my chest and watched Marley stammer with her words.

"Mall? Wha—? What mall? Girl, what are you talking about?"

"The mall you were just at with Kensley." I let that little bit of information simmer in before I added, "Mall St. Matthews."

"You got your information wrong." She guiltily turned away, releasing the hair-tie holding up her loose curls. They fell to her shoulders as she walked away from me and entered the kitchen.

I followed her. I had to find out what she was hiding. I wanted her to confess to what I already suspected. She was messing with Cash.

"I was there. I saw you with my own two eyes. What are you doing hanging out with Cash's sister? More importantly, why would you lie to me about it? You're supposed to be my girl."

The icy look in her eyes that she displayed when she finally turned to face me had me grateful of the island separating us. It was malice; a look that usually preceded hands being thrown or wigs being pulled. I'd never seen it displayed toward me, and at that moment, I became nervous.

"Am I?"

"Of course! We used to tell each other everything. Now, it's just different. You don't call me as much as you used to. We rarely hang out. What's the problem? What's the big secret?"

She smirked as the front door swung open. Santi's loud voice could be heard laughing, along with someone else. I turned toward the kitchen's opening, awaiting my baby daddy's arrival. He walked in along with Cash and stopped when he hit the doorway.

"What's up?" he said, to no one in particular. He walked over to Marley and kissed her cheek. Putting on a show, he positioned himself behind her and kissed her ear. "I missed you."

Give me a fuckin' break! He did that shit to make me mad. My chest heaved up and down as my internal temperature increased a few degrees. I was hot – literally. Crazy thing was, Cash appeared just as upset me. Just as quickly as it started, Cash broke that lovey dovey shit up quick.

"A'ight now. Y'all can do that shit when we leave. Santi, why don't you tell the ladies the good news."

"I've been in talks with a few people about opening my own spot. Like a gentlemen's club. I contacted the right people, checked things out, and today I found a place. It's a fixer upper, but the size and location are perfect. I just signed the paperwork. I'm officially a businessman."

"That's good," Marley mouthed. She could have tried a little harder to sound happy for him, but she didn't.

I, on the other hand was beaming inside. The more money Santi brought in, the brighter the future looked for my baby. Without a sibling to share it with, he or she would be set for life.

"Let's celebrate!" Santi yelled, entering the wine cellar adjacent to the kitchen. "What'll it be?"

"Ladies choice." Cash said, watching Marley open a cabinet and pull out four wine glasses. "What do you ladies have a taste for?"

"It doesn't matter to me," Marley sighed.

What was up with her? I didn't know that calling her out would fuck up her entire mood.

"Whatever y'all decide is cool. I'm not drinking."

Santi emerged with a vintage bottle of *Dom Perignon*, my favorite. That action alone put a smile on my face. He was thinking about me.

"Since when don't you drink?" he asked.

"Since I found out I was pregnant."

All the color drained from his face. "Pregnant?

"That's what I said."

"You're pregnant?!" Marley questioned, as if she needed me to say it again for confirmation. She heard me the first time, but to appease her, I repeated myself.

"Yes, I'm pregnant. That's why I came over here. I wanted to tell my best friend the good news in person."

Cash looked from Santi, to me, and back to Santi. He smirked and shook his head. "You hear that Santiago? Amaya's pregnant. Pop that bottle. There's two things to celebrate."

Marley looked me up and down. Her face was unreadable as she sat the wine glasses on the marble island. My gaze shifted to Santiago, still holding the vintage bottle of wine in his hand. Unlike Marley, I could read his face just fine. His eyes lowered to small slits as he peered back at me, full of emotion. It wasn't a happy look, or anything remotely close. Nah. It was rage and it was directed toward me.

18

MARLEY

*E*nvy spread through my veins like a deadly disease. How could Amaya be pregnant and not me? I was married with a whole husband and had yet to carry one of his seeds, but she... she was single and hopping from dick to dick and she's pregnant. This was not fair. I wanted to yell, cry and scream at Santi, but I wouldn't dare while Cashmere was here.

"Are you going to say anything?" Amaya quizzed with a scrunched face. She was glaring at me; trying to read my face. If she only knew.

"I'm just speechless. You didn't tell me you were seeing someone," I threw shade while sipping my wine. The way I was feeling, I was liable to drink the whole damn bottle. My nerves were on ten and I couldn't help but notice how pissed Santi looked. There were little beads of sweat on the tip of his nose and around his hairline. He was chewing the inside of his jaw and grilling the hell out of Amaya. What was that all about?

"So, will you two be the godparents?" Cashmere asked with a smirk. I could tell he found this to be very amusing which made Santi and Amaya both squirm. What was going on here? Did they know something I didn't?

That statement made Santi choke on his wine. I reached over and patted his back. Cashmere's smirk was replaced with tight lips as he watched me interact with Santi. I knew he was pissed, but we had to make things look normal. He would be in my ass about it later and I wasn't with the shit today.

"Thank you, Ley." Santi said then kissed my hand. I could feel the fire in Cashmere's eyes burning a hole in the side of my face.

Amaya loudly smacked her lips I whipped my head around and stared at her with a raised brow. My facial expression was asking if her she had a problem. She forced a fake smile and shook her head no. I don't know what was up with everyone today.

"Only if they would want too," Amaya finally spoke dryly.

"I'll pass," Santi spat while adjusting himself in the chair.

"Why? I would think you would at least consider it since you don't want a baby," I mumbled, but everyone heard me.

I desperately wanted a baby and at this point, I didn't care by who. Santi or Cashmere could knock me up and I would be just as happy. I wouldn't mind because Santi is my husband and I've always wanted children with him. Then, I wouldn't mind Cashmere because I knew he would take care of the baby and me. The only thing I would hate about being pregnant period would be the drama. I felt like once I got pregnant, shit would hit the fan and everything would come to light and I don't know if I'm ready for that.

"Please, don't start Ley. We'll have a baby when it's time. Right now, I'm just focusing on making sure we're straight." Santi groaned.

"Santi, we've been straight! What more do we need?" I yelled in frustration. This was a sensitive subject for me because I wanted it so bad. "What's *really* stopping you?"

I could feel the tension in the room begin to suffocate us all. Santi had his head in his hands and was mumbling under his breath. This was the shit I didn't have time for. As always, he was shrugging off my wants and needs like they didn't matter. I could feel my emotions getting the best of me and a dry, hard lump form in my throat. I refused to let any of them see me cry over this, so I slammed my hands down and stormed out the room. I grabbed my purse and keys and went to my first available car. I got inside and glanced at the front

door to see if Santi at least cared enough to come after me; he didn't. I
backed out the driveway and finally let the tears fall.

"Hello?" I sniffled.

"Go to my house," Cashmere instructed.

"I'm already here," I stated. I was laid out in his bed with only my
bra and thong on. I had a bucket of ice cream and was watching
reruns of *Keeping Up with the Kardashians*.

"I'll be there in ten. You need anything?"

"A drink."

"You know where I keep my stash. I'll see you in a bit," he said
then hung up. I wanted to fix myself a drink, but my legs felt like
heavy weights and stuck to the bed. I placed the ice cream on the
nightstand then snuggled under the covers while I waited for
Cashmere.

"Mmmm," I moaned rolled over on my back. I opened my eyes
and the room was pitch black. The clock on the nightstand read that
it was well after midnight. I didn't even realize I had fallen asleep.

"You taste so good," Cashmere growled in between planting kisses
on my inner thighs "Open up for me," He demanded and I obeyed.

I spread my legs, holding my thick thighs in my hands. Cashmere
inserted a finger in my wet canal while sucking my clit. I tried not to
squirm, but it felt so good. He continued to do that slowly; working
his fingers in and out of me while French kissing my lower lips. He
sped up the motion of his fingers and I felt my juices travel down the
crack of my ass. I shivered as he removed his fingers and replaced
them with his long, stiff tongue.

In one swift motion, he laid on his back and pulled me on top of
him with me sitting on his face.

"Ride my face." He instructed and slapped my ass. I happily did as
I was told and worked myself until I was ready to cum. "Lay on
your back."

"Ah!" I gasped as Cashmere filled my opening.

He kept a nice, steady pace as he kissed me. This wasn't an ordi-
nary kiss. I could feel the love he had for me as our tongues massaged
one another. He was handling my body with so much more care than

usual. He was making love to me; something Santi hadn't done in a long time.

"I love you, Marley." He whispered against my lips. The light scent of me on his lips kissed my nose and turned me on a little.

"I love you too, Cashmere."

I was in deep. I had fallen in love with my husband's boss right before his eyes and he didn't even notice. Not that we made it obvious, but it was just baffling how all of this transpired. It was never in my plans to step out on my husband, but I needed some love and attention; something Santi damn sure wasn't giving me. I know what Cashmere and I are doing is so wrong, but it feels so fuckin' right. I feel like this is where I'm supposed to be now; where I'm happy.

Cashmere pulled out of me and told me to get on all fours. I arched my back the way he loved and braced myself for his entrance. This was one of his favorite positions, so I knew he was about to be all in.

"Marley?" He hissed as he slid inside of me.

"Hmm?"

"Do you want a baby?" He questioned; catching me completely off guard. His paced picked up and I was having trouble finding my words. He slapped my ass and I yelped. "I know you heard daddy. Do you want a baby?"

"Yes, daddy!" I screamed. He wrapped his strong hands in my curly mane and began pounding me harder.

"You want daddy to give you one?"

"Yes!"

"Yes, what?"

My eyes rolled to the back of my head as I felt the wave of an orgasm flow through my body. My muscles tightened around Cashmere's shaft and that's when I realized he didn't have a condom on. I had been so wrapped up in his love making and didn't realize he never put one on. I couldn't protest because he felt so good and had me about to cum all on his dick.

"Fuuuuck!" He moaned as I released my juices and he did the same.

I laid on the bed and he cuddled up behind me and draped his arm over my sweaty body. The silence between us was calming as we caught our breaths. My mind traveled back to the words we had exchanged during our love making session and I decided to break the silence.

"Baby?"

"Yes?"

"Do you really love me?" I whispered.

"I wouldn't have said it if I didn't mean it, Marley. I know our situation is a little fucked up, but I can't deny the feelings I have for you." He expressed.

"Me either," I admitted. "I... I just don't want to hurt, Santi."

"Too late for that. Our feelings are involved in this shit now; there's no coming back from that."

He was right; I wasn't coming back from this. I was in love with Cashmere, but I just loved my husband. Over time I fell out of love with Santi. It was happening before Cashmere and I, but it helped dissipate my feelings over time. I had become okay with Santi never being home or putting me first because I was out doing me and it felt damn good. I had always put him first and catered to his needs while pushing mine to the back. Cashmere helped me put myself first again and showed me what I needed from my husband. That's how I fell in love.

"You're right," I agreed and snuggled closer to him. "Were you trying to knock me up?"

"You said you want a baby, right?"

"Yes."

"Then, yeah. I want you to be happy, Marley and if having a baby will make you happy, then I'm down. It was clear that Santiago wasn't with the shit."

It was crazy how this man would go the extra mile to make me happy when my husband didn't give a shit. He hadn't even called or texted to make sure I was fine, nor did Amaya. Damn! I couldn't believe she was pregnant. Her ass was being sneaky because she didn't tell me anything about a man. I was going to confront her about all the secrets she's been keeping and that stank ass attitude she's been having towards me.

"Do you think we're moving too fast? How am I going to tell Santi I'm pregnant and we haven't been having sex?" I panicked. "He's going to know I cheated."

"Don't worry about all that right now. We'll figure shit out once it gets there," Cashmere mumbled half sleep.

I agreed to drop to it. I wasn't pregnant now, so it was nothing to sweat about. Cashmere never worried about anything and that's one thing I liked about him. I had yet to see him sweat over anything and wish I could be like that. I'm starting to become like that with Santi and Amaya. I didn't feel the need to bite my tongue anymore, except about my affair. That needed to stay between Cashmere and I.

My phone chimed and it was Amaya texting me.

Amaya: We need to talk.

Me: Agree. Set the time and place and I'll be there.

I don't know what she needed to speak with me about, but I had a lot to say to her. As of now, I couldn't see where my friendship with her was going anymore. There was one point in time where we were thick as thieves; you never saw one without the other. She was different then, but over time she changed and I didn't know who she was anymore. I found her competing and judging everything I did. I never said anything because I thought I was tripping, but I see differently now. Maybe Cashmere was right about her.

19

SANTIAGO

I know I should have went after my wife, but my feet just wouldn't move. *Pregnant?* What kind of game was Amaya playing?

This wasn't our first time down this road. Amaya had been pregnant before; a few times to be exact. Each of those times we handled it in private. She went to the clinic, I paid for it, and that was that. We never involved Marley in what we had going on. Amaya kept her mouth shut, which was the sole reason our secret relationship was able to survive as long as it had. For her to pull this stunt in front of my wife of all people had my mind going haywire. Was she trying to get us caught? Better yet, why would she flaunt that shit in Marley's face? She knew Marley wanted a baby. She wanted *my* baby.

My eyes burned a hole through Amaya as the front door slammed behind Marley. I didn't care that Cash was still in the room with us. I wanted answers, and I wasn't going to wait for them.

"What the fuck was that?"

She had the nerve to play dumb. "What are you talking about?"

"You know damn well what I'm talking about! Why would you tell Marley that shit?"

"Because I am." She rubbed her flat stomach as if that was

supposed to convince me. "She's going to find out anyway. I can't hide it forever. Eventually I'm going to start showing."

"Bullshit! You didn't have to tell her a damn thing! You ain't having it!"

"Yes, I am." Her calm demeanor irritated me even more.

"No the fuck you ain't." I lunged forward, ready to shake some sense into her ass. Cash was faster, and grabbed me mid-lunge. "Don't play with me Amaya!"

"Who's playing?"

She casually walked away, opening my refrigerator as if the conversation was over. She produced a bottle water before closing the door behind her.

"Why are you doing this?"

"Doing what?!" It was her turn to catch an attitude. "What am I doing, Santi? I'm pregnant. So what! Life goes on. Regardless of what you say, I'm not getting rid of it. It's my baby and I'm keeping it."

Her word play had me confused. Her baby? Did that mean it wasn't mine? In the back of my mind I already knew the answer, but I had to ask anyway. I glanced back at Cash before turning to Amaya and asking, "Whose baby is it?"

"You're really going to ask me that question?" She stood quickly, causing the chair she was sitting in to fall backward. Approaching me, she continued. "You get around other people and you want to act brand new. The father of my baby is the same man I've been fucking for the past seven years. It's yours, nigga. Don't try to play me like that."

I could have sworn I heard Cash laughing behind me. When I turned toward him, he had a straight face and an unreadable expression. Normally, I would have been more tight-lipped in the company of others. Only a select few knew about Amaya and I, and that was simply by chance. At that moment, I really didn't care. I was a man. Marriage didn't equate to monogamy in my book. I loved my wife, and I also loved entertaining other women. As a man himself, I'm sure Cash could understand that.

Amaya's blatant disregard for my position had me wishing I could turn back the hands of time. How could I have been so stupid? I should have cut this chick off years ago. Lately, Amaya was acting less like my side piece and more like my main. Hell, she had already ran Talia off. Amaya beat the girl so bad that she quit answering my calls all together.

Everywhere I turned, Amaya was there. She followed me home, she did pop-ups at the most random of places. I started seeing her for what she really was – crazy! I was trying to distance myself from the madness, but instead, she brought the madness to me. How could she possibly think that shit was cool? Was she trying to fuck up my marriage? It seemed that way to me.

"You could've called and told me this shit," I snapped, taking advantage of Cash's loosened grip. I snatched free of his hold and waited for Amaya to justify her actions.

"For what? You're ignoring my calls, remember? How else was I supposed to tell you?"

"Read between the fuckin' lines. If I ain't answering your calls that doesn't mean for you to come over to my crib. You knew that shit would set her off. You can be mad at me all you want, but Marley ain't did a mothafuckin' thing to you. Why would you wanna throw that shit in her face? What? You think I'm gonna leave her because you say you're pregnant? That ain't happening, ma." I paced the floor feeling as if the room was closing in on me. If she didn't go through with it, what the fuck was I going to do?

"Yo, Santi. You gonna be straight?" Cash asked, snapping me back into reality. He'd been standing there quiet, making me almost forget he was even in the room.

"Yeah, I'm good."

He tapped at the screen of his phone before placing it back in his pocket. "A'ight, cool. I'll get at you tomorrow." He walked his own self out, but before the front door closed, I heard his voice in the distance. "Congrats again, Amaya."

The door closed before she responded. We were left alone; both filled with things that needed to be said. I started first, using a different tactic.

"We both know we ain't ready for a child, Amaya. I ain't ready. Deep down, you know you ain't ready either. Maybe somewhere down the line things will change. Right now, I just need you to trust me. You gotta get rid of it, Amaya."

"No! My mind is made up."

I was on her in seconds. Playtime was over. I gripped her shoulders tightly as I gritted my teeth. The tears beginning to stream down her face did nothing for me. I wasn't moved and I damn sure was going to let her know it.

"I ain't playing with you, Amaya. You're going to that fuckin' clinic."

"I'm keeping my baby!"

I moved with lightning-like swiftness. I pinned her against the wall, using my own body weight to hold her in place. Grabbing her chin in my firm grip, I forced her to look up at me.

"I ain't asking you. I'm telling you. Get that baby shit outta your mind. If I won't give my wife a baby, I damn sure ain't gonna let you have one. That shit would crush her and you know it. Marley is my wife, and when I'm ready, she'll be the one having my shorty. Not you. Listen to me, and listen to me good. Tomorrow, I'm going to call that clinic and schedule you an appointment. I'm taking you down there myself to make sure it's done. Do you understand me?" The muscles in my jaw clenched with every word. When she didn't answer, I tightened my grip and got right in her face. Spit flew from my mouth as I spoke. "I asked you a fuckin' question. Do you understand me?"

"Santi," she began, just above a whisper. Her floodgates opened, causing a waterfall of tears to cascade down her face. "Please don't make me do it."

I pushed up, causing the back of her head to bash against the wall. Her breathing increased as I manhandled her roughly. This bitch was trying my patience.

"Let me go," she started again, sobbing uncontrollably. "You're hurting me."

"I'ma do more than that," I threatened.

"It ain't fair!" Amaya belted at the top of her lungs. She tried to wiggle free, but I wouldn't let her go. "What makes Marley so special? If she was pregnant, you wouldn't say shit. But she ain't. I am. I keep getting pregnant because it's meant to be. Don't you realize that? You're supposed to be with me, not Marley."

I released the grip on her chin and took a step back. Frustration was coursing through me, and I feared what I might do. Never in my life did I want to hit a woman as bad as I wanted to hit Amaya. She was being unreasonable.

"So that's what this is about?" I finally asked after an extended pause. "Marley? You're doing this to hurt Marley?"

"I'm doing this for us!"

"There is no us! You can quit with that shit. You're crazy as hell if you think I'm going to be with you after this."

"But, Santi..."

Hearing those words got to her. She was starting to realize that I wasn't playing. Her game had backfired and now she wanted to plead her case. It was too late for that.

"Don't Santi me. You knew good and damn well what you were doing. Like I said, I'll make the appointment for you tomorrow. I'll call you with the details. Other than that, we have nothing else to talk about."

I wasn't trying to go to jail. If I stayed in her company, that's exactly where I would have ended up. To lessen the likelihood of that happening, I disappeared into my bedroom and threw myself across the bed. Staring at the ceiling, I replayed the events of the day in my head. I came home early to celebrate my new business venture. Instead, I was met with Amaya trying to get under my skin. Pregnant? What the fuck was I thinking?

"Santi," I heard Amaya's barely audible voice from my doorway. I closed my eyes, and silently counted to ten. "Can we talk?"

"Not now, Amaya."

"Please?"

She walked over to the bed and stood before me. I let out a loud sigh hoping that she would get the point. It wasn't safe to be that close to me. I could go from calm to savage in a matter of seconds.

Instead of taking heed to my warning, she ignored it, and stubbornly sat down beside me.

"You've made it clear that I'll never have you. Let me at least have a part of you. I want to keep this baby, Santi."

"No," I said simply, feeling sweat form around my forehead.

"She doesn't know it's yours, and she won't. I promise."

"We've been through this before. Amaya you already know how I feel about this. You knew how I was going to react when you opened your mouth. Why the fuck would you do that?"

"I was mad."

Now, I was just as mad. If not more.

"For?"

"How could you choose another bitch over me? You fed me a dream while wining and dining Talia's ass."

"I didn't wine and dine anybody," I defended, as if that made it better.

"Fine. You didn't feed her. You fucked her though."

I didn't deny it. It was the truth. I fucked Talia's young ass, and it was damn good too. I really wished that Amaya hadn't fucked that up for me. I could have used some her sloppy head at that moment. It was much better than listening to Amaya bitch about something she had no claims to. I wasn't her man. Thanks to her slick mouth, she wasn't my side bitch no more either.

"I knew you did!" There went the waterworks again. She needed to take that crying shit on somewhere.

"Amaya, go home. Please. You already caused enough trouble as it is. I don't know what's it's going to take to get myself out of this one."

That reminded me. I sat up and patted my pockets for my phone. I needed to contact Marley, and make sure she was straight.

"Marley. Marley. Marley. That's all you think about. Marley's not the one having your baby, I am! Fuck Marley! And fuck you too, Santi!"

Somehow, she miraculously matched the speed of Usain Bolt. I chased her out of the room, but gave up once she hit the stairs. She was gone, cursing both me and Marley on her way out.

I got Marley's voicemail, and hung up without leaving a message. I tried two more times while pacing the floor, but they both ended with the same result. For her to not answer my call, she was mad. It was going to take the Father, the Son, and the Holy Ghost to get back in her good graces. I decided to start with flowers. I called the local floral shop and ordered enough flowers to fill our room. Next, I dialed my personal contact at Davis Jewelers. Nothing says 'I'm sorry' like a piece of fine jewelry. As luck would have it, a new collection of custom pieces had just been delivered. I made an appointment to stop by the next day to find something that my baby would like. I just needed her to come home.

I called her phone again. This time, when her voicemail prompted me to leave a message, I pleaded for her to call me. It's all I could do. From here, it was a waiting game.

The only face I wanted to see was Marley's. I needed her to know that I heard her loud and clear. She wanted a baby, and although I was truthful when I told Amaya I wasn't ready, I was going to appease my wife.

I took my time showering, allowing the warm water to cleanse my mind, body, and spirit. I had to make some changes. If things continued the way they were, my marriage would be in jeopardy. I realized how my personal indiscretions were affecting my relationship with my wife. I loved Marley. She didn't do anything to make me stray. I was selfish. I wanted to live the fast life. Seven years of juggling two women and the only thing I had to show for it was a wife who wouldn't answer my calls and a thorn in my side hellbent on destroying what I worked so hard for. As the water cascaded down my body, I came to the conclusion that I had to put Marley first. That's the only way it was going to work. I had to make her my number one priority. Once I got everything squared away with Amaya, I was going to do just that.

20

CASHMERE

*B*etween all this shit with Marley and Kelsie, I needed a damn break. Ever since Kensley figured out who Kelsie was, Kelsie has been bugging the shit out of me to see her. I couldn't even give her an answer because I haven't talked to Ken about it since it happened. I can't lie, I'm avoiding the topic with her. Only because I don't want her to get attached to Kelsie and she go off and do the same dumb shit again. I would have to kill her for breaking Ken's heart.

"What are you thinking about?" Marley quizzed as she rubbed my head. I was laying in between her legs while we watched some movie on Netflix. She hadn't been home in two days and that was cool with me. I loved having her here to hold at night and wake up to in the morning. We had been going at it like some damn jack rabbits and not once did I pull out. I was doing whatever I could to get her pregnant and make her leave Santiago's no good ass.

"This shit with Ken and her mama. I don't know what to do anymore," I admitted with a sigh while running my hands over my face.

"Have you talked to Ken about it?"

"Nope."

"And why not?"

"I don't want her to get hurt," I said. "It's my job to protect her and I feel like if I let her have a relationship with Kelsie and she fails, then it will be my fault."

"Babe, you need to talk to Ken and see what she wants to do. I understand that you're hesitant and only want to protect her, but I think she is old enough to make this decision on her own. All this time she's thought her mother was dead and now, fifteen years later, she finds out it was a lie. Don't you think you owe it to her?" She advised and I agreed.

I knew Ken was probably pissed at me for lying to her all this time, but what else was I supposed to do? I didn't want her knowing that her mother was a drug addict who abandoned her to feed her disgusting habit. I wanted Ken to live a perfect life without one thing ruining it. I guess I can't protect her from everything, but I'll try my hardest to.

"You're right," I mumbled and sat up to face her. "Let me go holla at her."

Marley gave me a weak smile and put her small, soft hand on my face. I kissed her passionately and then went in search of Ken. I searched all over her side of the house and found her in her lounge room studying. She was deep into whatever it was and didn't even see me standing there. Her face was scrunched up and she was bobbing her head to the soft music that was playing in the background. I leaned against the door and admired my baby sister. She was so smart and beautiful. Why did Kelsie ever leave her?

"Ehm," I cleared my throat to get her attention. She glanced up and rolled her eyes when she saw it was me.

"What do you want, Cash? I'm trying to study," she spat dryly. I walked over and turned off her music then sat down beside her. She discreetly peeked over at me and continued working.

"What are you studying?" I questioned just to get the conversation started. When Ken was mad, I had to ease my way in to her space. She was like me and held up a guard with whoever she was mad at. Stubborn as fuck.

"A test for my AP English class."

"How's that going?"

She slammed her pencil down and folded her arms while grilling me. "What is it? I know you didn't come in here just to see what I was doing. Speak your mind, brother."

That was another thing; Ken knew me like the back of her hand. It was hard for me to hide anything from her because she could read me like a book. Since it had only been the two of us for all these years, we were closer than ever and could talk to each other about anything. Well, almost anything. She was the only girl who made me nervous and could talk to me rudely without getting slapped, but she would get put in her place. She was spoiled, but she wasn't stupid.

"First, I want to apologize for lying to you about your mother all these years." I started.

"Why did you lie?" She asked before I could continue. "And don't lie to me, Cash."

I leaned back in the chair and inhaled deeply. "Because, I wanted to protect you."

"Protect me from what? Her?"

I nodded my head yes. I had her full attention now. She was fiddling with her thumbs and shaking her leg. I knew she was scared to ask why, so I went on to explain.

"Ken, look. The reason I've lied to you all this time is because Kelsie was an addict. She was on drugs hard and I didn't want you exposed to that." I explained.

"I'm already exposed to drugs because you sell them, so what made her different?" She shot back and it caught me off guard. She made a good point, but Ken has never laid eyes on the shit I deal with. I've always been straight up with her about what I did for a living, but I've never had her around it like that.

"The difference is that she was using them; I sell. That's a big difference."

"I guess," she mumbled then shrugged her shoulders. "How did I end up with you if she's still alive?"

"I think she needs to be the one to tell you that," I answered.

"You mean... I can talk to her?" She breathed in shock and I laughed.

"That's up to you, Ken. I love you and I want to protect you from all that I can, but this is something you have to decide. Not me." I couldn't believe the words that were coming out my mouth. Marley had that damn effect on me to get me to see things her way and Ken noticed.

"Let me guess, Marley told you that?" She giggled.

"Maybe," I chuckled. "She was right, though. As bad as I want to tell you that you can't have any dealings with Kelsie, I can't do that. At the end of the day, she's your mother and if you want her in your life then I will have to accept that. No matter how hard it will be."

Ken jumped up from her seat and wrapped her arms around my neck. I hugged her back and prayed I was making the right decision. I would hate to kill Kelsie for fuckin' my baby over, but I would if that's what it came down to.

"Thank you, Cash. I want to talk to her and hear her side of things. I have so many questions that I need answers to and she's the only one who can provide them for me," she expressed and I understood where she was coming from.

"I completely agree. Now, I have another question for you."

"What is it?"

"How did you know she was your mother?" I interrogated with a raised brow. "From what I knew, you always assumed she was dead because that's what I told you. So, I'm confused." Ken was a smart girl, but there's no way she figured tha shit out on her own.

She sighed heavily and gave me big, round puppy dogs eyes before speaking. "Promise me you won't get mad?"

"You know I can't promise shit, Ken. I can't control my emotions."

"True, but I still need you to promise." She demanded with her hand out. We did our secret handshake and I waited for her to explain. "One morning, when she was standing outside the school watching me as usual. Curiosity got the best of me, so I walked over to her before the bell rang and asked her who she was and why was she always watching me. She never did answer; all she did was tell me her name and left it at that. So, I did my research and figured out she was my mother. I never said anything to you about it because I knew there was a reason behind why you didn't want me to know, so I waited for you to come to me first. Yeah, I was pissed because I couldn't believe you would keep something like that from me, but I got over it. This happened after I told you she was watching me."

I was speechless. I wasn't mad at her because I would have wanted to know why someone was watching my every move too. I just wish she would have came to me before. I could breathe a little easier knowing that now.

"Well, I'm glad I know now and you too. I will find a way for you to get in contact with Kelsie so y'all can meet up and talk," I told her and she smiled brightly.

"Will you come with me? I don't want to be alone with her yet," she admitted. "I don't know what to expect and of course, I need my protector there with me."

"I know you didn't think I was going to let you go by yourself," I smacked my lips and she giggled. "I have to see wha state of mind she's in before I even let her near you. She could relapse at any moment."

"Come on, Cash. Have a little more faith in her. From the scene she was causing here the other day, I think she's learned her lesson. I could see that she was genuine and just wants to be in my life; like a mother should." Ken expressed, but I still wasn't sure. Kelsie was going to show me she was for real this time or I would step in and change Ken's decision for her.

"Let's just take it one step at a time. I'm already fighting with myself on letting you make this choice on your own."

"I'll be graduating in two years, brother. You can't keep me on a leash forever," she stressed and rolled her eyes.

"I'll let you think that. Remember, your brother has more pull than you think. I'll have eyes on you no matter how far off to college you go. You can't escape this love," I teased and leaned over to kiss her forehead. I was about to get up and leave, but she stopped me.

"Wait! Since we're having honesty hour, there's something else I need to tell you." She breathed with a nervous expression painted on her face. I could already feel my head start pounding, so I sat back and closed my eyes with my fingers tips pressed together.

"Okay." I gulped. "I'm listening."

"I have a girlfriend," she blurted so fast that it took me a few seconds to process it. When I finally did, I stared at her with wide eyes and wiggled my ears.

"Come again?"

"I have a girlfriend." This time, she stated it with a little more confidence. "I'm bisexual."

"Are you sure?"

"What do you mean am I sure? I just told you I have a girlfriend."

"Yeah, I heard you. I'm just making sure you're not just going through one of those teenage girl phases where you're trying to find yourself," I explained. I mean, I couldn't control who she loved, but I wanted her to be sure this was who she truly was.

"Hmm, it may be. I never thought of it like that," she said more to herself than me, then shrugged. "Oh, well. I'm just living for the moment."

"At least I don't have to worry about you getting pregnant," I groaned as I got up from the chair. I leaned over and kissed her fore-head and she smiled. "Whatever makes you happy. Just know, I won't show any mercy just because you're dating a female. She will get interrogated and hurt if she hurts you."

"I know, Cash."

"You better. Get back to studying. I'm going to lay back down." I announced as I walked out the room.

"Thank you!" Ken yelled as I turned the corner. I just smiled and made my way back to my room. After hearing all that, all I wanted to do was go to sleep and forget all about it. After I finished handling business with Marley.

I peeked into the room and she was laying on her stomach;

knocked out. Her hair was all over her head and she was snoring. She had been sleeping a lot more lately and so have I. All we wanted to do was lay around, eat and sleep. I had a feeling I knew what it was, but I was going to wait for Marley to figure out. I decided not to wake her. Instead, I snuggled up behind her and was out in a matter of minutes.

21

AMAYA

*S*anti was heavily on my mind, but I refused to give in. Almost a week had passed, and we still hadn't physically laid eyes on each other. In the days since seeing him, he'd reached out twice, and that was only to tell me that he had scheduled my appointment. Well...Friday came and went. Santi may have thought he was calling the shots, but I had the final say. It was after all, *my* body.

To decrease the likelihood of me running into him, I'd been staying with my mother. She lived in Valley Station, an area Santi didn't frequent regularly. I had Armando lying to his boss about my whereabouts in exchange for the keys to my condo. I could only image the condition of my crib. Knowing my brother, there were probably bottles, drugs, and cum everywhere. Armando had one agenda, and that was to stick his baby maker into as many females that would let him. I shook my head at the thought of him getting it on in my bed. Fuck changing the sheets. I was going to throw the whole bed away.

I was sprawled out on my mother's couch, applying lotion to my legs when the doorbell rang. My mother was out getting her weekly Bingo fix, and Armando was MIA. I let the doorbell ring for a second time before standing to see who was at the door. Koda greeted me with a smile and opened his arms for a hug.

"What are you doing here?" he asked, inhaling deeply into my freshly washed hair. Just like my body, my hair matched the coconut scent of my favorite shampoo and conditioner combination. I let the excess suds seep down and cleanse my body.

"Housesitting," I lied. "Are you here for Armando?"

"Maybe. Or, maybe I'm here for you."

"Well, in that case..." I stepped back, allowing him entry to my mother's crib.

Closing the door behind him, I led him to the couch. Once seated, I picked up right where I left off and squirted lotion in my palm.

"Let me help you out with that."

He rubbed his hands against mine and removed the creamy concoction coating my fingers. Starting with my feet, he massaged the lotion into my skin, easing his way up to my ankles. His hand were soft; a stark contrast from the roughness I was used to. Santi had 'working man's hands', which I enjoyed caressing the full length of my body. Soft hands and all, Koda was a close second. He expertly used the skill God gave him and worked wonders on my calves. I welcomed the feeling of him venturing his hands upward, into my personal territory. I didn't stop him as his hands found my thighs and remained there longer than necessary.

"You want me to stop?" he asked, pausing to gage my reaction.

I was too caught up in the feeling to respond. He took my silence as permission to continue, and I let him. He scooted his body closer to me as his hands found the inside of my thigh. He massaged me ever so gently; softly squeezing at my sensitive area. The soft moan that escaped my lips brought a smile the size of Texas to his. It was hard not to become aroused with those sexy dimples staring back at me.

Bypassing my boy shorts and thong, his fingers found the slick folds of my womanhood. I gasped loudly.

"You okay?"

I nodded because I damn sure couldn't speak. The only thing I wanted at that moment was to feel him inside me.

He wasted no time at all. Reaching for the waistband of my shorts, he slid them off along with my panties. I lifted my hips to assist him. Koda removed a condom from his pants pocket before sliding them off. His boxers came off next, allowing his thick erection to spring free.

I made myself comfortable on the couch while he wrapped up and removed his shirt. I waited in nervous anticipation for him to handle this pussy any way he wanted to. Juices leaked from my body as I thought about how good Koda was going to feel. Then reality set in. Everything ain't as good as it looks.

Sex with Koda lasted all of three minutes, if that. There was no foreplay. No kissing. No touching. Nothing. He entered me roughly, pumping a few times to get his. He selfishly pinned me down, missionary style, preventing my body from moving.

"Koda," I called out, trying to get his attention.

He ignored me, panting like a damn dog with his eyes closed. He was zoned out; pleasing himself at my expense. For the life of me, I don't know how he worked up a sweat, but he did. I turned my head as a droplet of sweat fell from his forehead and landed on my cheek.

"Aww shit, girl," he sang proudly. "I'm about to cum."

All that dick and no stamina. Now I knew why he was single. No woman in their right mind would put up with subpar lovemaking. At that moment, I made up my mind. That was the first and last time that he would be getting in my pants. Hell, I could have saved him the trouble and rubbed my own clit.

"I hate to leave you like this," he said, reaching for his boxers, "But I gotta make a run real quick. Wanna ride with me?"

Riding was something I should have been doing, but not in a car. I declined his offer and started toward the bathroom. "No. What time is it?"

"Almost three."

"Shit, I'm supposed to meet up with Marley."

"Well, call me when you're done. I'll stop by and pick you up."

That nigga didn't even wash his ass before leaving. I, on the other hand, showered and changed into black romper and wedge heels. I pulled my hair back into a high ponytail and left to get things straight with Marley.

Although I had asked to meet up with Marley days ago, today was the day she finally found time to squeeze me in. We were meeting up at an Italian restaurant, and my plan was to set her straight. I was tired of the back and forth. It was time for the truth to come out.

I arrived first and was seated at a table close to the entrance. The evening crowd hadn't poured in yet, giving one-on-one attention with the waitress.

"Are you ready to order yet?" a young blonde asked, placing a basket of breadsticks in the middle of the table.

"Can I have some more time please? I'm waiting on someone."

She nodded and left me alone to review the menu. Marley strolled in shortly thereafter. She wore a simple maxi dress and sandals. Her hair was down, falling just below her shoulders. She looked a'ight, I guess. Without saying a word, she sat down opposite of me.

"Thank you for meeting me," I began, watching Marley's 'resting bitch face' peer back at me. "For a moment there, I didn't think you were coming."

"I wasn't." She sighed and placed her large tote bag beside her. "But I'm here, so talk."

"Do you want to order first?"

"No. I won't be here that long."

"Well in that case, let me talk fast." I flashed her a half-smile, hoping it would lighten the mood. It didn't. I nervously intertwined my fingers. "So, how are things going?"

"You really called me down here to ask me that?"

"I called you down here to see what was up with you. I haven't seen you since you stormed out like a child."

"What are you talking about?"

"You know good and well what I'm talking about. I told you that I was pregnant and you go off on Santi. That was my moment, and like always, you had to make it about you. What kind of friend does that?"

"Really, Amaya? You called me on some bullshit?"

"You left me hanging because you were in your feelings. That's what's bullshit."

"You know how hard that was for me. I've wanted to be a mother for as long as I can remember. I feel like you're doing this just to get under my skin. You've never talked about having kids. Never. Now all of sudden you're pregnant and throwing that shit in my face. How did you expect me to react?"

I gave her a long, bored look. I didn't give a rat's ass about her feelings at that point. Her issue was with Santi, not me.

"More like a friend, and less like a spoiled brat. It's not my fault Santi won't give you a baby. You're the one living in a fantasy world. That man has made it perfectly clear that he's not giving you a baby. Why do you think he hangs out in the streets so much? It's to get away from all your fuckin' nagging. He hasn't given you a baby in all these years, and you still won't read between the lines."

"You're pathetic!" She stood, clutching her tote in the process. "I don't know why I even wasted my time. Cash was right."

"And what's that supposed to mean?"

"You don't give a damn about no one but yourself. Everything is a competition with you. So, what? Now you think you've one-upped me? It's sad that your only mission in life is to be better than me. That's as pathetic as it gets."

"Spoken by someone who's had everything handed to her. If it wasn't for Santiago, you wouldn't have shit. Don't try to preach to me."

"Here we go again. Can we have a conversation without you mentioning my husband? Why is it that his name stays in your mouth?"

That's not the only thing, I wanted to say, but didn't. Instead, I turned things back on her. "Why do you care? It's not in yours. You're so far up Cash's ass that you've forgotten that you have a husband."

She laughed in my face, which further irritated me. "Santi and I are good. Any issues that we've had in the past have been squashed. As far as Cash goes, don't speak on things you clearly have no idea about."

"What's with the attitude? Face it, Marley. You're just jealous."

"Yeah. Okay. Humor me, Amaya. What could you possibly have that I would want?"

I leaned back in my seat, and rubbed the baby bump that hadn't formed yet. Her eyes fell to my midsection and stayed there.

"We'll see in about seven months." I beamed with confidence, knowing that I hit her below the belt. She didn't have a comeback for that one. Or, so I thought.

"I feel sorry for you...and that baby! Another child born to a single mother who just can't get right. You have nothing going for yourself. Laying on your back will only get you so far."

"You're one to talk. Ain't that how things started with you and Santi?" That struck a nerve. The large vein in her forehead that presented itself when she was upset was on full display. "You wanted him because of his money. You've been spreading your legs for seven years, and the only thing you got was his last name. Get off that fucking high horse of yours. You ain't no better than me."

"Santi wifed me because he wanted to. Nobody forced him to do shit."

"That's all he did. This is me you're talking to. Don't think I forgot about all the times you called me crying; wishing your man was home. Pull that marriage shit on someone who doesn't know any better. Your home has been broken for years. You have a piece of paper tying the two of you together. That's not a marriage. That's called friends with benefits."

"Why do I even bother with you? You're not even worth my time. Grow the fuck up, Amaya."

She took a few steps in the opposite direction, but I wasn't done yet. "Leaving so soon? Well in that case, tell Cash I said 'Hello'." Her straightened hair swung around faster than she did.

"What the fuck did you say?"

"You're so quick to point out everyone else's flaws but you can't see your own. Last time I checked, adultery was a sin. What are you getting out of the deal, hunh? Is Cash selling you a dream? Or are you just fucking him for free?"

"If you keep running your mouth I'm going to forget that you're pregnant."

I shifted my weight to one foot and crossed my arms over my chest. I knew Marley; maybe better than anyone else. The one thing in life she wanted was a baby. Because of that, I knew she wouldn't touch me. No matter how bad my mouth became, she wouldn't lay a hand on me. She wouldn't risk harming a child – even mine. Knowing that fed my ego. Too much time had passed with me standing in her shadows. My friend was now my enemy. It was time to take the gloves off and hit her right where it hurts.

"You think you're so much better than me. Well, I got news for you, Marley. Just like you're sneaking behind Santi's back and fucking Cash, he's sneaking behind yours and fucking me. This is Santi's baby."

I didn't get the reaction I wanted. I expected her to pop off at the mouth and deny that her man was even interested in me. I had slick comebacks and details waiting to be divulged if prompted. Instead, she shook her head and smirked.

"When you find a man that loves you, I mean truly loves you, everything else is irrelevant. Santi ain't even worth the headache. You can have him." Securing her tote on her forearm, she tossed her straightened hair over her shoulders and left.

After everything was said and done, Marley didn't even care. My plan had backfired and I was left looking like a fool.

22

MARLEY

I was heartbroken. It was taking everything in me not to go back in there and beat that damn baby out of Amaya! How could she? How could they do this to me? I knew some shit was going on, but I chose to ignore it. *All the fuckin' signs were in front of you, Marley!* I can most definitely say they took my kindness for weakness. I was weak, but not anymore. That's why I was able to just suck shit up and walk away from Amaya without pouncing on her fake, wannabe ass. I wouldn't dare lay hands on her while she's pregnant, but that didn't mean I couldn't touch Santi.

"Hey, baby." He cooed into the phone.

"Where are you?" I asked, trying to hide the tremble of anger in my tone. I wanted him to think everything was all good and dandy.

"I'm about to go into this meeting with Cashmere at his house."

"Oh, I wanted to see you." I fake pouted. "I wanted to talk to you about the other day. I've had time to sit and think about it." I wanted to puke.

"I can come straight home afterwards, Ley. I miss you so fuckin' much," he damn near cried and I rolled my eyes hard as hell.

"I miss you too. See you then."

I hung up and sped to Cashmere's house. The more I thought

about it, the sicker I felt. The two people I loved more than anything had betrayed me. How long has this been going on? Ha! This bitch actually got pregnant by *my* husband. *My* husband gave her a baby and couldn't even give me one! His own damn wife! This all made sense now. His late nights and her lavish gifts from an unknown man. They had been playing me this whole time, but I had something for their asses.

I made it to Cashmere's and hopped out my car. I used my key to get in and switched straight to his meeting room. I knew he would be pissed at me for interrupting while he's conducting business, but what I had to handle was far more important and I knew he would understand.

I barged into the room and all eyes fell on me. Santi was sitting there with a bewildered expression etched on his face while Cashmere was glaring at me with a raised brow. I sat my purse down and stood there with my hand on my hip while grilling Santi. He stood up and came over to me.

WHAP!

I slapped his ass so hard that his lip started bleeding. He clenched his jaw and looked at me out the corner of his eyes. In the background, I could see Cashmere stand up and I knew he was ready just in case Santi tried to strike me back. He wasn't that stupid.

"How could you do this to me? To us?" I whispered on the verge of tears.

"What are you talking about, Ley?" He growled, then roughly gripped my arm and pressed his lips against my ear. "This is not the time or fuckin' place for this. I don't know what your problem is, but you need to go home and wait for me."

"Is there a problem?" Cashmere's voice boomed and I jerked away from Santi. I stepped back and I could feel Cashmere's eyes studying me.

"No, she was just leaving." Santi tried to dismiss me and I laughed.

"I'm not going any fuckin' where until I get some got damn answers! So, this meeting is over and y'all can reschedule!" I demanded and looked at Cashmere who snapped his fingers and cleared the place. Santi looked back and forth between the two of us and his frown deepened.

"The fuck was that?" He asked Cashmere who just shrugged his shoulders.

"Is Amaya carrying your baby, Santi?" I blurted and he froze. All the color drained from his face and he couldn't even look at me.

"Hell, no! What makes you think that?" His voice squeaked and he was looking down at his shoes. I pushed him and he stumbled over the chair.

"Why keep lying? She already told me, dumb ass!" I screamed and kicked his side.

"Ley, stop!" He shouted, scooting away and standing while still keeping some distance between us. "Come on! Let's not do this here. We can go home and talk about it," he suggested with fear laced in his tone.

"No, muthafucka! We're about to settle this right now! Is she really carrying your baby, Santi and don't lie!" I stomped over to him and looked him dead in the eyes. A part of me wanted him to say she was lying and she just wanted to get under my skin, but I knew better. When I saw the tears fall down his cheeks and he dropped his head, I fell to the floor and let out a gut wrenching cry.

I was hurt beyond what words could express. All the time and love I had invested in Santi was for nothing. I wasted years of trying to be the perfect wife and do what I thought would be best for him. I always put him first, no matter how I felt about it. I just wanted to make him happy. And this was the bullshit I got in return. Good thing I decided to do me.

"I'm sorry, Ley." Santi had the nerve to say.

"You're sorry? That's it? That's all you can say?" I scoffed and shook my head. "I shouldn't even be surprised." I picked myself up off the floor and dusted myself off. He still didn't look at me, so I raised his head with my hand and smacked him once more. I gazed into the eyes that I had fell in love with and no longer felt what I used to. My love for Santi was slowly dissipating and this situation helped me see that. "I hope she was worth you losing me because I'm done, Santi. If you didn't want me anymore, that's all you had to say and I would have let you be. Instead, you chose to hurt me to the core. How long have I been begging you for a baby and you go and knock my best friend up?"

"It wasn't supposed to happen like this, Ley. I've tried to break it off and focus on working things out with you, but she would always threaten to tell you and I couldn't bear the thought of losing you," Santi sniffled then finally looked at me. He looked pitiful, but I couldn't feel any sympathy for him. He had brought all this on himself and now, he had to deal with the consequences.

"You should have thought about that before you went sticking your dick in her!" I screamed in his face. "You're so damn selfish. You two deserve each other. I'll be sending someone to get my things. Be ready in court because I'm coming for every got damn thing you got! She doesn't deserve the shit I worked hard for."

"The shit you worked hard for?" He spat like the words were poison. The only thing you did was spend my money and sit at home and nag. Don't act like you were perfect."

"Huh. So, tell me how you really feel? Are you saying that I play a part in why you couldn't be a fuckin' grown man and keep your dick to yourself? Like I agreed to the shit? Don't play me like that, Santi. That was a choice *you* made!" I snapped with my finger in his face. "I worked hard to keep our marriage! Something you didn't give two shits about! I worked hard to be your wife. I was there to love you, hold you down and lift you up when times got hard. I was there! Where the fuck were you?"

I couldn't stand the sight of him anymore, so I got myself together and switched to the door with confidence. Santi was a piece of shit and I should have realized that from the start. I can't believe I was so blind and it was only because I loved him. His true colors were out now and so were Amaya's. I could sit here and blame myself for being stupid all day, but what good would it do? At the end of the day, they were in the wrong. I was too, but they didn't know that.

"Don't you dare leave, Ley! We're not done talkin'; I won't let you leave me!" Santi barked and I didn't even blink. I rolled my eyes and placed my shades on. I wouldn't allow him to see me cry again.

"There's nothing you can say to make me forgive you. Like I said, I'm done. I deserve better."

I jerked the door open and jogged to my car. I parked my car around back and went back inside to Cashmere's master bedroom. I sent him a text letting him know I stayed then powered my phone off. I didn't feel like being bothered with anyone. I needed time to myself so I could think. Stripping from my clothes, I dragged my feet into the adjoining master bathroom and ran some water in the huge tub. I dropped in a bath bomb and watched the tub turn a pinkish blue.

Climbing inside, I slid down until the water was covering my neck. I laid my head back on the neck pillow and cried as memories of Santi and me flooded my brain. We had so many good times together in the beginning. It was like I was floating on cloud nine and no one could bring me down; only Santi.

I can remember when things first started going down and I would always vent to Amaya about it. I thought she was being a good friend and shoulder to lean on, but that bitch was using all that shit to her advantage. She used me and I can only imagine for how long. It had to be for some time now because I could see that her feelings were involved. *Conniving bitch!*

I heard the bathroom door open and shut. I didn't open my eyes because I knew it was Cashmere. His cologne greeted me before anything. I inhaled his scent deeply and started to feel secure. He always made me feel warm and safe. My feelings for Cashmere were deep; deep to the point where I knew I loved him. He was everything that my husband should have been. Santi betrayed me with someone I considered family. That let me know that our marriage was simply a piece of paper. It didn't mean shit to him, so it didn't mean shit to me.

Cashmere lifted my body, climbed in the water and then sat down with me on top of him. I buried my face in his neck and let the tears fall freely. He didn't say anything. He just stroked my back with his strong hand and held me tight. This was all I needed and I was thankful that he was giving it to me. We stayed like that until the water turned cold and I had no more tears to cry. Cashmere turned the shower on then helped me inside. He washed my body while placing soft kisses wherever he could. Once he was done washing both of us, he helped me out the shower and put some lotion on me before I laid in the middle of his bed. He rolled in beside me and held me tightly.

"You were right about her," I whispered. "She was never my friend."

"And that's not your fault. None of this is. You were just the victim of a fucked up situation," he stated. "Any thought of something you did needs to be erased right now. You did what you were supposed to as wife and friend, but didn't get the same in return. All this shit is on them."

"I know," I sighed. "I can't help but feel guilty about what we're doing. Amaya is catching on. She's been throwing you up a lot lately."

"Why feel guilty? I understand that you're still married, but y'all haven't been *together* in some time from what you tell me. Fuck what anyone else has to say. Amaya needs to worry about her own damn self and keep my name out her dick sucker," Cashmere barked and I giggled. "I'm about to ask you something and I need you to be straight up with me, Marley. Don't lie."

The tone of his voice worried me a little, so I sat up and turned to face him. He was laying there with a slight scowl on his face and worry lines waving his forehead. I could see that something was bothering him.

"What's wrong, Cashmere?"

"Are you going to take Santiago back? I know that's hard for you to answer right now, but I just need to see if your heart is in the same place as mine."

His question caught me off guard, but my mind was made up. My heart was no longer with Santi. I had fallen out of love with him and I was ready to close that chapter of my life. I knew it was going to hurt and I would have days where I missed him, but we had outgrown each other. He made that decision when he stepped out and so did I.

I wish things could have ended differently, but that's just how life goes sometimes.

"No, I'm not." I answered confidently and he tried to hide the smile that was tugging at his lips. "I deserve much better than how he's been treating me these past few years. I was no longer a priority in his life and he chose what he wanted. He can beg and cry all he wants, but I'm done."

"I love you, Marley. Let me be the man to make you happy again and fix all the pieces he's broken within you." He expressed while gazing into my eyes. "I'll do whatever it takes to show you I will always put you first and love you to no end. I know it's going to take some time, but I swear you're worth the wait."

Tears filled my eyes as I listened to him express his feelings. I've never seen Cashmere this vulnerable. His words were like music to my ears. I had fallen so hard for this man and I was so happy with him. He made me forget about all my worries. He's what made all this shit with Santi and Amaya lighter.

"I love you too, Cashmere. Let's just keep taking things one step at a time. Deal?"

"How about we start in Costa Rica? I could use a little break from work and you most definitely need a getaway," he suggested and I happily agreed. We decided to make plans when we woke up. All the crying and screaming I did had me drained and I just needed to sleep these feelings off. Wrapped up in Cashmere, I fell into a deep sleep and dreamed of what the future could be.

23

SANTIAGO

I ain't one to show my emotions, but that shit hurt my heart. Never in my wildest dream did I imagine Marley ever leaving me. I knew the possibility was there, but in the back of my mind I never thought she would actually do it. She had me sitting in that big ass crib of ours alone, listening to those stupid love songs. I shed a tear or two before hitting up my bar and drinking my sorrows away.

It's been almost a week and I still haven't heard from Marley. She cut me off and left me at my weakest point. Marley made it perfectly clear that she was done, but I tried anyway. I called her phone to the point where she could have involved the law. Some may say that my actions were a form of harassment, but who cares! That's my wife. Until the paperwork is in and the ink dries, I still have a chance.

Then we have Amaya. When I see her ass, it's on! The way she handled our situation can't be forgiven. That was some malicious shit. All she had to do was be the good little bitch that I thought she was. Yeah, I was mad about Talia, but eventually I would have found my way back to Amaya. That's how it always happens. I get mad, stay away for a while, then slip back up in her panties. No biggie. Of course she just had to push this shit as far as she could. I guess she thought that if Marley found out, I'd catch her on the rebound. Not happening. Not only did she tell Marley about the baby, she met up with my wife and named me as the father. It's a wrap. You never run your mouth to the wife. Since she did, I'm bustin' her fuckin' head when I see her. That bitch ruined my life, and she's gonna pay for it.

I chose to brighten my mood by buying something new. Knowing that I had money and could buy anything I wanted always made me feel better. I ended up driving into a car dealership with my six month old Maybach and driving out in a sporty new Aston Martin. I called two of my boys to drive my Maybach home while I cruised around in my new ride. I rode up down Broadway, teasing the city with my new toy. Let's face it, not too many people could afford a luxury vehicle like this. In the midst of everything goes on, there was one thing that was constant – my money.

The first order of business for the day was to check on my new club. I drove to the location and parked on the street. The parking lot was being repaved, preventing me from parking closer. I hopped out the car with my keys in hand, and admired the progress that had been made thus far.

The brick building had been power washed, removing the buildup of mold and dirt collecting around the foundation. Broken windows were replaced, and a large sign had been mounted above the entrance. *Ley Santi*, which I decided to name the place, was right on track to be completed within the eight week time frame. Now, I just needed to see the inside.

Strolling in, I was met with workers performing a variety of different tasks. Two men sanded the walls on opposite sides while three more people worked on installing the hardwood floors. The last time I checked, they hadn't even started yet. They were now more than twenty-five percent complete.

A wide smile formed on my face as I rubbed the stubble growing out of control on my chin. The place wasn't complete yet, but it was well on its way and I was happy about that. Finally, something in my life was going right.

"How's it looking?" a male voice asked behind me. I turned around to see my contractor smiling ear to ear.

"Hey, Charlie. It's lookin' good. I stopped by to see how things were going. I must say, I'm impressed."

"We try to complete our projects before the expected time frame. Our clients like that. Word of mouth is our best form of advertising and we strive to keep our clients happy. That way, they'll use us again and tell their friends."

I nodded and scanned the room once more.

"What's going on over there?" I asked, pointing to the spot where the bar was supposed to be located. The cherry wood floors had been installed in that section, but the bar was nowhere to be seen.

"I wanted to talk to you about that," Charlie began, clearing his throat. The tone of his voice changed. I knew bad news was coming.

"I received a call this morning. The bar is currently on backorder. I was on the phone with the warehouse for almost an hour. They're completely out of stock."

"So what does that mean?"

"Well, we have two options. We can wait under the order comes in, which is expected to be almost twelve weeks."

"Hell naw! Three fuckin' months? That ain't happening," I complained. "I ain't pushing back the grand opening. The date is already set."

"We do have another option. I found a suitable replacement that I think you would like. It can be delivered by the end of the week."

"Okay. Let's do it." I trusted my contractor's opinion. I didn't need to see it to know that it would work. Charlie knew my vision and if he thought it was acceptable, that's all I needed to hear.

"It's gonna take us over budget about a thousand dollars."

"Damn. Are they making it by hand?" I spat sarcastically. "Why is it so expensive?"

"Quality, Santi. You get what you pay for."

I nodded and agreed to the changes. Charlie was on his phone within minutes, making arrangements for the new bar with expedited shipping. I followed suit, removing my phone from the pocket of my jeans and calling Cash. I also had shipments to secure.

"What's up?" he grumbled into the phone.

"Damn, you busy?"

"Something like that. Hold on a minute. My girl is sleep and I don't want to wake her."

Cash and I were cool, but his personal life remained private. He didn't disclose those intimate details. A girl? This was news to me.

"I'm back," he stated, returning to the line. "What do you need?"

The dismissive tone in his voice momentarily caught me off guard, but I relayed the reason for the call to him anyway.

"That shit sold like hotcakes! I'm almost out. How soon can I get more?"

"Sorry, my man. I'm dry right now."

What? Dry? Impossible.

"Come on now, Cash. This is me. I'm sure you can work your magic and get me what I need."

"I know you've been watching the news. Border patrol is knockin' people left and right. I took a huge hit off that shit. I don't know when I'm gonna be back up."

Damn. There went my plans. I hated reaching out to someone else, but I couldn't let my customers down. Cash's prices were right up my alley. Everyone else was trying to tax a muthafucka.

"A'ight. Let me know if something changes."

Click.

I removed the phone from my ear and brought it to eye level to confirm what I already knew. That nigga hung up on me. What the fuck was up with him? I shook that shit off and glanced one last time at the workers before exiting the building.

I climbed in my ride and drove around; burning gas for no reason at all. I made a few phone calls to check on my 'other' business before finding myself sitting in my driveway. It was Friday evening, and I had nothing to do. I was halfway up my driveway when my cell phone rung. It was Armando.

"Talk to me." I spat into the phone.

"Shit, I was just checking on you. Ain't nobody seen your face in a few days. You a'ight, nigga?"

"I'm still breathing, so I'm good."

"You don't sound good. You sure everything's okay?"

I wondered if Amaya had told her brother about what had transpired between us. Then I heard the genuine sincerity in his voice and knew that he was unaware of the situation. It's amazing how Amaya keeps her mouth closed for some, and has loose lips with others. Why was I even thinking about that bitch?

"I'm sure. What do you have going on for the night?"

"You already know. Hoes! Koda and I are going to the strip club. You wanna roll?"

"Sure. Why not?" It's not like I had anything else to do. "Which one?"

He disclosed the address and meeting time. I agreed to meet him at The Godfather and ended the call. As I entered my empty house, I was reminded that my wife wasn't there. She usually greeted me with a big smile and fresh home cooking. Instead, I was met with darkness and complete silence. *Damn, I missed that woman!* I didn't realize how good I had it until she was gone.

After a nap and a quick shower, I was almost ready to hit the club. Pulling my hair back off my shoulders, I examined myself in the mirror. I kept it simple in a Polo shirt and dark jeans. My sour mood didn't warrant anything fancy. I was going simply to get out of the house. I could have easily out dressed anyone around me, but why bother? I wasn't trying to pick up anyone. My attire didn't matter.

I arrived a little after ten. We were supposed to meet at nine, but as usual, I was late. Instead of going straight to the club like I planned, I made an last minute detour to Smitty's. Surprisingly he was still there, and hooked me up with a shape up and a fresh trim. I looked like a totally different person when I left. I was back to my old self; at least on the outside.

I doused myself with Eternity cologne before walking into the club. I should have known it wasn't my kind of scene as soon as I stepped through the door. Besides Armando and Koda, I was the only other person in there with a little color to their skin; if you know what I mean. I walked over to them and sat down as two big breasted, flat ass women struggled to shake what their momma didn't give them.

"Where you been?" Armando asked, juggling two big titties in his face.

"I had to get fresh first. What y'all drinking on?"

Koda raised his bottle in my direction. "Dos Equis. Want one?"

"Naw, I'm good."

I'm pretty sure you can figure out how my night went. I donated a few hundred dollars, just for the hell of it. Other than that, it was a long, boring night. The only takeaway I received was what not to do when I opened my own spot. I was not going to hire anyone who couldn't dance. Hair twirling and grabbing titties just didn't do it for me. I wanted bad bitches who could drop it low and spread it wide right in my face. Men liked that shit. Hell, I know I did. I also wanted bitches who could work their mouth piece. You know, talk a nigga out of everything in his pockets. My girls couldn't be scared to sell a nigga a dream. It was all in a day's work.

When the club closed, the three of us walked to the parking lot together. I was parked next to Armando and Koda was a few spots over. As they bragged about the numbers they'd collected, I tried Marley's number again. I knew it was a lost cause, but I tried anyway. Imagine my surprise when I heard an automated male voice recite 'The subscriber you have called is not in service.' What the hell! She changed her number.

I didn't say anything as my bruised ego led me to my car. I climbed in and sunk down in my seat. Fuck! I hit the steering wheel and sighed. How could she do this to me? We took vows. For better or for worse. That's what she said. We both did. Now that the worst was upon us, she just up and left. What happened to 'in good times and bad'? It was bad now, but if given the chance I could make it better. *Until death do us part.* I remembered reciting those words clearly. I meant that shit. I still do.

Armando tapped on my window, knocking me out of my trance. I rolled it down to see what he wanted.

"Man," he sighed, gritting his teeth in frustration. "My fuckin' car won't start."

"You want me to take a look at it?" I grabbed for the door handle, but he objected.

"Naw. It's been acting up for a few days. I didn't get around to taking it to the shop. Fuck!"

"So what are you gonna do? You need a tow?"

He glanced at his BMW and then back to me. "Yeah. Let me call my buddy. He got his own truck. I'll have him tow it to the crib."

Armando made his call while I sat patiently. That's when I noticed Koda's car was no longer in the parking lot. He'd already driven off, leaving me to play the waiting game with Armando.

"He said it's gonna be a few hours. He's busy tonight."

"Damn," was all I could say. I looked at the clock in the dashboard. It was two in morning. "You staying and waiting?"

He thought about it before dialing his friend's number again. "Aye, I'ma go ahead and go home. Is that cool?" He waited a moment before continuing. "A'ight then. The car will be sitting here. I'll hide the keys for you."

He directed me to his mother's house. I'd never been there before, so it was up to Armando to show me the way. She lived in the boondocks; all the way out Dixie Highway in no man's land.

"Second house on the right," Armando instructed. I pulled into a paved driveway and put my car in park. "Good lookin' out. I'll get at you tomorrow."

The long drive back down Dixie Highway had me nodding off at the wheel. I wasn't a young cat no more. My body was tired. I felt the car swerve and a loud horn blasted behind me. I was up now. The car trailing my ass pulled up beside me. The windows were tinted so I couldn't see whatever message the person was trying to get across. I focused on the road, not trying to get into any shit at that moment. I just wanted to get home, take my clothes off, and fall in my bed. Unfortunately for me, it didn't happen that way.

I heard a phone ringing in close proximity to me. It wasn't my normal ringtone. It was Armando's phone, and it was sitting in the passenger's seat, lighting up in an array of different colors.

"Shit," I sighed, making a U-turn in the middle of the street. I couldn't go all the home with the man's phone in my car. What if that was his boy telling him something about his car?

Retracing my route, I found myself on the same dark street that I had previously abandoned. Before I could turn into the driveway, the car in front of me beat me to it. I wasn't paying much attention at first, but as I focused in on the license plate with the words THAT BIH displayed on it, familiarity kicked it. I knew that car well. I should. I paid for it. It was Amaya.

I parked on the dimly lit street a few houses up and slipped out of the driver's side. With lightning-like swiftness, I crept toward her like a thief in the night. Taking her sweet time, she emerged from the car, not knowing that I was now hiding behind it. As she stepped out and pushed the door closed, I made my presence known.

"So this is where you've been hiding?" I emerged from my hiding place and walked up on her.

Her eyes widened in surprise as my face came into view. "Santi! Wha-wha-what are you doing here?" she stuttered backing herself into the car.

WHAP!

I wanted to put my fist through her skull, but I backhanded her instead. "So you thought you could hide from me?"

WHAP!

I smacked her again, this time with more force. She spun around in a half-circle, losing her balance in the process. Her legs gave out under her, causing her to fall to the ground. My eyes saw more than they should as her legs flew open and exposed her bare ass under her short dress. I didn't feel the slightest bit of guilt as she grabbed the side of her face and sobbed uncontrollably.

"Santi," she cried. "I'm sorry."

I grabbed her violently and pulled her to her feet. "Don't try to apologize now. It's too late for all that." My large hand gripped the sides of her face and pulled it mere inches from mine. "You fucked everything up."

"I'll make it up to you, I promise. I'll get the abortion. I'll even tell Marley it was all I lie. Please, just don't—"

I did something I never said I'd do. I didn't see her as a woman at that point. She was an enemy; which meant no holds barred. I hit her. Not those slaps that barely stung my hand either. I'm talking about balled fist, straight to the dome. My closed fist connected with her face. Blood spat from her mouth as her eyes rolled back in her head and her body went limp. That one hit was powerful, sending her straight to la la land. She was out cold, falling hard to the ground. Still, I showed no mercy. Fuck with me, and the payback is ten times worse.

I repeatedly kicked her stomach. It was a free abortion in my book. After that day, I didn't care if I ever saw Amaya again. I was breaking all ties, and that included the life growing inside her.

She came to by the second kick and attempted to shield her stomach.

"Ahh," she cried out in pain. "Stop! Please stop! Please, I'm begging you!"

I gave her one last kick to her side for good measure before lowering myself to the ground next to her. "I don't ever want to see your face again. You're dead to me. You better not say shit to nobody or the next time you see me you'll be looking down the barrel of my gun."

She continued crying like that was going to help the situation. Everything that happened to her, she brought on herself. I didn't give a fuck about any of it. I was all out of fucks to give.

Calmly, I rose to my feet, wiping away the sweat forming at the bridge of my nose. I tossed Armando's phone toward her sore body and walked to my car at a snail's pace. At that moment, I didn't care who saw me. If anyone was bold enough to run up on me, they would be dealt the same fate. Muthafuckas were going to learn who I was. Playtime was over. Amaya was a prime example.

24

CASHMERE

I rolled over and wrapped my arms around Marley. It was the middle of the day and we were both still in bed. We had got back from Costa Rica the evening before, and were trying to recover. It was a nice little get-a-way that we both needed. She had her moments where she would cry and I just let her. How could I tell her not to when she had been with Santiago damn near all her life and she had considered Amaya a best friend? All I did was comfort her and let her get it out.

"You up, baby?" I quizzed as I kissed her cheek repeatedly. She hid under the covers and giggled while I stretched.

"I am now," she yawned. "I think I could literally sleep for two days."

"Do what you want. I wish I could, but I have to get back to it."

"I do too," she stated and sat up. "Let's order something to eat. I'm starving."

"What would you like?"

"A nice fat, juicy burger." She hummed while licking her lips.

Here lately, she had been eating everything in sight and sleeping whenever she got a chance. In Costa Rica, she took a nap after almost every activity. She would blame it on the sun draining her, but I knew different.

"Okay. Let me go see if Ken wants something."

I walked to the other side of the house where Ken and her girl-friend, Cena were studying. Cena was a good girl as well. Her and Ken were in the same AP classes and some of the same colleges were looking at the two of them. I was beyond proud of the young woman Ken was becoming, but I wasn't ready to let her go.

"Would y'all like anything to eat? Marley is about to order some-thing and I'm going to go pick it up."

"Will you stop by Taco Bell? I want a gordita crunch," Ken placed her order.

"What about you, Cena?" I asked.

"May I have the same, please?" She questioned with a weak smile.

"Sure. I'll be back in a few," I informed them and went to find Marley who was hovered over the toilet spilling out her insides. "You okay, baby?"

I got one of her hair ties and wrapped her hair up for her. I put some toothpaste on her toothbrush and ran cold water over a face towel. A few seconds later, she was done and brushing her teeth. Her skin was pale and her eyes were red.

"Thank you, babe. I just got sick all of a sudden," she noted after she was done. "Did Ken decide what she wanted?"

"Yeah, I'm going by Taco Bell. Go ahead and order our food so I can pick it up on the way back. Do you need anything from the store?"

"I need a lot, honestly. I'm going by Santiago's house one day this week to get some more of my things. I can't function properly without certain stuff," she groaned as she scrolled through her phone.

"Move in with me."

"Move in? I don't know about that, Cashmere. I know you're used to having your own space and I don't want to invade. I already feel bad for being here this long," Marley confessed.

"You're my woman, right?"

"Yes."

"Then, why would I have a problem with my queen moving in? It's more than enough room and Ken would love to have you here every day and so would I. I've grown so accustomed to you being here that I don't want you to leave. Well, I'm not going to let you." I decided with a smirk. "I'll be calling someone to go get your things while I'm out."

"What if I don't want to move in?" She teased with a sly grin. "Who said I didn't want to be by myself?"

"I did," I chuckled. "Come give me a kiss so I can go."

She waltzed over to me and kissed me deeply. It was crazy how I had grown so attached to her. She had me missing work and letting Murder oversee things. That wasn't like me, but I was loving this time with her. Eventually, I was going to get back on my shit. As for now, I was going to enjoy Marley.

"Don't take too long," she demanded. "I'm starving."

"You want to ride with me?"

"No," she declined. "I'm going to lay back down. I'm still not feeling too well."

I nodded my head and went to go fetch our food. I called and made arrangements for a moving company to go and get all of Marley's things. I hope she didn't think I was playing because I wasn't. She had been spending all her time at my house anyways, so it only made sense. Plus, I didn't want her to leave. It felt good as not being lonely.

On the way home, my thoughts drifted to this little sit down Ken and I were having with Kelsie tomorrow. I wasn't sure how things were going to go, but for the sake of Kensley, I want it to go smooth. Anytime she brings Kelsie up, I can see the excitement and desperation in her eyes for her mother. It pains me because I wish Kelsie would have got her shit together a long time ago, but if she did, then I wouldn't have Ken and I wouldn't trade raising her for anything in this world. No amount of power or money amounts to the love I have for my little sister.

~

"COME ON, CASH! I'M DRIVING," Kensley yelled from the garage. I heard a car start up and I sighed.

"What are you doing?" I interrogated as I peeked my head out the door. Ken was sitting in the passenger seat of my brand-new Audi with a mischievous grin plastered on her face.

"I said I was driving," answered with a shrug of her shoulders.

"Not my new whip, Ken. You can drive anything else but that," I fussed.

"Pleaseeeee, Cash! I swear I'll be careful. You'll be in the car with me, so I have no choice." She giggled with big puppy dog eyes and pouty bottom lip. I rolled my eyes because she knew what she was doing.

"Let her drive, baby. I trust her," Marley added her two cents as she walked up behind me and laced her arms around my waist.

"Aren't you supposed to be on my side?" I joked while shaking my head. "You can't move in if y'all are going to be double teaming me all the time."

"You can just stay on my side of the house," Ken told Marley and they laughed. "So, what do you say?" Ken asked me again.

"I guess, Kensley."

"Thank you, Cashmere."

"Mhm." I went to grab my keys and wallet from Marley.

"Stay calm, Cashmere." Marley instructed. "Give her a chance."

"I'll try," I said honestly then kissed her. "The movers should be bringing your things soon, so don't fall asleep."

"I'll try not to," she fake yawned and giggled. I kissed her once more then went to get in the car.

"Don't fuck up my car," I demanded.

"I'm not." She carefully backed out the driveway and headed to the restaurant. I watched as she tapped her fingers against the steering wheel and chewed the inside of her bottom lip.

"Are you nervous?"

"I am," she admitted truthfully. "I have so many questions that I'm scared to know the answer to."

"But, you want to know the truth, right"

"Yes.

"Then, don't be scared to ask. I'm going to be sitting right there with you. I'm not going to say anything because this is something you need to do on your own, but just know you're not alone." I assured her and leaned over to kiss her forehead. She gave me a comfortable smile and focused on the road. The rest of the ride to meet Kelsie was quiet. We were both consumed in our own thoughts I wish I knew what she was thinking.

Minutes later we pulled in front of *Porcini Restaurant*; one of Ken's favorites. She killed the engine and sat there with a distant glare in his eyes. She was nervous and I couldn't blame her. All I could do was try to keep her calm.

"It's going to go fine, Ken. Stop worrying." I tried to ease her mind. "Remember, I'll be here too."

She took a deep breath and released. "You're right. Let's go."

We got out the car and she grabbed my hand. I opened the door for her and the waitress led us to where Kelsie was already sitting. When she saw us, her eyes lit up brightly and she stood up to greet us.

"I'm so glad y'all came," Kelsie stated with a smile. "I waited for y'all to order."

I can't front, Kelsie looked like she was cleaner than the last time we saw her. She looked good and I knew it was because of Kensley.

"How are you?" Kensley was the first to spark the conversation after our drinks arrived. I wasn't speaking because I was just here for support.

"Good, good." Kelsie answered. "How are you? How's school going?"

"I'm good. School is great. I made a thirty on my ACT test, but I'm aiming for higher next time. I want to get a full ride to the college of my choice," she beamed proudly. Kelsie listened in amazement as Ken filled her in on all her AP classes and extracurricular activities. Her eyes were filled with shame and guilt and I figured it was because she realized that she missed out on an amazing daughter. It wasn't too late.

"I'm so proud of you and I know Cashmere is too. I hate I missed out on all those things," she stammered with sadness in her voice.

"So," Kensley gulped. "Why did you miss out on my life?"

An awkward silence filled the space between us. Kelsie's eyes traveled to me and I held my hands up in surrender. This was on her. Even though Ken already knew why, she just wanted to hear it from the mouth of her mother. She wanted to know why Kelsie chose drugs over her.

"I made some very poor choices in my life," Kelsie started with her head down. "It started when your father left me. You were only about two or three. I fell into a deep depression and turned to drugs. Being high was the only way I could function and live life daily without him. He was the air that I breathed and I would have done anything for him. He didn't give me a reason for leaving, he just left and I think that's what hurt the most. My addiction got so bad that I could no longer care for you. Well, I let my addiction make that decision for me. I wasn't strong enough to fight it. It consumed my body like a deadly virus and I let it control me for thirteen long years."

"That night I saw that boy trying to rape you was when I really made up in my mind that I needed to fight this demon back. I checked into a rehab center and got clean. I did this not only for myself, but for you. I want to be the mother you missed out on all these years. I know I can never make it up for all the times I missed, but I want to start somewhere. Kensley, I am so sorry for walking out on you. I'm sorry for choosing drugs when I should have chosen you. I'm sorry for not being strong enough to fight until now. Whether you believe it or not, I love you and I always have. I know it may take some time for you to come around or you might not come around at all. I have to accept whatever decision you make because I brought this on myself. All I can do is pray you give me a chance and show you just how bad I want to be in your life."

"I owe you an apology too, Cashmere. I'm sorry for leaving my responsibilities as a parent on you. Even though you knew how your mother felt about me, you stepped up and took raised your sister like your own when you didn't have to. I can't thank you enough for doing all that you have done for her. Kensley, you are truly blessed to have such a loving and caring brother like Cashmere. I will never deny that. I owe him my life for taking on my responsibilities."

By the time Kelsie was done talking, her and Ken were both in tears. I can't lie and act like her words didn't touch me because they did. She was speaking from the heart, and I felt that shit too. She did what I thought was the impossible and changed her life for the better. For Ken. How could I interfere with that? It was time for me to step back and allow her to be the parent that she was supposed to be.

"The only thing you owe me is being a mother to Ken. I know it's not going to happen overnight, but I'm willing to let you try. That is, if that's what Ken wants." I said and looked at Kensley. "The ball is in your court."

Ken didn't respond. She just got up and held her arms out to Kelsie who immediately burst into a loud sob as she embraced her. I knew Ken had her mind made up before time; she just needed to know if she was making the right decision and I could honestly say that I believe she was.

25

AMAYA

*K*arma's one bitch that I can't stand. She comes around when you least expect it, fucking everything up in the process.

As I laid in the small, uncomfortable bed, I had time to reflect on my life and the people in it. I talk a good game, but I'm not proud of a lot of the decisions that I made. I reacted before fully thinking things through. It proved to be my downfall. I was wrong, and not just for messing with Santi either.

I didn't have a positive role model to mirror myself off of. My mother was just like me; chasing a married man who strung her along for years. He was Armando's father, and the love of her life. My father died when I was young. Shortly thereafter, my mother met Roc, and Armando came along. He won over her heart in just a short amount of time and eventually moved us all out of East Acres projects. For years, I looked up to him. He treated my mother like a queen, buying her any and everything that she wanted. He didn't discriminate, either. Because he was with my mother, he treated me like a daughter, I called him dad, and wanted desperately for the two of them to make things 'official.' That would never happen. His wife put an end to that. She threatened to divorce him, and blast his personal indiscretions to everyone at the law firm he managed.

I didn't know it at the time, but Roc had a wife and three kids at home. I put that man on a pedestal and he was playing both women. The irony! Like me, my mother didn't give up. She claimed she didn't know about his wife, but I'm not so convinced. Looking back now, there were tell-tell signs that I should have picked up on; like Roc only coming around in the evenings and on weekends. I was young though, and it wasn't my business. Roc was still my dad, and even after the big blow up with his wife, he continued to come around.

My mother had it in her mind that he would leave his wife. That's what he promised to do. Their relationship carried on for a few more years before she was served with an order of protection. Roc's wife was on him again, threatening divorce if he didn't leave my mother alone. I don't know what was so different about that particular time, but Roc chose his wife and their family over us. Unlike the times before, Roc left and never returned. He cut us all off, including his own flesh and blood.

It's funny how people are so quick to judge and give their opinion. My mother's name seemed to be in everyone's mouth, and everyone had something to say. Roc's wife was this innocent victim who had been cheated on and embarrassed within the community. Yet, all the negative attention was directed at my mother. She was a whore. A homewrecker. A tramp. You name it. That woman didn't know my mother from a can of paint, but wanted the whole city of Athens to turn their backs on her. What about Roc? He's the one she exchanged vows with. He was her husband, and after tarnishing my mother's name, she stayed with him. For the life of me, I don't understand it.

Without Roc's financial help, we were well on our way back to the projects. That's the real reason why we moved to Louisville in the first place. My mother did have a friend in the Bluegrass State who we visited. After our little vacation was over, my mother all but begged to stay. In reality, we didn't have anywhere else to go.

Knock. Knock.

Jennifer, my day nurse, entered without my permission, and made her way to the bedside. "Good morning, Amaya. How are you feeling today?"

"I feel like I look. Terrible."

"You do not look terrible. Even though you're all banged up, you're still pretty."

Who was she fooling? I was lying in a hospital bed, barely able to move. Even the simplest of tasks were harder than they should be. I cringed inside when I felt a cough creeping up my throat. I even tried to control my breathing because the pain associated with inhaling oxygen into my lungs was almost too much to bear. I had two black eyes and a broken nose, but it was my fractured ribs that made it hard to breathe. Thanks to a collapsed lung, I had a chest tube draining the air to allow my lungs to re-expand. There was nothing pretty about me at that moment, but I appreciated her attempt at making me feel better.

"Thanks," I mumbled.

"How did you sleep?" She made her way to the head of the bed and placed a hand on her thick hip.

"I didn't. That other nurse ain't like you. She comes in every hour on the hour for nothing. Every time I dozed off, she kept waking me up for bullshit. I hope her old ass ain't gonna be here tonight."

"Oh, hush." Jennifer mouthed, and grabbed for the computer discreetly hidden in the wall. "Ethel is one of the best nurses we have. She doesn't mean any harm. She's all about patient care. She wants you to be as comfortable as possible."

"I'll be comfortable when I get some sleep."

"Well, after I'm done with you, you can do just that. Are you having any pain?"

"What do you think?"

She gave me a hard side-eye. "On a scale of one to ten, how would you rate your pain?"

"Ten."

"When's the last time you had something for pain?"

I closed my eyes and bit my tongue. I needed all the help I could get at that moment and popping off at the mouth wouldn't be a good idea. The large wall clock hanging in front of me had been stuck at noon since I arrived almost a week prior. The blinds were closed and I had no idea if it was day or night. How would I know when I got pain medicine? She had my electronic chart at her disposal, yet she chose to ask me a dumb question.

"I don't know. Maybe a few hours ago."

She checked my chart. "It looks like you were given morphine less than an hour ago. That didn't control your pain?"

"No," I responded, frustrated that I had even been asked the question in the first place.

"Okay. I will call the doctor to see if something stronger can be ordered. In the meantime, let me document your vitals."

She didn't have to do much. The numerous machines that I was connected to gave her a general overview of how I was doing. She punched the keys of the computer mounted on the wall. When she was done, she pushed the computer back inside its secret hiding place.

"Did the chaplain come see you last night?" she asked, taking a seat at the edge of my bed.

For the past three days, the same nurses rotated twelve hour shifts. Before Jennifer left, I had a mental breakdown, and she comforted me with her kind words. She felt that I was going to have another episode when she left, and put in a request for the chaplain to talk to me.

"Yes, he came."

"And?"

"He said God had a different plan."

"What's your take on that?"

"It's bullshit."

"How so?"

"Look at me, Jennifer. Do you really think that God's plan was for me to be viciously attacked. I could have lost my life."

"But you didn't."

"My baby did."

"And that's unfortunate." She repositioned herself on my bed and turned toward me. "Losing a baby is hard. Believe me, I know. My husband and I have been trying to have a baby for three years now. Every time I get pregnant, I miscarry. I know how you're feeling, but you have to push forward."

"I don't know if I can do that," I said honestly. "My situation is a little different from yours, Jennifer. The father or your baby didn't beat the living crap out of you because he didn't want the baby."

"So, why won't you cooperate, then?"

I had disclosed the details of what brought me to the hospital with staff once I arrived. The police were called, but I refused to give them Santi's name. Call me crazy, but I still loved him. Jail was the last place that I wanted him to be.

"I don't know," I whispered. "I just...I just don't know."

"No one deserves to be beat on, Amaya. If you don't take anything else from what I'm saying, know this. Regardless of anything you do, or anything that you've done in the past, nobody deserves what happened to you. Know your worth."

"You wouldn't be saying that if you knew everything I've done."

"It can't be that bad."

"Wanna bet?"

She peered down at the watch gracing her small wrist. Standing to her feet, she pushed the only chair in the room toward my bed. "I got time. Let's hear it."

I lost my confidence as she sat mere inches from me. How could she possibly understand? She was beautiful, with smooth caramel skin and light eyes. More importantly, she was married. I was a side chick. There was no way I could justify my actions.

"I'm not here to judge," she began, picking up on my indecisiveness. "We've all made mistakes. The way we handle those mistakes is what matters."

I took a deep breath, and released the pain with a long sigh. "I've been with this guy for seven years. He's married." Nervously, I intertwined my fingers, but Jennifer didn't say anything. She just listened. "He was my friend's man. Well, actually her husband."

"And you thought that was okay?"

"You said you weren't going to judge!" I snapped, becoming defensive. "You're judging me already."

"I'm not judging you, Amaya. I just want to see where your head is. I apologize if you took it that way. Go on, continue."

"Mar—" I stopped myself before divulging Marley's name. "My friend gets everything she wants. She's never had to work for anything; it was all handed to her. I didn't expect them to last as long as they did. I didn't feel bad at all for what I was doing. He wanted it just like I did."

"And now?"

"You see how things turned out. I'm sitting in the hospital and she's out doing her. It's just not fair. It ain't even like this is the first time I got pregnant. The only thing different is that this time I stood my ground. I refused to get an abortion and this is the result."

"Are you finished?" she calmly asked, pulling at a piece of lent on her navy blue scrubs.

"I guess."

"Think about what you just said. Your friend? Is that how you do your friends?"

"I should've just kept my mouth closed. You don't understand."

"It's not that. Think about it from another point of view. What if you were married to that man, and your 'friend' did what you did. How would you feel? There's no way that you can honestly tell me that you'd be cool with that. If you did, there's something seriously wrong with you."

I remained quiet.

"From the outside looking in, it seems like your issue is with this friend of yours. You're upset because she's doing her. What is she supposed to do? She's been betrayed by two people who were supposed to be in her corner. Life doesn't stop because we've been hurt. She's supposed to move on, and so should you. Think of this as a life lesson and take some time to find you. She wasn't your friend, Amaya. She was an acquaintance. A friend is someone you love and have a mutual respect for. You don't do what you did to a real friend. Think about that."

"Of course you're going to take her side." I was done with the conversation by that point. Jennifer could saunter her ass on out of my room and help someone else for all I cared.

"You just don't want to hear the truth. Would you feel the same way if she wasn't your friend?"

"No."

"So, why do you care, then?"

"I don't."

"It's written all over your face. Once you're honest with yourself, you can move forward. Until then, you're going to have a hard life." She eased her slim body to a standing position and pushed the chair back to its rightful place. "I'll call Dr. Monroe about that pain medicine."

As she opened the door to leave, I had one last question to ask. "How do you know so much, Jennifer."

She turned to me and smiled. "I was once in your position. I was young and dumb; searching for love in a man that couldn't give me nothing that I couldn't give myself. I found my worth and now I'm happily married. It's a whole lot better on the other side, Amaya. You should try it."

I watched the door well after she left. She was right. Nothing good had come from my bad decisions. I lost a friend, and somewhere along the way, I lost myself. Closing my eyes, I attempted to sleep my guilt away. Unfortunately, the knock at the door prevented that from happening.

"Come in." I waited a few seconds for my visitor to appear.

Koda strolled in with a bouquet of red roses. "I brought you these," he said, placing them on my beside table. "I thought they would cheer you up."

I managed a smile as he made his way to me. The scent of his 3AM cologne hit my nostrils and stayed there. I took in his appearance; basketball shorts, oversized t-shirt, and Nike sandals with black socks. Typical Koda.

"You look good," he lied.

"I look like shit and you know it." I ran a hand through my wild, untamed hair.

"You could never look like shit, Amaya. You're the most beautiful woman I know."

Something about the way he said that rang true in my mind. Koda dug the shit out of me, and I knew it. I'd been stringing him along for months, waiting for my chance to be with Santi. All the while, Koda was waiting for his chance to be with me.

"Thank you," I blushed.

"So, when are they gonna let you out of here?"

"Hopefully in the next day or two. I can't wait to get home and get in my own bed."

"Or, you can rest comfortably in mine."

"That's nice of you to offer, but I don't want to intrude."

"Until we find out who did this, I'd prefer to keep you close. I already feel like shit knowing I wasn't there to protect you."

A neighbor found me on the ground and alerted Armando. After I was transported to the hospital, my brother called Koda and went around the neighborhood looking for the perpetrator. What they both didn't know, was that they were on the payroll of the man they were trying to find.

"Don't beat yourself up about it. It is what it is. He'll get his. Until then, I just want to forget this ever happened."

"I'ma see to it that he gets his. I just wish I had a name. A real man doesn't beat up on a woman and leave her for dead. He's a piece of shit; whoever he is."

I thought about Jennifer's words. I had a man, a single man, that wanted to be with me, yet my own personal demons were preventing me from moving forward. I had already fucked up my relationship with Marley. There was no way she was going to forgive me for what I had done, but I had to move on. Maybe Koda was the person I was supposed to be with. His sex wasn't all that, but that could be corrected. Why was I holding myself back from a good man? For Santi? He showed me his true colors when he beat my ass. It was time to stop worrying about other people and focus on what was important. Koda could help me do that, but I had to be honest with him first.

"I know who did it."

His eyes widened in surprise. "Who?"

"I hope this doesn't change how you feel about me, but I want to tell you the truth. I've been seeing someone for a few years now. He's the one that did this to me." The muscles in his jaws twitched as he stood over me. "I kept our relationship a secret because I didn't want his wife to find out."

He turned and paced the floor, rubbing his hands over his fresh fade. I wasn't trying to hurt him, but in order for me to move forward, I had to get it all out.

"There's more," I continued. "I was pregnant."

"Wait. What? Amaya, you're pregnant too?"

"Was. I *was* pregnant. That's why he did this to me. I refused to terminate the pregnancy and that's why I ended up here."

"That's fucked up, Amaya. Here I was thinking we had something going and you fuckin' around with another nigga. That shit's foul."

"I know," I mumbled with tears forming in my eyes. For the first time in my life I spoke my truth. "I was wrong. I've made a lot of bad decisions, but that in no way reflects upon you. You've been nothing but good to me, and I appreciate everything you've done. I want you to know that I'm sorry. From the bottom of my heart, I apologize. I will understand if this changes the way you feel about me, but I don't want to get into a relationship with skeletons in my closet. I'd rather for you to know now, then to find out later."

He sat on the edge of my bed, but didn't look at me. "At least you told me yourself. I appreciate that."

"So what now?"

"I don't know. I got a lot to think about, but the offer's still open. You can chill at my crib until you're back on your feet."

He sat quiet for a while, directing his attention toward the tile floor below. I knew he was hurt, and I was the cause of it. It wasn't easy, but I already felt like a weight had been lifted from my shoulders.

"Who is it, ma?" he finally asked, turning to face me. "Do I know him?"

"Yes," I said reluctantly. Closing my eyes, I mouthed, "Santiago."

He was out the door within seconds.

26

MARLEY

stood at the steps of the place I once called home and smiled. I was going to miss this place. This was my first home with Santiago and we shared some great memories here, but the bad outweighed the good and that's why we were in this predicament now. Looking at the doormat underneath my pumps made me smile even harder. I remember being so happy about getting us a doormat with our last name on it. I wanted everyone to know we lived here as husband and wife. That was many years ago; the good old days.

I stared down at the divorce papers in my hand and knew I was making the right decision. As much as I loved Santiago, this was something I had to do. No longer was I going to let him step all over my heart like a doormat. I had allowed him to do so for far too long and it was time I stopped torturing myself and be with a man who appreciates all of me. Oh, how I wish Santiago was that man. I wanted my marriage to work so bad that I put up with his bullshit for years. That was just how much I loved him. If only he loved me the same.

Inhaling deeply, I rang the doorbell then stepped back. It took a few seconds for Santiago to come open the door and I must say; he looked like shit. His locs were full of lent and unkempt. He always kept his hair done because appearance was everything to him, but I guess not now. He had huge, crust filled bags under his low, red eyes. He wore nothing but a dingy, oversized white wife beater, Calvin Klein boxers and a robe. His socks were mismatched and he wreaked. The mixture of alcohol and loud kissed my nose and I wanted to puke. My smell had been sensitive lately and I could smell him loud and clear.

"Ley, what are you doing here?" He quizzed as he tried to fix his appearance. He stood up straighter and tied his robe. He picked a few pieces of lent out his dreads then rubbed his eyes and smiled weakly.

My heart went out to him because he looked so bad without me. Or maybe it's because of Amaya. Either way, my soft spot for him hated to see him like this. It seemed as if he couldn't function and if he hadn't eaten in days. Sadly, he brought this all on himself.

"I was just coming to see if you would sign these," I stated while handing him the papers. "I thought it would be better if I delivered them myself."

He studied the papers with a deep scowl etched on his face. I waited patiently as he read over them and then grilled me. He didn't say anything; he just stared as if he was trying to read me. What he didn't know was that he didn't know me anymore. Santiago didn't know the new Marley. His glare didn't make me bow down or weak anymore. I was simply unbothered. Only Cashmere had that affect now.

"What are these?" He questioned through gritted teeth.

"Divorce papers. You can read."

"What the fuck, Ley! Why are you doing this?" He had the audacity to ask like him not sticking his dick in Amaya was a problem. He knew why I was doing it.

"I'm done. I'm not in love with you anymore, Santiago and it's pretty obvious that you feel the same about me."

"Of course, I'm still in love with you! You are my wife; why wouldn't I be?"

"Stop with the bullshit. You fell out of love with me when you decided to go stick your dick in my ex best friend and got her pregnant!" I screamed with spit flying in his face. "How are you going to sit here and tell me you were in love with me when obviously, you were in love with *her*." I didn't think I would get upset, but listening to the lies he was pushing through his teeth pissed me off. It brought out emotions I wanted to keep hidden. I didn't want him to know it got to me as bad as it did.

"I loved you both," he sighed.

"There was no way you could have loved me because if you did, you never would have hurt me." I spat. "How long?"

"How long what?"

"How long were y'all going behind my back? It had to be for some time if you loved her," I breathed while shaking my head at him. The thought of him actually loving her and telling her the things he was only supposed to tell me pained my heart. He was only supposed to love me.

Santiago rubbed his hand over his face and sighed in exasperation. "Would you like to come in and talk about this?"

"No, thank you. I won't be here much longer," I implied with a smirk. This conversation was taking longer than I thought it would. "Now, answer the question."

"Seven years," he sighed and I felt like all the wind had been kicked out my body. I let out a gut wrenching laugh to mask the pain I was feeling.

"Seven years. Seven fuckin' years you were out here playing me like a fuckin' fool. Seven years of my life wasted on you. I could be somewhere building a family with a nigga who deserves a woman like me! One who would appreciate me. I loved you so much, Santiago. I put you before everything. My life revolved around you and Amaya's conniving ass knew that. I would sit and vent to that bitch about you and she would always ask me if you were cheating. Now, I know why. Guilt was eating at her ass and she was scared I was going to find out. I was too dumb. No, I was in love and only saw the good in you when everyone else saw the bad. I'm glad I can finally see you for who you really are. A weak ass man."

The look on his face was priceless as I finished my statement. It felt so good to get that off my chest. Now, I felt like I could truly move on and be happy. Santiago knew how I felt and he would have to live with that on his conscious every day. He was the reason our marriage ended.

"I'm so sorry, baby. I never meant for any of it to happen. Let me work this shit out, Ley. Please," he begged and a few tears splashed his cheeks. "I can't live without you. I know what I did was fucked up, but I swear I'll be the man you want and need me to be. I won't put work before you; I'll always put you first. I'll do whatever it takes to make you happy again and fall back in love with me."

Everything he just said, he meant it. It all came from his heart. I was touched that he was willing to fight so hard for me, but I wasn't moved. The damage was already done and there was no coming back from that. Eventually, I knew I would forgive him and Amaya. Despite the things they had done, I still loved them both. That type of love didn't just disappear overnight. Like I said before, I'm done.

The reason I am so sure of not wanting things to work with Santiago has a lot to do with how I feel about Cashmere. I can't deny that. Cashmere was there when Santiago should have been and that's how I was able to completely fall out of love with my husband and fall in love with him. Now, if Cashmere wasn't in the picture, do I think I would want to work things out with Santiago? I'm not sure. Either way, I don't think I would be able to stomach the things he's done.

I know that I've done wrong too. Two wrongs don't make a right, so I couldn't sit here and act perfect knowing I went against my vows as well. I never would have if Santiago was doing his job as a husband. I'm not saying that makes what I did right, but I wouldn't have found comfort and love in another man if he had done his job.

"I love you, Santiago. I always have and I always will, but I just can't do this anymore. I accept your apology; I do. My heart just isn't ready to forgive you. You hurt me so bad that it's going to take me some time to bounce, but with the help of my man I'll be able to."

"Your man? You already moved on, Marley?" He barked and threw the papers down.

"You did. So, why couldn't I? Please, Santiago. Just sign the papers so I can go," I pleaded. I had somewhere I needed to be.

"Who is he?"

"Sign the papers."

"I'm not signing a damn thing until you tell me who the fuck he is!" He yelled and I laughed.

I sent a text and waited until I heard a truck pulling up behind me. I spun around on my toes and smiled when I saw Cashmere. He was looking scrumptious in a dark gray business suit and a navy tie. His hair was freshly cut and lined up, making me cream a little. He caught my eye and winked before swaggering our way.

"What's up, Cash. What you doing here?" Santiago asked with a frown.

"Here to check on my woman," Cashmere stated calmly then wrapped his arm around my waist. We engaged in a deep kiss and he smiled at me. I could see the love in his eyes for me and it made me have butterflies. "I love you, baby."

"I love you too," I cooed.

"What in the fuck is this?" Santiago questioned through gritted teeth while pointing back and forth between Cashmere and I.

"You said you wouldn't sign the papers until you knew who my man was. Well, here he is." I beamed. I wasn't trying to make him jealous. I just wanted him to see that someone was appreciating what he didn't.

"I see. So, you weren't any better than me, huh? You were out here fuckin' and suckin' right along with me. You're no angel in this, Marley. You've been sitting here downing me; making me feel like shit when you were out here being promiscuous. My boss? Might as well say we're even," Santiago scolded while taking a few steps closer to me with his fists balled up. I stepped back and Cashmere stepped in between us with his hands resting in front of him.

"That's not the right thing to do, Santiago if you want to continue breathing. I know shit looks bad, but it is what it is. Marley is my woman now. No hard feelings; it just happened." Cashmere explained in an even tone. I knew he was trying to refrain from going off because of the way Santiago stepped to me. He didn't play about the women in his life; especially Kensley.

"Get the fuck up out my face with that bullshit. You're fake as fuck, Cash. You ain't no real nigga. You did some pussy ass shit. You took advantage of knowing what was going on and did some foul shit. I don't have respect for snake ass bitches like you," Santiago snapped with a clenched jaw.

"Is that the way you talk to the man that feeds you?" Cashmere chuckled and shook his head. "Don't do this to yourself, bruh. You and I both know you don't want these problems."

If we weren't out in the open, I would have fucked Cashmere right then and there. I love hearing the way his deep, baritone voice trembles when he's talking with authority. He's always so calm, but I know that's just the calm before the storm.

Santiago nodded his head and backed up. He knew that if he even attempted to touch Cashmere then he would be dead on sight. I nudged Cashmere and glanced down at the papers.

"Sign the papers, Santiago and there won't be any problems." Cashmere demanded.

"I'm not signing a go-" Santiago started, but was interrupted by Cashmere jacking him up by his throat. Santiago punched Cashmere in the jaw and Cashmere threw him. They stood there glaring at one another and if looks could kill, they would both be on the floor. I walked up behind Cashmere rubbed his arms with my face pressed against his. I could feel his body becomes less tense and his breathing slowed down.

"It's okay, baby." I assured him with a kiss. "We can just settle it in court."

Now, Santiago was no punk by any means. He has never been the type to let anyone come at him sideways. He wasn't with the bullshit. Even with him knowing what Cashmere is capable of, he still wouldn't back down from him. They would be going back and forth until one of them were dead and with the power Cashmere had;

Santiago would be dead in a split second. I didn't want that, so I had to calm Cashmere down before things for ugly. If I didn't calm him, then I would have had to call Kensley to do it. One glance at her and he would simmer down.

Cashmere popped his neck and sighed in exasperation. I knew he was fighting with himself to calm down. I continued to whisper in his ear and he finally cracked a smile.

"Let's go. I have a surprise for you," I told him then turned my attention to Santiago. "I'll see you in court. Bye, Santiago."

Cashmere and I walked away, hand in hand. Santiago didn't even protest, he just walked away and slammed the door behind him.

~

Later that night...

"Here you go." I sat Cashmere and Kensley's plates in front of them and went to retrieve my own. I had a surprise for them that I could not wait to give them. I knew they would be just as excited as I was.

"This looks delicious," Kensley complimented as her mouth watered. "And it smells good too."

"You know anything my baby whips up is good," Cashmere stated with a smirk. I sat down with them and we prayed. Dinner seemed to go by slowly. Even with us talking and laughing, I was still anxious. I was bursting with excitement on the inside.

About thirty minutes later, we were all finished. We cleaned the kitchen and retired to Kensley's movie room to watch a movie. While they got situated, I went and got their surprises. When I walked back in the room, I handed it to them and they both looked at my funny.

"What's this?" Ken asked. "It's not anybody's birthday."

"I know. I just wanted to give y'all something in appreciation for accepting me," I said with a smile. I watched as they simultaneously ripped their way to their cards. Once they opened it up, a smile tugged at Cashmere's lips and Kensley jumped up screaming.

"Oh my gosh! I'm going to be an aunt!" She squealed and

embraced me tightly while jumping up and down. "Ooo, can I help name the baby and plan the baby shower?"

"Of course," I giggled and beamed at her excitement. I glanced towards Cashmere who had his head down. I kneeled down next to him and lifted his face. I couldn't believe he was actually crying. "What's wrong, baby?"

"I'm just happy to be starting a family with you and giving you what you want," he managed to get through tears. "I swear I'll never hurt you, Marley."

"I know, Cashmere. I love you so much."

"I love you more, Marley. And my baby," he cooed as he rubbed my flat stomach.

After everything I had been through, I still managed to come out on top and happy. I was finally having the family I have always wanted. Life always had a funny way of showing you things. It can changed in the blink of an eye. You just have to be strong enough to handle whatever it decides to throw at you.

27

SANTIAGO

I had the worst luck in the world. My custom bar was damaged during the shipping process and now I was back to square one. I squeezed the bridge of my nose and sighed in frustration. All I wanted to do was get my shit up and popping. Why was that so hard?

"I'm working on it," Charlie stated, hearing the frustration in my voice. "I found a new company that could possibly offer us a replacement for the replacement." He chuckled as if that shit were funny.

"I ain't with the games, Charlie. Is this place local?" I turned down a side street and parked off to the side. The only thing I had going on for me was my business, and I took that shit seriously.

"No, they're in California, but there's a warehouse over the bridge in Indiana. I've had success finding things there in the past. It's wholesale, so the price is right, but you're not guaranteed to find what you're looking for. It's sort of like finding a needle in the haystack, but when you do, it's well worth it."

"A'ight," I huffed into the phone. "So, what are you doing tomorrow?"

"My son has a football game and—"

"Fuck all that. We're going to that warehouse you were talking about. What time do they open?"

"I think around nine, but Santiago," he began swallowing hard. "Tomorrow is Saturday. We didn't discuss anything about working weekends. I have plans. I can't miss my son's tournament."

"If you want to be paid for your services, I'd advise you to get your priorities straight. I'm sure the little mothafucka will have other games. This club is important. Everything else can wait. Is it going to be a problem?" I heard a hint of indecisiveness in his loud sigh. "If you think this is too much for you, I'm sure I can find someone to finish what you've started. Now, let me ask you again. Will it be a problem?"

"No, sir," he spat.

"Good. I'll see you tomorrow." I ended the call and threw the phone in the empty seat next to me.

I resumed my route and entered I-264. I was trying to find something to get into. Well, actually I was just trying to clear my mind. Every time I found something that was remotely interesting, my mind would drift back to Amaya. I found out from Armando that she was in the hospital. Suburban Hospital to be exact. He told me that he found her laid out in their mother's driveway. Someone roughed her up pretty bad, and in addition to her physical scars, she had a couple broken ribs. She also had a collapsed lung, but I didn't care about all that. I wanted to know about the baby. Hopefully I did enough damage to prevent its birth.

"She gonna be a'ight?" I asked Armando when I heard the news.

"Yeah, man. I can't believe somebody really did that to her. I mean, it's a dumb muthafucka out there somewhere waiting to meet his maker. You don't fuck wit my blood and get away with it."

"I know that's right." I fed Armando's ego, knowing damn well he couldn't bust a grape. He wasn't shit if he didn't have a pistol in his hands. Even then he wasn't much competition.

Thankfully he had Koda. That nigga just didn't give a fuck. Nothing bothered him. He swept that shit under the rug as if it didn't even faze him. Those are the crazy muthafuckas you have to worry about. The type of muthafucka that unleashes their wrath when you least expect it. Koda can laugh with you one minute and send you to an early grave the next.

I quizzed him about her whereabouts and asked them if they had any leads.

"Naw. Her stubborn ass won't say shit. She won't tell me who did it. Hopefully Koda will have some better luck."

"Koda?" I felt a hint of jealously brewing. "For someone who's just a friend, he's spending a lot of time with her."

Amaya wasn't my bitch anymore, but I wasn't going to sit around while someone else in my crew had her. Fuck that! It was bad enough that Cash had already dipped into my cookie jar. It wasn't going to happen again.

"He's been checking for her for a while. He's just as fucked up about the situation as I am."

"What do you mean checking for her?" I sat up in my bed, feeling betrayed by one of my own. I guess I finally understood how Marley felt knowing I had been with her friend.

"You didn't know? They've been messing around for a few weeks now. I thought you knew."

"No. I didn't know."

My mind returned to the day at the park. The same day I met Talia, Amaya was chilling with Koda. I didn't think anything of it. She did little shit like that when she was upset and trying to get under my skin. Besides, Amaya was dialing my digits again the very same day. Koda couldn't have been that important. Now I was finding out that things were deeper than I thought. I needed to have a talk with Koda. My sloppy seconds were off limits.

"Damn. I really thought you knew, Santi. I figured you two were on the outs again, and she was trying to find something to pass the time. I warned Koda about my sister. I told him that she's after one thing and one thing only. It's a chance he's willing to take. I hope he knows what he's doing."

"Did you tell him about me?" I asked, surprising myself with the question. I'd never confirmed my relationship with Amaya to her brother, but after finding us in various compromising positions, he had to know.

"Naw. That's not my place," he said simply. "I don't think Amaya said anything either. Koda would've asked if she had."

I lied to Armando and told him that I would check on Amaya later. He disclosed the hospital and room number before hanging up the phone. I actually contemplated going up there. It wasn't going to be a social visit either. I wanted to make sure that the job was done.

I swerved onto the shoulder, knocking myself back into reality. The conversation with Armando had taken place yesterday, and today was all about business; new business that is. I didn't want to hear anything else about Amaya, Koda, or Armando for that matter. Once my shit was up and running, I was permanently axing all of the out of my lives. I didn't want or need Amaya anymore. I felt the same way about her minions. They could all be someone else's headache. I got all that I needed out of them and now I was done.

Marley is someone else I was done with. The only difference was, she made the decision for me. I still can't believe she served my ass with divorce papers. Fuck her too! She ain't nothing but a hypocrite. How the fuck is she gonna be mad at me when she was doing the same thing? Fuck her and her man? I wish nothing but pain and heartache on both of their asses.

I sighed loudly. I knew I had fucked up. Lashing out was the only way I could express myself. I had a big ass crib, too many cars to count, clothes, jewelry, other material shit, and still I was by myself. I wasted years of my life on a woman who ran off with my boss of all people. My fuckin' boss! Who does that? I ought to drive over there and fuck them both up off GP. On second thought, nah. They can have each other. In the game of life, everyone is replaceable. Marley is getting old anyway. I need me a pretty young thing that can keep me youthful. Let's face it. I ain't getting no younger either. I wonder if Talia would give me another chance. Amaya's out of the picture, and I ain't had that warm gushy in a minute.

I called Talia's number. Surprisingly, she answered.

"Hello?"

"Long time no hear, beautiful. What are you up to?"

"What do you want Santi?"

"Damn, it's like that? Is that for us?"

"Dealing with you is trouble. Trouble that I don't want. I shouldn't have to look over my shoulder for crazy mothafuckas trying to get at me just because of you. I'm too pretty to be fighting. I will if I have to, but I don't like being put in that situation."

I changed my route, heading back down to the West End. If Talia really didn't want to be bothered with me, she wouldn't waste her time on the phone. I wasn't the smartest man in the world, but something about me was keeping her on the phone.

"I'm done with all that. I've been done with ol' girl. You ain't got nothing to worry about. I just wanna see you. I miss you. Do you miss me?"

"No," she said with a chuckle. I knew she was lying.

"Well, I miss you. He misses you too." I licked my lips as if she could see me through the phone.

"Who's *he*?"

"My dick," I announced as if she didn't know. "He misses that mouth of yours.'

"Oh really," she cooed into the phone - just like I knew she would. "Is that right?"

"Yep! So right that I'll be there in about fifteen minutes to pick you up. Bring some clothes. You're chilling with me for a few days."

"I can't right now," she complained. "I got my son."

"Bring him too," I blurted out. For me to have invited her child to come with us, I really wanted some pussy.

"Naw. His father will be here soon. Give me about an hour and I'm all yours."

"Promise?" I asked, removing the phone from my ear and glancing at the caller interrupting my conversation with Talia. It was Armando.

"I promise."

"A'ight then. Call me when you're ready." I ended her call and answered Armando's. "Speak to me."

"Where you at?"

"Don't be asking me no shit like that! What the fuck is wrong with you? It don't matter where I'm at," I chastised.

"A'ight then, my bad. I guess you ain't interested in this easy lick I just stumbled upon. I'll holla at you later."

"What are you talking about?" My curiosity was piqued.

Armando went on to divulge the news of a lifetime. Some nigga fucked over the wrong broad, and after Armando smashed, she told him everything. Her nigga operated a stash house not too far from Talia's crib. It was estimated to be enough in there to keep us straight for a while. The best part came when I found out who the supplier was – Cash. I knew the shit was gonna be A1.

"What time you thinking about rolling out?" I asked.

"Shit, right now! Koda and I have been watching the spot for a few hours now. Ain't nobody in that bitch. I just sent one of those fiends to knock on the door. Ain't no movement or nothing. We're going in."

"I'm on my way."

That's all I needed to hear. I had been trying to figure out what I was going to do. Now that the secret was out between Cash and Marley, he didn't have to use the lie that he was 'dry' anymore. I knew that shit didn't sound right. He just didn't want to feed my pockets anymore because he was too concerned with feeding my bitch. It's all good though. Armando came through, and gave me a plan B. I would be back in business in no time. At least, that's what I assumed.

I parked two blocks down the street and called Armando's number.

"We're already inside. Koda and I are bagging this shit up now. I got Pluto and Man on lookout duty."

"Cool." I scanned my surroundings one more time before running up the three stairs leading to the concrete porch. I nodded toward Pluto as I opened the storm door and pushed the heavy wood door open.

I wasn't even in the door good before I was grabbed from different directions. The dim lighting made it hard to see, but I could feel rough hands.

"What the hell is going on?!" I yelled to no one in particular. I was met with a swift kick to the groin area, causing me to topple over in pain. "Ahhh!" I yelped.

"What's the matter, hunh? You can dish it but you can't take it? Fuckin' pussy!" I knew that voice. My eyes trailed the floor until her shoes came into view. Slowly, I traced the length of her body until our eyes met. Amaya leaned on Koda for support, but that didn't stop the angry scowl from spreading across her face. "Look at you. You're fuckin' pitiful."

My pride wouldn't keep me down. I rose to my feet, shaking off the pain. I was too consumed with Amaya to notice the bodies collecting around me.

"Fuck you, bitch!" I spat.

A solid right hand connected with my jaw knocking me into another universe. I saw stars – literally. I don't know who delivered the blow, but as I slowly came to, I was surrounded by niggas on top of niggas. They swarmed around me, taking turns kicking and punching while I tried desperately to escape. Realizing it was no use, I did what any person in my position would do. I covered my face with my hands and took everything they gave like a soldier. My body was on fire, and I could taste the saltiness of my own blood, but I didn't dare let them see me sweat. I held my cries inside and gritted my teeth as they tried to work me over.

"Pick that nigga up," Armando demanded.

I was pulled to my feet; each arm held by a goon that I'd never seen before. Quickly I glanced around. Besides Koda, Armando, and Amaya, I didn't know of the niggas eagerly waiting for their verbal cue to take me out.

"You ain't nothing but a bitch," Armando began, taking small strides in my direction. "Let that nigga go. Let's see how bad he is going up against a man."

My arms were freed, but I didn't have the strength to fight. Armando knew that. Regardless of how I felt, my mouth was bad. I didn't bow down to no one. The only man in the room was me. Fuck it! I was going out with a fight.

I spat toward his face; laughing as the blood tinged phlegm, narrowly missed his opened mouth.

"You muthafucka!" The butt of his gun caught me in the jaw. Losing my balance, I dropped to one knee.

"Stop playing with this mothafucka and get it over with," Koda barked. "He ain't worth the time you spending on his ass."

"None of y'all mothafuckas are gonna do shit to me. Ol' weak asses," I turned to Armando, standing firm with his gun pointed directly at me. "What you gonna do with that? Hunh?"

To add insult to injury, I turned my back to him, giving him an easy shot. Extending my hands to the side, I tested his bitch ass.

"Yeah, that's what I thought." I confidently turned back around. I expected to see Armando's unsteady hands trying desperately to hold on to the gun. Instead, it was Amaya, with Koda right behind her. The smirk disappeared from my face.

"Think again, muthafucka!"

I didn't have time to react before I was sent to meet my maker.

EPILOGUE

. Epilogue
Cashmere
One year later...

My heart swelled with pride as I watched Kensley walk across the stage. She was able to skip her junior year and go straight to being a senior. She was doing so well with her academics that school thought she would feel more challenged in a higher grade. They were right, and of course, Kensley graduated on top. She was number five in the her graduating class and number ten in the state. I was beyond proud of all that she had accomplished thus far. I know she has a bumpy road ahead of her, but she will get through it with ease. I have faith in her.

Kensley scored a thirty-four on her ACT the first time; two points away from having a perfect score. She was disappointed at first because she felt as if she didn't do her best. Marley and I assured her that that was *her* best and she should be proud of herself. She got a full ride to the University of Louisville and I was so glad that she stayed close to me. I would have been heartbroken if she would have left. Nah, I'm lying. I just would have moved with her.

"I'm so proud of you, baby!" Kelsie exclaimed as she handed Kensley her flowers and balloons then embraced her tightly. She was beaming with pride and I knew she was proud.

Since our talk that day at the restaurant, things between them had been going great. Kelsie stayed on track of keeping herself clean. She had a job, car and now, she was about to get her own place. Things were looking up for Kelsie and I knew it all was because of Kensley. Kensley changed her life for the better and vice versa. There were times that Kelsie would be desperate for a hit and Ken would be right there coaching her through her mini breakdown. I love how their relationship had blossomed into something so beautiful.

"Thank you, mama. I'm so glad you could be here. I honestly never thought you would be here to see me graduate," Kensley expressed while crying. "I'm just so happy you're here."

They cried some more and fixed Kensley's makeup to take pictures. I wasn't the photogenic type, but I was smiling hard as hell for my baby girl. This was a major milestone and she had succeeded a year early.

"I'm super proud of you, Ken! I can't wait to see what the future holds for you," Marley cooed as she hugged my baby sister.

"I have to thank you for helping me get through this year. It was tougher than I thought it would be, but you were right by my side helping me along the way. Thank you," Kensley cried and her and Marley hugged again.

"I know you're going out with your friends tonight, but I need you to follow us somewhere right quick." I informed Kensley and she started pouting.

"But, Cash! We were about to go eat first," she whined.

"It won't take long, Ken. Come on. We parked right beside you."

Ken said bye to Kelsie and her friends then followed behind Marley and me. It was obvious that Ken was mad, but she would get over it. We had something for her that would make all that anger disappear. She just didn't know it yet.

"I'm so excited," Marley gushed. Ken followed behind us as we rode to our destination. "She's going to be so happy."

"I know," I chuckled. "Anything to make her smile. Kensley has always been a great kid, so I didn't mind doing this for her. She deserves it and more."

"You're right, baby. You're such a great big brother. Ken was really blessed with you."

"Thank you, babe."

We made it to our destination and got it. We waited for Ken to get out and come over to us. When she did, her face was buried in her phone and she was sporting a frown. She didn't even look up, so I cleared my throat.

"Yes?" She sighed in exasperation, glaring at me.

"So, what do you think?" I quizzed with a smile, knowing she wasn't going to take the hint.

"It's beautiful, but I don't know who we're here to see."

"No one." Marley chuckled, further enraging Ken.

"Then, why are we here?" Ken asked as calmly as she could. I was still her brother, so it was fun picking with her and getting under her skin at times.

"Marley and I have been thinking about moving, so we wanted you to check this place out with us and get your opinion. I wanted us to move closer to campus so you wouldn't have to stay there," I told her and she rolled her eyes.

"I appreciate you thinking enough of me to move closer to school, but couldn't this have waited until tomorrow?" Ken pouted. "I could be eating right now."

"No, it couldn't. Now, come on and look inside." I demanded and she obeyed with an attitude.

"Why are you messing with her, Cashmere? You know she's ready to go be with her friends," Marley whispered in my head and giggled.

"I'm just trying to make her sweat," I whispered back.

It took us all of fifteen minutes to tour the entire house. It was a nice five bedroom, three bathroom home with a pool, jacuzzi and tennis court. The back patio was huge and so was the kitchen. It was a nice first time buyer home.

"So, what do you think?" I asked Ken.

"I love it. It's beautiful, but why down size? We have plenty of room at the our house. I don't mind driving back and forth every day," she answered while Marley produced a set of keys she had hidden behind her back. It was finally becoming clear to my baby sister. She stared at the keys for a long moment without saying anything. Eventually, she found her voice and looked up at us with tears in her eyes and her hand over her mouth.

"Is this... Is this *my* house?" Ken stammered as if she was choking on her words.

"That's right." I chuckled. "Welcome home, Kensley. I couldn't think of anything better to show you how proud I am of you. You are truly an amazing young woman and deserving of all this and more. I hate to let you go, but I know you can handle being on your own. I'm always a call away."

I got choked up because I realized that it was really time to let Ken go and be on her own. It came too fast and I didn't have time to prepare for this moment. I don't think anything ever prepares a parent or loving guardian for it. Life doesn't stop just because a person is in their feelings. It sure didn't stop for me.

"Thank you so much, Cash! I promise I'm going to continue making you proud," Kensley cried as she wrapped her arms around me and jumped on me like she used to when she was a little girl. I sat there in her foyer, holding her like she was five years old again. I reminisced on the old times and a lone tear slid down my face. I was letting go.

MARLEY

"Happy birthday, Kash!" Cashmere and I squealed as we walked into the zoo.

A year ago today, we welcome our son Kash into the world. Kensley and I were praying for a girl, but Cashmere won and got his namesake. He bragged about it for weeks until I broke down crying one night. The pregnancy hormones had me tripping, but I was tired of him picking on me. After that, he promised me he would give me a girl; no matter how many times it took. It wasn't going to work like that for me. Three strikes and we're done.

Kash was the light of our lives. He was such a happy child and I believe it was because he was in a household with two parents who loved him dearly and each other. Ever since I told Cashmere I was pregnant, our relationship has been going nowhere but up. I was falling in love with him more and more every day and I was beginning to think I was ready to try marriage out again. I would know when the time was right.

We took a few family selfies then went on our adventure through the zoo. It was fun seeing Kash's little face light up at all the different animals. By the time we made it to the last animal enclosure, Kash was knocked out in his stroller. Cashmere and I decided to just grab something to eat on the way home since Kash would most likely be sleep for a few hours and we didn't want to wake him. As we were leaving, we ran into someone I thought I would never see again.

"Hey, Marley." A pregnant Amaya greeted me with a warm smile. She looked stunning in a long maxi dress that hugged her small, round belly. She was glowing.

"Hey. How are you?" I asked politely.

"I'm good. And you?"

"I'm great."

"Awww, he's adorable! What's his name?" She gushed as she gawked over a sleeping Kash.

"Kash. He's something special," I beamed as I stared at my baby boy. "Do you know what you're having?" I questioned her.

"A girl," she stated proudly. "Koda and I were both hoping for one. It took a while conceiving after my miscarriage..."

There was an awkward silence resting in between us. I had heard all about Santiago beating the baby out of her and in turn, he paid with his life. I hated he had to die behind his actions because I felt he didn't deserve that. They could have just beat him severely instead of killing him.

"Listen, I've been wanting to apologize to you since I snapped on you at the restaurant that day. I'm sorry for not being a best friend. I'm sorry for going behind your back and messing around with Santiago. To be honest, I was just jealous and wanted what you had. Instead of trying to take what was yours, I should have went and found my own. I'm sorry for that. Marley, I hope you can find it in your heart to forgive me," Amaya expressed through tears. "I've been fighting with myself on whether I should reach out to you or not, but I always talked myself out of it. Seeing you now, I couldn't let this opportunity pass by."

"Amaya, I forgave both you and Santiago a long time ago; Lord, rest his soul. I couldn't be happy in my relationship if I continued to harbor ill feelings towards the two of you. I may have forgiven, but I will never forget. You and him hurt me beyond what words can express, but Cashmere was there to help me get through it. I didn't only lose my marriage, but I lost a friendship that I thought would have lasted a lifetime. I accept your apology and wish you and Koda nothing but the best. It was good seeing you, Amaya. Take care."

I walked away without looking back. It felt as if the weight of the world had been lifted from my shoulders. Finally, I got the chance to tell Amaya I forgave her. I had been wanting to do that for some time now. I only felt it was right so that we could both move on with our lives.

After Santiago's burial, I stayed behind and told him I forgave him too. I took his death a little hard and thankfully, Cashmere was understanding of it. Since we were technically still married and he had a will, I inherited everything he had owned. The house, the cars, the money, even the new club; all of it was mine. I ended up splitting everything with his mother. I had more than enough and I knew she could put better use to it than I could.

"You okay?" Cashmere asked as I pushed Kash to the truck that was waiting for us.

"Yeah, I just saw Amaya."

"How did that go?" He quizzed as he got Kash situated in his car seat and helped me inside.

"Good. She apologized and of course, I accepted and told her I forgive her too. I feel so much better now, baby."

"Can I make you feel even better?" He teased and kissed my cheek.

"Cashmere, Kash is right here asleep." I giggled.

"I don't mean that, naughty woman. I mean this," he said then handed me a small box. I opened it to find a huge engagement ring inside. My mouth dropped and I gazed at him with wide eyes and he smiled brightly. "Marry me, Marley. I feel like this is the perfect time. I'm the happiest I've been in forever and I want to you to have my last name. I vow to be the best husband and father to you, Kash and anymore of our little babies. I want to spend the rest of my life with the perfect woman. That woman is you."

"Yes! Yes, I will marry you!" I squealed then hopped in his lap and kissed him deeply.

I was ready for this new chapter in my life. I had two doors close and two more open. Life couldn't get any better than this. I fell for a Louisville savage, but I got my happy ending.

AMAYA

*F*inally, it's happening. I'm going to be a mother and I am scared to death! Koda has been right by my side the whole time, but he's a man. No matter how supportive he is, or how much he goes over and beyond to cater to my every need, he'll never truly understand how I feel. He will never know what it feels like to have a life growing inside him. Thankfully, I have Karlita. She's Koda's younger sister, and just happens to be due a month after me. I don't know how I could have gotten through these last few months without her. She has been a God-send.

Koda and I are great. He's still out there doing his thing, and I... Well, I'm playing my role. I went to his place after leaving the hospital and never left. It took a while for him to stop questioning everything I did, but over time the trust was restored. He stopped treating me like a roommate, and I moved from his spare bedroom to his bed.

The sex... Oh my God! I gave him a few lessons in the art of love-making and he's been breaking my back ever since. Koda just needed a little guidance, that's all. He's a thugged out cutie with a heart of gold. What can I say? He grew on me. So much so, that when he got down on one knee and asked for my hand in marriage, I didn't have to think twice. Of course I said yes! That's my baby!

Ironically, I still think about Santiago a lot. He lost his life at my hands and that shit still haunts me. The workers did one hell of a job cleaning up after the fact. No evidence had ever been found connecting me to the murder and it was now a cold case. Some would say I got away with murder. I look at it as my second chance.

Jennifer's words weighed heavy on my mind. She wasn't just my nurse; she was a voice of reason. She made me realize that I was foul. As hard as it is for me to say that about myself, it accurately describes my past behavior. I spent my whole life blaming everyone else when I was the one with the problem. I felt as if life owed me something. Everyone was privy to some secret good fortune and I was doing everything I could to find it too. I fucked up relationship after relationship trying to find what didn't exist. I wasn't happy because of my own personal demons. It had nothing to do with anyone else. It was all me.

Determined to make a change, I did what many people in the African American community are afraid to do...I sought help. Yep! I found a counselor who changed my life. She made me dig down deep and find the root of my problem. It all stemmed from my childhood. My father was never around and my mother was out doing her. I practically raised Armando, which forced me to grow up fast. Then, there were my looks. I wasn't the most attractive, but I had a good heart. People just weren't checking for me the way I wanted them to. I was teased constantly and suffered from low self-esteem. After I transformed from an ugly duckling to a beautiful swan, people started noticing me. I enjoyed the newfound attention. Guys who were once off limits were now throwing themselves in my direction. I wanted what I wanted and that was that. I didn't care who got hurt in the process. Hell, I'd been hurt my whole life. My father abandoned me. My mother neglected me. I survived; everyone else would too.

My counselor helped me change my whole thought process. Some people don't learn and grow from their mistakes. I guess you can say I'm one of the lucky ones. I made peace with myself and now I can move forward with a clear conscience. I told Koda everything and for some strange reason, he's still by my side. We have a little girl due in about four months. I've wanted this for so long and now I have a man who wants it just as much as I do.

I see Armando every now-and-then. He found him a big booty stripper chick and followed her to Cincinnati. I was skeptical at first. He was trying to turn a hoe into a housewife and I didn't want that for my brother. Instead of telling him how I felt, I bit my tongue. I'm the last person who should judge anyone. He says he loves her. That's all that matters. They have twins that were born a few weeks ago. My niece and nephew are just the cutest! So far, so good. They're happy. I'm happy for them.

My mother passed away about nine months ago. We were finally building our mother-daughter bond when she was killed during an attempted robbery. The police have no leads. It's my karma; I've accepted that. I took Santi away from the world and my mother was taken away from me.

Shortly after that, I met Karlita. Koda introduced us at one of his family's gatherings. We instantly clicked. She reminded me of Marley. It didn't take long for a friendship to develop. We've been rocking with each other since the day we met.

I saw Marley the other day. She was at the zoo with her son. She has a son; can you believe it? I didn't have to ask who the father was. Cash couldn't deny that boy even if he tried. He's a spitting image of his father with a little bit of Marley thrown in.

Marley looked beautiful as always. I was surprised when she approached me. After everything I had done, she still spoke and that says a lot about her character. It was bittersweet. I wanted to pull her into my arms and beg for her forgiveness. I just wanted my friend back. I wanted the sister relationship that we'd previously had, but again, everything's not about me. Marley has to be open to that. I doubt that it will ever happen, but I can't dwell on it. At least I got the chance to apologize for all the wrong I had done. She said she forgave me. I hope that's true.

"You ready?" Koda asked, grinning from ear-to-ear.

"As ready as I'm gonna be."

"She better be ready!" Karlita's voice rang out behind me. "I didn't get dressed up for nothing!"

"I'm ready!" I reassured.

"Good, let's go. They're waiting for us."

Koda entered the courtroom with Karlita's boyfriend, Benny. It was Koda's idea to make our union legal before the baby was born. I wanted to wait and have the wedding of my dreams, but Koda had other plans. He didn't want his daughter born out of wedlock, and I couldn't blame him. Besides, my section would have been small anyway. I didn't have a host of relatives and friends to fill the pews of a church.

As I grabbed the door and took steps towards my future, Karlita grabbed my arm. "Amaya, wait."

"Yes?" I questioned.

"I wanted to give this to you." She handed me a small box wrapped in a bright pink bow. "Open it," she commanded.

My eyes widened in surprise when I saw the box's contents. It was a beautiful sapphire necklace. Tears immediately filled my eyes. Even with less than a day's notice of our plans, Karlita found time to think about me.

"Koda gave me the chain when I graduated from high school. I bought the pendant this morning. I hope you like it." Nervously, she smiled and turned her attention to the floor.

"I love it!"

Her smile reminded me so much of Koda. She shared his same hazel eyes and butter complexion. Karlita was short and petite with a cute mole resting above her pouty lips. Her stomach was just as round as mine, and protruded from her black wrap dress.

"You're welcome," she stated confidently. "Oh, I borrowed the box. Now you have your something old, something new, something borrowed, and something blue all in one."

"Thank you, Karlita!"

"No, thank *you*." She helped me fasten the necklace around my neck. "Thank you for making my brother happy. He loves you, and I do too. You've been like a sister to me and in a few minutes, you will be. I wish you two nothing but the best."

I hugged her tightly. I tried and failed miserably at not ruining my makeup. I was just so damn emotional. Karlita's words meant more than she knew. In a time that I should have been missing Marley, I was actually happy. Karlita was about to become family, I was marrying my best friend, my skin was flawless, and I couldn't have been happier. I had so many positive things going on and Marley wasn't a part of any of it. We were both thriving... Apart. Maybe that's how it was supposed to be all along.

~ The End ~

A NOTE FROM THE AUTHORS

A lot of people may think that Amaya didn't truly get what she deserved. She was just as much to blame for the situation as Santiago, yet she had a happily ever after. That was intentional. In life, we all make mistakes. We all have something in our lives that we regret; however, life is about growth. It took getting handled by Santiago for her to realize that.

This book was not meant to glorifying cheating. We both value the sanctity of marriage, but let's face it – things happen. Cheating is nothing new, and it plagues marriages on a daily basis.

While Santiago's 'punishment' was extreme, it just goes to show you how unforgiving the game can be. Friends can become foe without hesitation. When you choose to engage in that type of lifestyle, you have to be prepared for the repercussions. No one is invincible.

Marley was wrong, too. She became emotionally detached from her husband and allowed Cashmere to step into his place. Sometimes we are so consumed with what other people are doing that we do not realize that we're no better.

Now Cashmere.... Whew! That man was everything. He knew what he wanted and went for it. He slipped right into the crack in Marley and Santiago's marriage and stayed there. Was he wrong for that?

You see, you have to look at the big picture. Yeah, Santiago cheated on his wife, but Marley cheated too. Because Santiago cheated first, does that make Marley better than Santiago? Not at all. It's all about perception.

Some people are rewarded with second chances. For Marley and Amaya, they were able to find love and learned a valuable lesson in the end. Sometimes true love comes with a price.

Thank you for reading! We would love to hear from you. Be sure to leave a review to let us know what you think!

CPSIA information can be obtained
at www.ICGtesting.com
Printed in the USA
LVHW04s1439040518
576004LV00011B/554/P

9 781717 352422